THE WAKEFIELD DYNASTY

7

GILBERT MORRIS

A
GATHERING
of
EAGLES

TYNDALE HOUSE PUBLISHERS, INC.
Wheaton, Illinois

Mor

Library of Congress Cataloging-in-Publication Data

Morris, Gilbert
  A gathering of eagles / by Gilbert Morris.
    p.   cm. — (The Wakefield dynasty ; 7)
  ISBN 0-8423-6237-1 (softcover)
  I. Title.   II. Series: Morris, Gilbert.   Wakefield dynasty ; 7.
PS3563.08742G34   1998
813'.54—dc21   98-20311

Printed in the United States of America

04   03   02   01   00   99   98
7   6   5   4   3   2   1

CONTENTS

6/01
Insp

To Amos and Helen Funderburk—

You two have made my life brighter.
Of all the couples I have ever known,
you two are one of them.

THE MORGANS

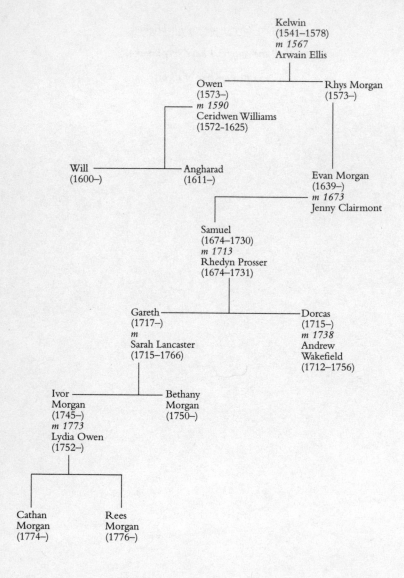

Kelwin
(1541–1578)
m 1567
Arwain Ellis

Owen
(1573–)
m 1590
Ceridwen Williams
(1572-1625)

Rhys Morgan
(1573–)

Will
(1600–)

Angharad
(1611–)

Evan Morgan
(1639–)
m 1673
Jenny Clairmont

Samuel
(1674–1730)
m 1713
Rhedyn Prosser
(1674–1731)

Gareth
(1717–)
m
Sarah Lancaster
(1715–1766)

Dorcas
(1715–)
m 1738
Andrew
Wakefield
(1712–1756)

Ivor
Morgan
(1745–)
m 1773
Lydia Owen
(1752–)

Bethany
Morgan
(1750–)

Cathan
Morgan
(1774–)

Rees
Morgan
(1776–)

WAKEFIELD DYNASTY

THE WAKEFIELDS

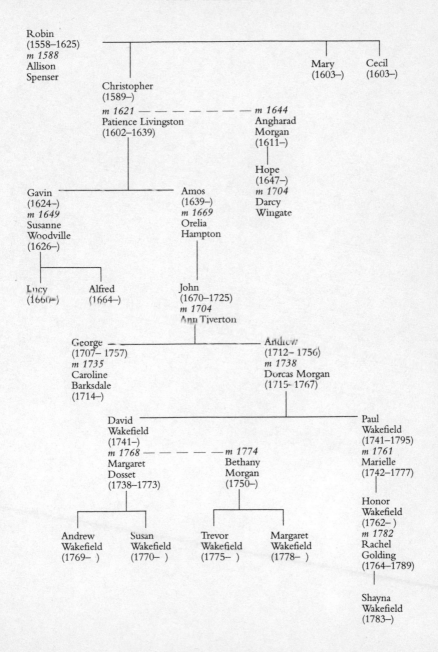

Robin
(1558–1625)
m 1588
Allison
Spenser

Mary
(1603–)

Cecil
(1603–)

Christopher
(1589–)

m 1621 — — — — — — — *m 1644*
Patience Livingston   Angharad
(1602–1639)   Morgan
                             (1611–)

Hope
(1647–)
m 1704
Gavin   Amos   Darcy
(1624–)   (1639–)   Wingate
m 1649   *m 1669*
Susanne   Orelia
Woodville   Hampton
(1626–)

Lucy   Alfred   John
(1660–)   (1664–)   (1670–1725)
                          m 1704
                          Ann Tiverton

George — — — — — — — — — — — — Andrew
(1707–1757)   (1712–1756)
m 1735   *m 1738*
Caroline   Dorcas Morgan
Barksdale   (1715–1767)
(1714–)

David   Paul
Wakefield   Wakefield
(1741–)   (1741–1795)
m 1768 — — — — — *m 1774*   *m 1761*
Margaret   Bethany   Marielle
Dosset   Morgan   (1742–1777)
(1738–1773)   (1750–)

                                                   Honor
                                                   Wakefield
                                                   (1762–)
                                                   m 1782
Andrew   Susan   Trevor   Margaret   Rachel
Wakefield   Wakefield   Wakefield   Wakefield   Golding
(1769–)   (1770–)   (1775–)   (1778–)   (1764–1789)

                                                   Shayna
                                                   Wakefield
                                                   (1783–)

Cousins

Part ONE 1 8 0 0

A BALL FOR SHAYNA

Great clouds of steam rose from the copper tub as Lucy McDougal, a short, wide-hipped woman of twenty-five, emptied a large bucket of boiling water into it. Then, with a red face and a trace of scorn mingling with her Scottish accent, she said, "Now, I don't doot but that you'll get your death o'cold and go to an early grave!"

Shayna Wakefield lay immersed in the soapy water, her auburn hair tied up to keep it free from the suds. She slipped farther down, luxuriating in the hot water, and smiled up affectionately at the maid. It was an argument that occurred every time she had a bath—which was more regularly than most of her acquaintances. Picking up a handful of frothy bubbles, she blew them, watching lazily as they sailed upward, cleared the edge of the tub, and landed on Lucy's dress. "You say that every time I take a bath, Lucy, and I'm not dead yet. Bathing never hurt anyone."

"It destroys the natural oils of the body," Lucy said firmly. This was a theory she had devised and devoutly believed—almost as firmly as she believed in the articles of faith from her Covenanter ancestors. Putting her hands on her hips, she sniffed, her nose twitching with irritation. "It's naught a healthy thing. I can't imagine the prophet Elijah taking a bath. It's naught in The Book!" This, for Lucy, was the end of the argument. If something wasn't in "The Book"—the *Holy Bible*—then it was not worthy of her attention. Picking up a soft brush, she continued, "But if you must risk your life, I'll scrub you down."

Shayna sat up in the lovely suds and leaned forward, enjoying every part of the bathing. She collected soaps and lotions and had learned that the one she was currently enjoying came from Castile, in Spain. As Lucy scrubbed, Shayna thought of the ball that was to come.

As a matter of fact, Shayna Wakefield thought of balls quite often. They occurred in the romances she delighted in, and now she was to have, for the first time, one of her very own! She had been preparing for this event for weeks, buying new clothes, inviting as many guests as her father would permit.

Now she straightened up abruptly. "That's good enough, Lucy. You're going to take all my skin off."

"I'll go get your clothes laid out. You can't lie in that tub all day. Hurry up now!"

"All right, I'll hurry!"

As Lucy left the room, Shayna once again slid lower in the water. Taking a soft cloth, she moved it across her face, but she was not thinking of the bath now. She was thinking about the critical point she'd reached in her life.

"Seventeen years old!" Speaking the words boldly, Shayna laughed. "If Lucy hears me talking to myself, she'll think I've gone crazy. But it's not every day a girl passes into womanhood. That's what I am! Seventeen years old—and a *woman!*"

After dreaming more of the ball, she reluctantly grasped the edge of the tub and pulled herself up. Taking a large, fluffy towel, Shayna rubbed furiously until her skin glowed pink. Then, tossing the towel aside, she left the small bathroom and hurried into her bedroom.

Shayna's fourteen-by-sixteen bedroom had light blue carpet with white flowers and rose-and-blue floral wallpaper and curtains. Many gilt-framed pictures decorated the walls. She loved the gray stone fireplace and the massive cherry furniture, especially the canopied bed covered in blue and white and edged with blue fringe. A wardrobe and mirror dominated one wall and a dressing table covered in delicate white fabric took its place beside the bed. The entire room was made for the comfort of a young woman accustomed to luxuries. The cost of the furnishings would have fed the village where she shopped for a year.

Lucy, who had been picking lint from a dress that lay across the bed, looked up with alarm, then threw up her hands. "Not a stitch on," she cried out. "Come along and get into these clothes before you catch your death." Lucy picked up a white cotton chemise, pulled it over Shayna's head, tied it, then held out lace pantalets for her to step into. After tying them around Shayna's waist and slipping a loose shift over her head, Lucy started on the multiple petticoats—one flannel, one cord calico, and then three starched and flounced ones to support the weight of the gown.

Lucy picked up the dress and held it up with an expression of disapproval. "It's a mortal sin, it is—spending this much money on a *dress!*"

But as Shayna slipped into the gown and allowed Lucy to button it up the back, she was not concerned about the expense. As the daughter of Sir Honor Wakefield, she rarely knew what her clothes cost. She was spoiled and cared not one wit that it was so. Now she pulled away from Lucy impatiently and went to stand before the mirror. The reflection she saw satisfied her entirely.

Her long auburn hair, still done up from her bath, was tinted with copper lights, a legacy from Marielle, her Indian grandmother. But as far as Shayna could tell from the portraits that hung all over the castle, the Wakefields had the same auburn color. From her father, who was one-quarter Ojibway, she'd received her high cheekbones and oval face. From her Jewish mother Shayna had inherited smooth skin that was darker than most English ladies'. Although Shayna could remember her only faintly, she knew her mother had been beautiful and, somehow, in that mysterious alchemy of birth and blood, had passed down that beauty to her daughter. But neither of Shayna's parents had her dark green eyes.

Her jade silk dress, too, was a triumph. With its dark beauty set off by white lace around the bodice, short puffed sleeves, a white silk underskirt, and an overskirt tied up with large white bows, the dress was a vision to behold.

"Well, if you're through admiring yourself—," Lucy began, only to be interrupted by a knock on the door. She whirled and went to open it. "Oh, Sir Honor, she's just finished dressing!" Then, with praise in her voice but not enough so that Shayna might grow vain, Lucy said, "She'll do very well, I suppose."

"Do you think so, Lucy?" a deep voice responded. "Let me have a look."

The man who entered the room was six feet two inches tall. His striking face featured a widow's peak, dominant chin, and direct gray blue eyes. At thirty-eight, Sir Honor Wakefield had lost little of his athletic figure. Now he ran his hand quickly over his chin as his daughter waited for his approval.

"Well," he said slowly, noticing that she was expecting a great compliment, "I suppose it will do."

"Oh, Papa," Shayna said, her face falling with disappointment as she turned away from him, "is that all you can say?"

Honor grabbed her shoulders and swung her around. "I was just teasing you!" Then he stepped back, smiling. "Let me see. . . . You look very much like your mother. I can't say better than that."

"You've never said that to me before!" Shayna said, delighted, for she knew her father thought of no woman other than Shayna's mother. When he lost her mother, Shayna was only six. Everyone had expected him to marry again, for he was wealthy and famous, yet he had not. Secretly Shayna was glad, for she had received his full attention. As she kissed him, she whispered, "That's the nicest compliment you could pay me. She was beautiful, wasn't she?"

"Very beautiful." Honor Wakefield thought of the time Rachel Golding came into his life. She had been only a year older than Shayna was now. One look at her and Honor had lost his heart. It had been a storybook romance, for she had fallen in love with him too. Honor had told the story often to Shayna: how his bride-to-be's parents, well-to-do Orthodox Jews, had determined that Honor and their daughter would not marry. But then Marielle, Shayna's grandmother, had won Rachel to faith in Jesus Christ. When Rachel and Honor married, her parents held her funeral and cut her off.

"You look just as she did on the day I first met her, Shayna," he said, sadness in his eyes.

"You miss her very much, don't you, after all this time?"

"I think of her every day."

Shayna hugged her father hard. "Well, you've got me, Papa."

Honor Wakefield squeezed her. "I won't for very long with you looking like that. All the young bucks in the country will be lining up to ask for your hand in marriage."

"I hope so." Shayna smiled back at him.

Shayna and her father were not only close in appearance but also close in heart. They'd spent as much time as possible together. But since he had chosen to go into the navy, he was absent for long periods, sometimes for many months, and she wept every time he left. Honor Wakefield now thought of those missing years and regretted them even more.

As if she could read his thoughts, Shayna asked, "Will you be leaving soon on a voyage, Papa?"

Honor nodded reluctantly. "I'm afraid so. But this won't be a long one—no more than two months. I'll be going in the *Leopard*. It'll be her last voyage; then she'll be sold or broken up."

"I wish you didn't have to go," she said. Then, seeing the pain in his eyes, she added hastily, "But it won't be long."

"When I come back, you and I will take a trip. Maybe we'll go to Spain or some exotic place like the settings of the romances you always read. You'll meet a handsome Spaniard down there and fall in love. But then he'll die and you'll spend the rest of your life wearing black and never looking at another man."

"Papa, what a terrible thing to say!"

"Well, isn't that what happens in the romances you love so much?"

"More than that!" Shayna defended herself quickly, for she knew her father was more of a realist, as was quite natural for a captain in His Majesty's navy.

Honor Wakefield knew well that life was not all romance—a fact he realized Shayna had yet to discover. He had kept her carefully shielded so that she had not brushed against harsh realities as other young girls were often forced to do. Now he wondered if he had done the right thing. *It might have been better,* he thought, *if I had let her endure a few hard knocks. She'll have to someday and when she comes out of this nice little world I created for her, she's going to be shocked, I'm afraid.*

Aloud he said, "I have a present for you. Does that surprise you?"

Shayna, knowing he was teasing, only smiled.

Bringing out a small box, he handed it to her. "Happy seventeenth birthday, Shayna."

Shayna lifted the lid, and there, nestled in the box, was a necklace of stones that burned like emerald fire. The size and beauty of it took her breath away. With eyes shining more brightly than the stones themselves, Shayna exclaimed, "Oh, Papa, it's lovely! It must have cost a fortune!"

Honor Wakefield chuckled and took the necklace. "That's the

first time you ever worried about what anything cost. Here, let me put it on."

After he fastened the clasp, Shayna looked in the mirror.

"The necklace was your mother's. I've been keeping it until your seventeenth birthday," Honor said, looking down at her fondly. "You look beautiful, my dear."

"I can't thank you enough, Papa."

"Well, let's go down if you are ready. I expect Trevor will be here soon."

"Yes, I've saved him a dance."

"Just one?" Surprised, Honor examined his daughter and noted her expression, aware that he might not know her as well as he thought. *It was simple enough when she was six,* he thought, *but now at seventeen she has her secrets.* "Aren't you anxious to see your cousin?"

"Of course I am, Papa. I'm always glad to see Trevor."

Trevor Wakefield, David and Bethany Wakefield's son, was Shayna's second cousin since David and Paul Wakefield, Honor's father, were twins. Although Paul had died five years earlier, the two families were still close. A successful novelist, David lived in London but kept a cottage nearby where he, Bethany, and the family came during the heat of the summer. For a long time, Trevor, who was eight years older than Shayna, had been like a kind brother to her. He had taken her places and, indeed, had filled a large gap in her life during her father's long sea voyages. So it was no secret, at least to those close to the Wakefields, that Trevor had, within the last year, fallen hard for Shayna. Trevor, who was in his studies at Edinburgh and would one day be a physician, had never before been particularly interested in any young women—which surprised everyone, for he was winsome and good looking, though quiet. Many young women and their mothers had planned elaborate strategies to draw him into their nets, but all had failed. The previous summer, when Trevor had spent several months at home, he seemed to see Shayna as a woman for the first time. She had blossomed most exquisitely and Trevor had gone back to Edinburgh with his head and heart full of thoughts of Shayna Wakefield.

Seeing her father was waiting for a reply, Shayna changed the subject. "Come along. We'll be late."

As the two went downstairs, Honor Wakefield wished desperately that he had a wife, someone to share the responsibility of raising Shayna. *I'll have to talk to Bethany about this to see how Trevor feels.* Honor knew his Aunt Bethany had spent much time with Shayna, becoming almost like a mother to her. His thoughts raced as they left the room and went down the staircase, joining the already milling guests amidst the music and babble of conversation.

⬥

"Well, I must say you look *almost* as handsome as your father."

Trevor Wakefield looked across at his mother, whose eyes twinkled with humor. At fifty, Bethany Morgan Wakefield looked twenty years younger. Her hair was still black, her dark blue eyes clear. When she looked at David Wakefield, her husband, sitting next to her in the carriage, he turned toward her. After a moment, she told him with a grin, "No, I believe your son looks even better than you do."

Trevor laughed. "I can't believe you're saying that. You always said Father was the best-looking man in the whole world."

"Well, you get your good looks from him and some from me. That makes you doubly blessed," Bethany Wakefield replied, a trace of her father's Welsh lineage in her speech. She had been very much in love with David ever since she had first met him as a child, and now she reached out and patted his hand. "What do you think? Are you excited about the ball?"

"Well, I'm anxious to see how Trevor behaves. A man in love is apt to do foolish things, you know." He saw Trevor's face redden, for even at the age of twenty-five Trevor was still amazingly shy. Some considered him almost backward. But his reticence stemmed not from lack of wit or intelligence; he simply was born with a quiet streak and talk like this always embarrassed him.

"You shouldn't tease the boy! Shayna's a fine young woman, and she'd make a good wife for him."

"Mother, I haven't even asked her yet!" Trevor protested, leaning back on the coats. At an even six feet, one hundred and eighty-five pounds, he was strongly built. He had reddish chestnut hair, an olive complexion, blue gray eyes, a short English nose, wide mouth, and thick eyebrows that he had to trim. A deep cleft in his chin gave him problems when shaving but added attractiveness to his face.

"I think it's good for a man to marry a younger woman. Shayna's young enough to be trained," David added innocently, with a wink at Bethany.

"Why you—!" Bethany exploded, her temper rising. "Are you saying that you trained me?"

"Certainly. That's why I married someone younger," David continued, smiling.

Trevor returned the grin. "You'll never get the best of him, Mother! These writers are just too quick for mortals like you and me." Actually, Trevor was proud of his father's success as a novelist, as was his mother. Trevor knew that it had not always been easy for his parents, for David Wakefield had a checkered history. He had been born, so everyone supposed, heir to the title of Marquis of Wakefield. Then in a most strange and astounding case, it had been proven that his brother, Paul, was the real heir to the title. As a result, David, who had married a woman who did not love him, had to make his own living and had known extreme poverty. And yet, in spite of all this, Bethany Morgan had continued to love her childhood friend. After David's first wife died, the two had married and their marriage had been the best that God provides for a man and woman.

Up to this time Margaret Wakefield, Trevor's attractive and alert twenty-two-year-old sister, had said nothing. Now she said, "Don't worry, Brother. All you have to do is get rid of some of your inhibitions and Shayna will fall into your lap."

"What do you mean by that?" Trevor demanded.

Margaret touched her black hair to make sure it was in place. "I mean she's very romantic. I think the only thing that would please her is if you came in wearing a dark mask and announced that you're the masked avenger, like one of her romance heroes."

"I'm hardly likely to do that!" Trevor said tersely. But he had no chance to say more, for the carriage pulled up.

As they got out, Bethany asked, "Why did you say that to Trevor?"

Margaret cocked her head toward her mother. "Because it's true. You mind what I tell you, Mother! He'll have to do something more than talk about his medicines and operations to win Shayna Wakefield!"

As the four stood before the Marquis of Wakefield's home, Bethany and Margaret were, as usual, a little intimidated and awed. David was not, for he had grown up in this magnificent three-story manor house of gray stone. As they walked up the double set of steps and onto the porch toward the large, decorative front door, the women admired the corner-tower turrets, large windows, and steep gabled roof.

When they entered the hall, music wafted on the air. They were greeted by the marquis, Honor Wakefield, who shook hands with his Uncle David with great pleasure. "Uncle David, it's good to see you. Bethany, I never saw you looking better. And you, Margaret, how lovely you look!"

"How are you, Nephew?" David asked, looking handsome in a double-breasted black tailcoat, white linen shirt, gray-and-black cravat, and gray waistcoat. His loose-fitting trousers were tucked into black leather boots. "Quite a crowd we have here."

"Yes, I had to stop Shayna. She would have invited half of the county if I hadn't stepped in."

"There she is," Bethany said.

Margaret peered at her distant cousin. "What's that around her neck?" Then she eyed her host and smiled. "I take it that's a trinket you gave her for her birthday."

"I must plead guilty. But a girl's only seventeen once," Honor replied. Then, looking at Trevor, he said, "You'd better go get in line. She's besieged by these young fellows from the neighborhood."

"Yes, sir, I'll do that at once."

As Trevor moved off, Bethany noticed that Honor looked anxious, even troubled. But she knew this was no time to discuss whatever was bothering him.

Meanwhile, Trevor stood along the wall of the gold-leaf-and-flower-etched ballroom, watching Shayna as she danced with a tall, fair-haired young man. Somehow the beauty of the room— the ceiling scenes of cherubs, the alabaster floor that reflected the mirror-backed sconces and flickering candles, the chandeliers; verde fireplace with silver candlesticks; and scarlet, gold, and blue damask chairs—depressed him. As he took a crystal glass of punch from one of the white-clothed tables, he mused, *It's probably not the best idea in the world for a poor not-yet doctor to come courting the daughter of a marquis. That silver service alone would pay my wages for a year!* The fact that Trevor was not good at parties since he had spent more time studying anatomy than learning how to dance didn't make him feel better. Staring at the unknown man who was laughing down at Shayna, he thought, *He can dance better than I can, but I'd like to see him dissect a corpse!* As he realized how ridiculous his comparison was, he smiled inwardly. Trevor did have a sense of humor, but it was subtle. Able to see the discrepancies between what appeared to be and what actually was at such events, he was amused rather than grieved by society.

Finally the dance was over, and he intercepted the two as they left the floor. "Happy birthday, Shayna."

"Oh, Trevor, I'm so glad you've come!" Shayna indeed was glad, for she liked Trevor very much. Reaching out her hand, he took it as she said, "Do you know Mr. Leslie Carrington? Mr. Carrington, my cousin, Mr. Trevor Wakefield."

The two men exchanged greetings, and Carrington asked, "You're cousins, you say?"

"Distant cousins," Trevor said quickly.

"Trevor's studying to be a physician, and he'll be the best one in Scotland, too," Shayna put in proudly.

"Oh, I'll be coming back to England when I finish my training."

"Mr. Carrington is a lawyer."

Trevor acknowledged this, and the three chatted for several moments before Trevor asked Shayna, "Can I have the next dance since I missed the first one?"

"Of course."

"Don't forget," Carrington said as the two moved off, "the next one you promised to me."

"It's so good to see you, Trevor. You must tell me all about your studies," Shayna queried.

Trevor, with a straight face, began saying, "Yes. Well, we had to trepan this man. First we shaved his head and then we cut—"

"Trevor, what a thing to talk about!" Then she saw the humor in his eyes. "Just enjoy the dance."

"I can't dance. You know that."

"Well, I can and you can learn if you'd only put more time into it."

Trevor could not argue except to say he did not have much time. He was blatantly determined to become the finest physician in the British Empire. This took study, for the courses were arduous and his teachers were strict.

The two went through the figures of the dance and when it was over Trevor surrendered her again to young Carrington.

The rest of the evening was rather dull for Trevor. He stood around until Bethany came over and scolded him, forcing him to dance with some of the other women. "Look, there's Ann Hargrave over there. She needs a partner."

"She always smells like garlic."

"I don't care what she smells like. Go dance with her."

"Yes, Mama."

Trevor danced with Ann, then with several others, and even managed two more with Shayna. She was, he saw, ecstatic with the dance. *She was meant for things like this and I cut a poor figure. I've got to learn how to dance better and to talk about some of these subjects even if they bore me to death.* Trevor had resolved such things before, but he had never been able to follow through on them.

The ball had been going on an hour and a half when David interrupted Shayna. "Would you spare a dance for an old man?"

"Of course, Uncle David!" Shayna led him to the floor. "I wish you could teach Trevor to dance as well as you do."

"He's never been interested much in that, but I'll have a word with him." As they enjoyed the dance, Shayna's eyes narrowed. "Who is that young man who's just come in?"

Glancing in the direction of the entryway, David responded, "I'm surprised at you! You don't know your own relations? That's your cousin, Cathan Morgan." The five-foot ten-inch newcomer, dressed in an army uniform, wore a high-collared scarlet jacket with purple lapels and cuffs, a crimson sash, and white kerseymere culottes. Black leather boots and silver lace epaulets with tassels completed the stunning outfit.

"Why, I would never have known him," Shayna responded.

"When was the last time you saw him?"

"It must be ten years ago. We were just children. He was visiting you."

Cathan Morgan was the son of Ivor Morgan, Bethany's brother. Since Ivor had been in the army for thirty-four years, he and his family had moved around considerably, even going overseas for long periods.

"Come. I'll have to introduce you. He'll never know you. You were a little girl with scratches on your knees the last time he saw you."

As the two approached the black-haired, athletic-looking young man, he called out, "Good evening, Uncle David."

"Good evening, Cathan. It's good to see you again. I believe you know this young lady."

"I don't believe I do!"

"You two have short memories," David said wryly.

"I'm Shayna, Cathan." Seeing his shocked reaction, Shayna put her hand out quickly. "Don't worry. I didn't know you either."

Cathan Morgan was tanned and well built, with a wedge-shaped face and dominating chin. But for all his clean-cut, handsome features, what struck Shayna most were his penetrating, almost hazel eyes.

Cathan covered his surprise smoothly. "Then I expect I'd better have this dance so that we can renew old acquaintances."

Shayna nodded and took his arm. Inside, her heart was thudding and she was thinking, *He's the finest-looking man I've ever seen!* Aloud she said, almost repeating her earlier words to him, "You really didn't know me, did you, Cathan?"

"Of course not. You were a little girl the last time I saw you. I compliment you on the change."

"Thank you. You've changed, too. You're in the army?"

"Up until recently. I'll tell you about it some other time. Right now I want to know about you."

Although Shayna Wakefield did not yet realize it, Cathan

Morgan satisfied most of her dreams about romance. He was a soldier, had traveled the world, and had a daring, reckless quality. As she compared him with the young men of the neighborhood, who had never traveled more than a few hundred miles and were rather phlegmatic in their acceptance of daily life, he came out looking favorable. And as he pressed her arm more tightly than customary, something in her stirred to meet the challenge in his eyes. She surrendered herself to the pleasure of the dance and without meaning to, found herself dancing again with him. Peter Gilcrest should have had the dance, but Cathan had simply maneuvered him out of position and swept her away. "You didn't really want to dance with that fellow, did you? He looked so boring."

"You're awful!"

"So I've often been told, but *you're* not awful. I'm most pleased to find my childhood companion grown into such a beautiful woman."

Against the wall, Honor and Bethany Wakefield stood watching the pair. "That young fellow's changed a great deal," Honor said. "I would never have known him. What's he been doing? In the army, is he?"

"Yes—at least he was. I'm a bit concerned about him and so is Ivor."

"What's the trouble?"

Bethany did not want to prejudice Honor against her nephew, but she had to be honest. "Oh, he's not at all like Ivor! My brother was always the steadiest man in the world—still is, for that matter. And Cathan's not like his brother or two sisters either, who are all doing well. Somehow he just hasn't found his way. I guess his name—which means "battle" in Welsh—suits him very well. He's been fighting most of his life. His mother would tell me how he used to come home from school bruised and battered because he always took on the big bullies. No matter how many times they thrashed him, he would stay with them until he got the better of them."

"Sounds like he's cut out for the army."

"I suppose so, but still we worry about him. I just got a letter from his mother. She's worried because he's left the army and now she doesn't know what he's going to do."

"How old is he?"

"Twenty-six."

"It's time to choose his profession. Trevor, for example, is almost finished with his training." Honor shook his head. "Very difficult for a young man these days."

Bethany glanced over at Trevor. "Honor, look at Trevor. He looks absolutely miserable."

"He doesn't like balls any more than I do."

But Bethany was not dissuaded. She approached her son and asked, "What's wrong with you, Trevor?"

"Nothing. Why should anything be wrong?"

"Your face looks like you've bitten into a wormy apple! Now, I think I know you pretty well. You're jealous of your cousin Cathan."

Involuntarily Trevor looked over to where Cathan and Shayna were dancing. "Well," he said matter-of-factly, "he's a romantic fellow. Just look at him. He's a great dancer and I can't dance at all. I'm nothing but a clumsy cow."

Out of the blue Bethany Wakefield said, "Go over and throw him out the window!"

Shocked out of his apathy, Trevor stared at his mother. "What did you say?"

"I said go throw him out the window! That would catch Shayna's attention," she said wryly. "She's obviously entranced by his uniform because she's read too many storybooks about dashing young men. Trouble is, being dashing doesn't pay very well. So go throw him out the window."

"Mother, you're ridiculous! I can't do that! Let's face it—I'm a rather dull fellow."

A swift argument rose to Bethany's mind but stopped before it reached her lips. *Why, he really means it! Somehow I've failed to get across to him that he's not dull—only quiet.* As she watched Shayna interact with the officer across the room, she thought resentfully, *She's a fool if she doesn't see any further than that red uniform!*

Meanwhile, Cathan Morgan knew the ball was ending. He was an expert at strategy and had learned how to maneuver not only troops but also young women. And Shayna Wakefield, he had quickly learned, was naive. So, using only a few of his skills, he had led her to a darkened alcove off the main room, then into a room lit only by a few candles. Then he said, "I can't tell you what it means to a poor soldier to come and find someone like you."

"Do you say that to all the girls?" she quipped.

"Oh yes," he said. "But I don't always mean it as I do now." As his intense eyes probed hers, the candlelight touched a scar on his lower-right cheek.

"How did you get the scar?"

"I was in a raiding party off the coast of San Luis on a small boat. . . ." He continued to tell the story, for he could tell she yearned for adventure. And the story was true enough, although he magnified his own part in it.

"What a wonderful life you've led," she said with admiration.

"No, I've missed it all. You grew up and I wasn't here to watch you."

Shayna did not know how to respond to that, nor to the fact that he had pulled her close. She knew he was going to kiss her and she did not resist. She had been kissed three times before, but nothing as demanding as this. As the kiss continued, her arms crept around his neck.

Finally she drew back and started to speak. Then, conscious of a shadow that had fallen, she turned toward the door. Trevor

Wakefield had stepped into the room and she saw from his face that he had seen the kiss. "Oh, Trevor . . . !" she whispered.

Trevor Wakefield stared at the two, then said in an even voice, "I just came to say good-bye." He was gone before Shayna could reply.

"He saw us kissing," Shayna said, shocked.

"Yes, he did. I remember Trevor." Noticing the look on Shayna's face, he said, "He was jealous. Are you two engaged or anything?"

"Oh, no!" Shayna said quickly, feeling horrible because of what had happened. She did not want to hurt Trevor. But she had no time to think further for Cathan took her hand, kissed it, and pulled her close again.

"He's probably a fine fellow," Cathan said, smiling, "but he's had his chance." And then Cathan kissed her again.

Shayna remained in his arms for a moment before she came to her senses. Then, feeling their actions were somehow improper, with an effort she wrenched herself away. "I've got to go say good-bye properly to Trevor."

As she slipped away, Cathan Morgan stood in the darkness. "Well, well," he said, stroking his chin, "things *have* changed. A beautiful girl just seventeen—with a rich father, no less. We'll be seeing a lot of each other, Miss Shayna Wakefield!"

AN EXTENDED VISIT

D avid Wakefield leaned back in his chair, admiring the room. With its green carpet, red-and-green striped wallpaper, pine mantel on the fireplace, and cherry-wood clock next to a walnut bookcase and desk, it had been one of his and his brother, Paul's, favorite rooms at Wakefield. *I spent some good times here when I was Master of Wakefield,* David thought. He glanced up at the brass chandelier and then toward the sampler of the Lord's Prayer that hung on the wall above a Pembroke table.

Sitting behind the desk, Honor, the Marquis of Wakefield, was twirling a large globe, stopping it from time to time. Frowning, he said, "I don't know what's going to happen to England in the future."

"You mean about Boney?" David asked, using the nickname usually accorded to Napoléon Bonaparte. David himself was not a political animal, but he knew that Honor, as an officer in the Royal Navy, was aware of events all over the world.

"Yes. The man's a monster! He'll be satisfied with nothing except to rule the world!"

Honor Wakefield spoke the truth, for ever since the French Revolution and the rise of Napoléon Bonaparte, Europe had been involved in a ferocious struggle. At first, as the revolution swept across France and the Bastille fell to the mob in 1789, England stayed free of the struggle—until France declared war on Britain in 1793. Then England joined a coalition that included Austria, Prussia, Holland, and Spain.

As Honor spoke of armed engagements, invasions, and thousands of men being killed, David tried to assimilate the scope of the war that seemed to be sweeping over the civilized world.

"Horatio Nelson, our best admiral, pretty well saved us last year," Honor continued. "France had gotten strong in the Mediterranean so the Admiralty sent Nelson to deal with them. It was a high gamble, for if Nelson hadn't found them, the French could have come right into the English Channel and up to the Thames. Then we would have lost the war. But the Admiralty picked the right man. Oh, it was a glorious battle!"

"You were there, weren't you?"

"Yes, commanding the *Leopard.*"

"Well, thank God for men like Admiral Nelson," David said.

"Indeed, for we are in need of a leader like him in the days to come," Honor responded grimly. "The navy is England's only hope since Napoléon seems to be able to pull off victories on land. So it's up to the navy to protect the country so that Napoléon can't get his men on our shores. The problem is that the navy is scattered over the world doing convoy and blockade duty, mounting attacks, and carrying troops. All Napoléon's admirals have to do is find one time when the British fleet's scattered and they can walk right up and knock on the front door of Wakefield Manor." Honor then switched the subject and asked David the question that had been troubling him for years. "Does it ever bother you at all, David, this matter of the title?"

Surprised, David replied, "You mean because I'm not the marquis?"

"Yes. It must have been frightful for you. One day you were the Marquis of Wakefield, with all the power and money, and the next day, by a jury's verdict, you're out on your ear. And my father got the title, the money, everything. You can't tell me you didn't resent it a *little.*"

"I don't think I did, Honor. I never wanted the title, but your father did. And I wanted him to have it. As a matter of fact," he said slowly, "I tried to see to it that he got it back when Father died. But it couldn't be done."

"But you lost everything in one stroke."

"It's not the good times that make men, Honor. I'm sure you must know that, as a military man. How would you like to go into battle with a crew of men who had never lacked for anything? A group of landlubbers, like me, for example. Would that suit you?"

"No!" The word exploded from Honor Wakefield's mouth. "It would be suicide! But that's a little different."

"It's not different at all. The one thing I wanted was to be a writer. I could never do that when I was the marquis because I was busy with the estate's affairs. Then when I was, as you've put it, 'thrown out on my ear—'" David smiled to show there was no ill will—"I was forced to do that which I had always wanted to do."

"It must have been hard."

"Well, I didn't miss many meals—I just had to postpone a few," David continued thoughtfully. "But God was preparing a wife for me. When I was free to marry, Bethany was right there and the children loved her already."

"You've had a happy marriage, haven't you?" Honor said, longing in his voice. "I envy you finding a wife like Bethany."

"You've never thought of remarrying?"

Honor had been asked many times why he had not married again and still he could not give a satisfactory answer. It would have sounded foolish to his own ears—almost like something out of Shayna's romance novels—to say, "I loved Rachel so much that a marriage with any other woman would seem hollow." So instead he said to the man he loved and trusted as he did few others, "I never found a woman I cared to share life with after Rachel died."

Then they turned to other subjects. Finally Honor said, "I've been meaning to ask you about Trevor. I haven't seen him since the ball."

"No, he went back to Scotland to take up his studies again."

"I wish he could study in London. We don't get to see much of him here. He practically grew up in this place. He's almost like my own son."

"We feel the same way about Shayna. She's a dear girl—"

When David broke off, Honor said quickly, "I think I know what's troubling you. It troubles me, too. I've been hoping Trevor and Shayna would make a match of it."

Relief washed across David's face. "Bethany and I have talked about it. It would be a little bit like our own marriage. She was a Morgan and married me, a Wakefield. They're only second cousins, of course, and we love Shayna."

"It was going very well, I thought." Honor picked a walnut from a dish, then tossed it back on the desk. "She's been seeing too much of her cousin Cathan. I know he's your relative, David, but I'm . . . apprehensive."

"To tell the truth, so am I. The Morgans are good people. Gareth Morgan is the finest man I know."

"He's getting along now, isn't he?"

"Eighty-three, I believe, but still preaching. Still goes out on his horse to ride twenty miles in bad weather to some church. I don't see how he does it. His son, Ivor, is a good man and a fine soldier," David said.

"But from what I've heard and seen, Ivor's son, Cathan, is not stable."

"What does Shayna say about him?" David queried.

"Oh, she's head over heels infatuated with him. And he's still wearing his red uniform—which he has no right to wear, I understand. He's left the army, hasn't he?"

"Yes. I don't know all the circumstances, but I don't think he left under the best conditions."

"I'd like to know about that. Would you give me his commanding officer's name?"

Feeling a little guilty, David supplied the name. But he and Bethany had talked about this and they had agreed it would be only fair to give Honor whatever information they had about Cathan. "It may have been something quite justifiable," David reminded Honor.

"I trust so." Just then the sound of dogs barking caught Honor's attention and he hurried to the window. "Come look at this!"

Rising from his chair, David went to stand beside his host and watched as the stablemen brought out two horses. One of them helped Shayna into the saddle; then Cathan Morgan swung astride the powerful bay with an easy motion. Both laughing, they left the stable yard at a fast gallop. At a loss for something to say, David commented, "He rides well."

"Oh, I'm sure he does! He does everything well physically. He's very fit, but there's more to a marriage than riding a horse." Finally Honor said heavily, "I wish you'd talk to Trevor."

"And say what exactly?"

"Tell him to get down here and do some serious courting! I've never seen Shayna like this—and I can tell young Morgan has experience with women."

Sighing, David said, "Trevor's not good with women. He spends his time in libraries and with medicine. He's an amateur where women are concerned."

A hard light leaped into Sir Honor Wakefield's eyes and he spoke between clenched teeth. "Well, Cathan Morgan isn't an amateur and that's what bothers me!"

Shayna's face was flushed with pleasure as she pulled up her mare and turned to her companion. "Let's race to that grove over there."

"All right," Cathan said, smiling. "I'll give you five lengths."

At Shayna's command, the mare shot out, quickly achieving a dead run. Shayna was a fine rider, having been taught first by her father and then by Michael Devon, who had served in the cavalry until coming to work under her father as steward. She looked back over her shoulder and shouted, "Come on! You can do better than that!"

Cathan was holding his horse back carefully. He had rarely ridden such a fine animal, but he had no intention of winning the race. He allowed the stallion to come up within a length and a half, but then pulled him back so that Shayna reached the grove of trees first.

"You're a fine rider, Shayna! I never saw better for a woman."

Shayna flushed at his compliment, not knowing how easy it was for him to please her. "Come along. I want to show you something." She led him to a ruined house with nothing left standing except a few walls and a broken chimney that rose some ten feet. "This burned long ago," she said, "but they had a beautiful garden and the flowers are still there."

Slipping off his horse, Cathan tied the animal to a sapling, then helped Shayna down, holding her a little longer than was necessary until she protested. "I just want to be sure you're safe," he said, winking at her. He tied her mare and then followed her into a grove of ancient fruit trees. Once inside, they were in an open space, paved with weed-choked stone. Circled by yew hedges, the area had beautiful red-and-yellow flowers. Shayna took his hand in her excitement, leading him toward another spot. "This was the tower. They took the stones away to build something else."

"And it must have had a princess at the top. Is that what you have imagined?" Cathan asked, taking in Shayna's beauty. Her riding habit, consisting of a burgundy waistcoat, white frilled lawn shirt, and voluminous skirt, made her an even more delectable sight. Her hair, loosened by the ride, hung down her back.

"Come, sit over here," she invited. "I'll tell you a story about this area and then you can tell me about another one of the battles you've been in."

Cathan was willing, so they found an old stone wall, sat down on it, and talked for the next hour. Cathan had to admit that, although Shayna was ignorant about the ways of the world, she had a freshness and a wonderful way with words that he liked very much.

"Now, tell me about a battle," she insisted.

"All right. We were cut off at Toulon. The French had two whole divisions and we had only a few battalions. . . ."

Shayna sat there entranced, her eyes growing large as he described the battle in graphic terms and related how they had to cut their way through the French line with swords and whatever weapons were at hand.

Finally he ended his story with, "I was lucky to come out of that one. I've got a scar that goes from here to here on my chest, sliced wide open by a French lieutenant."

"What happened to him?"

"We buried him the next day. It was his death or mine."

Impulsively Shayna put her hand on his chest at the place he had indicated. He was wearing only a thin shirt and she could feel the firmly muscled flesh underneath. "Right here?" she asked.

Putting his hand over hers and holding it tight, he leaned close and whispered, "Right there." As a handsome man, Cathan had known many women—he had no scruples about taking love where he found it. But Shayna was different. He had arrived in the county with a heaviness on his mind, for he no longer had a

27

profession and was not sure what to do next. But because of Shayna, he had been able to put his troubles away and enjoy himself.

Now, with their faces close in the quietness of the glade, he saw her lips soften and she began to breathe heavily. As the lilac fragrance of her hair and clothes broke through his armor, he was suddenly aware of the deep, lovely fire of this girl. Although young and immature in many ways, she had a rich, impulsive spirit.

Caught up and yet disturbed by the presence of this young Welshman, Shayna resisted for a moment, saying, "No, you—you mustn't" as he reached to draw her into his arms and kiss her. Then, stirred by his caress in a way she could not explain, Shayna's body melted against his. Yet as his hands pressed her closer, she pulled herself away with a sheer act of will and stood to her feet, remembering Bethany's warnings about men. He rose with her, seeing it would be unwise to proceed further.

"You're very sweet, Shayna," he said gently, then kissed her hand. "I think we'd better go back now."

Shayna was glad he let her break off easily, for she knew she could not trust herself. She felt vulnerable and helpless against his touch. As she got on the mare and they made their way home, she said almost nothing. When they arrived, he helped her down, the touch of his hand burning into hers. "I'll see to the horses," he said, smiling. "It's been a good day."

"Yes, it has."

❦

Two days after this ride, Honor came to Shayna's room. When she opened the door, surprise leaped into her eyes. "What is it, Father?"

"Just a little talk if you're not busy."

"No, I was just reading."

"Another romance?"

Shayna flushed. "Yes, but don't make fun of me."

"No, I won't. . . . Shayna, I've been meaning to talk with you. I got a letter from Trevor and you got one too, I think."

"Yes. It was mostly about how he's doing at the hospital."

"Very well, I understand." It was not what Honor had hoped Trevor would write. He wished Trevor would take the advice that he had sent through David and try to come take Shayna's mind off Cathan. Now he said casually, "We haven't seen much of Trevor since his studies take most of his time. I was thinking we might invite him down."

"That would be nice. We always enjoy Trevor."

Since Shayna loved having guests, the lack of excitement in her voice disturbed him. Now he well knew that her whole mind was taken up with the handsome young Welshman.

Honor made a quick decision. "I've decided we're going to London."

Shayna's eyes widened with surprise. "To London! Whatever for?"

"Oh, I've got to see to the *Leopard*. There are always a thousand things to do. It's her last voyage, but I want it to be a good one. I'd like for you to go with me. Maybe we can do some things there."

"But we have a guest."

Honor Wakefield wanted to say, "A guest who's paid an extended visit." Instead he said, "He's welcome to come with us, of course. I expect he has business." He knew this was not so—or at least expected it.

Shayna's fertile imagination began to work on what he had said. "That would be wonderful, Papa. I haven't been to London in six months. When will we leave?"

"Tomorrow morning, I think, if you can be ready that soon."

"Yes. If you'll excuse me, I think I'll go tell Cathan."

Displeasure soured Honor's face as he watched his daughter

run from the room. "That didn't work out exactly like I antici-pated," he muttered. "But surely the fellow will *have* to go somewhere. I'll have to do something about him before the *Leopard* sails. I can't leave her alone with him." He thought for a moment. "I'll talk to Bethany. She can help, I'm sure." Still, he was unusually apprehensive.

Realizing that the source of all his troubles lay with Cathan Morgan, Honor said, "Blast the fellow! I wish he were still in the army—and halfway across the world!"

Three

A WEEK IN LONDON

I think you might enjoy this, Cathan. I come here at every opportunity when I'm in London—which isn't often enough."

Cathan had been striding alongside Sir Honor Wakefield and now glanced up at the bleak granite building that lay ahead of them. He was not familiar with London but had become more so in the two days they had been there. After lunch his host had said to him, "I'm going to take a fencing lesson. You might find it enjoyable."

Now as they walked up the steps, Honor shrugged. "It doesn't look like much, but then I don't suppose it has to. Sometimes a pretty rough sort comes here."

"I enjoy a good contest, Sir Honor," Cathan remarked. The two left the portico and entered into a large room where they immediately heard the ring of steel on steel and the cries of the contestants and smelled sweat and alcohol.

"Ah, it is good to see you, sir!" said a tall, mustached man with a heavy French accent, coming over to greet the two. Having just left a contest, he wore a protective guard over his chest. He bowed toward Honor. "We have been deprived of your presence, Lord Wakefield, for too long."

"Thank you, Maurice. May I present Monsieur Cathan Morgan."

"Monsieur Morgan." Maurice bowed again. "You are wel-come, sir."

"How's business, Maurice?"

"Very well, thank you, sir." He gestured toward the matches that were going on. "They come more and more to prepare for the service, I suppose."

"How do you feel," Honor said, grinning at the Frenchman, "preparing Englishmen to fight your countrymen?"

"France is my country, but I hate Napoléon! He has made a mockery of France; the quicker he is defeated, the better I shall like it. Then we can get back to being honest, noble people once again."

"I will do all I can to help in that line. Now, perhaps you would lend me one of your instructors—"

"Nonsense. I will try a round with you myself." Turning to Cathan, Maurice nodded. "Lord Wakefield is very fine with a foil. He has everything necessary—strength, balance, and most of all, audacity." He considered Cathan as a possible customer. "Will you not try a contest, sir?"

"Yes," Honor said quickly, "you must have become very proficient in the army."

"Ah, monsieur is a soldier! Then it will be doubly interesting. Come, you know where the quarters are for changing."

Fifteen minutes later both men emerged from the room where they had left their street clothes. Now they wore black tights and padded white coats. "Which of you gentlemen will be first?" Maurice asked.

"You go ahead," Cathan told Honor. "I'll watch."

The two men squared off, saluted one another, and then began to play with the foils. As Maurice called out encouragement from time to time, it was obvious to Cathan Morgan that his relative was, indeed, very good. Finally, when Maurice cried out, "A touch! I do confess you have improved, sir. You have been practicing," Cathan's eyes narrowed.

Honor Wakefield knew full well that the owner had politically declined to win the bout. He smiled briefly, saying, "You should practice a little more yourself. Another then?"

"Very well, sir!"

This time the bout went somewhat longer, and Maurice managed to touch his opponent's chest. "Touché!"

Sweating and panting, Honor turned and said, "That's enough for me. Now you, Cathan."

"I shall wait until our instructor regains his breath."

"It is nothing," the Frenchman said with a smile. He had been a fencing expert for many years and Sir Honor Wakefield was one of his most affluent clients. Although he had no knowledge of Cathan's skill, it never occurred to him that he would have any difficulty. "If you are ready, sir?"

Cathan pulled the wire mesh over his face and assumed a position—right leg forward, left leg back, his arm behind him.

He did not advance but waited for Maurice to come toward him. As the blade shot out, he easily turned it aside, then made a move that was parried by the instructor.

"You are very fast, sir! Very fast, indeed!"

Maurice was surprised by the young man's agility. He had seen at once that Cathan was strong. This was good, since a powerful right wrist and arm were necessary to direct the sword. However, Maurice had always felt that strength was not the chief factor in swordsmanship. It was in the heart where true championship swordsmen were born.

For a time Maurice moved to Cathan's left, then to his right. Finally deciding he had allowed Morgan enough leeway, he lowered his sword and drove straight at him. The blades flickered and the clash rang as the two men moved back and forth. Maurice stopped suddenly, for he was almost touched by the button on the end of his opponent's foil. With a start, he thought, *I must be careful. This man knows his business.*

Cathan Morgan's face was smiling behind the wire mask. He could have won the contest easily but preferred to keep his true skill under wraps for the moment. Time and again Maurice drove for him and he parried easily. Fencing was an active sport and Cathan could see that Maurice, who'd probably been fencing for hours, was tiring. Nevertheless, Cathan waited until the Frenchman made a lunge, then he turned the sword aside and touched Maurice's chest, bending the sword in a complete arch. He did not cry out touché but merely stepped back and waited.

Maurice pulled off his mask and stared at Cathan Morgan. "I congratulate you, sir. You are an excellent fencer! You have had much practice and very good training."

"I have had very fine teachers."

"Would you care to try another match?"

"As you will, sir."

Three times Maurice tried—and failed—to break through Cathan's defense. Finally he took off his mask and let his sword dangle toward the floor. "I confess, I have not seen such skill in England. You are worthy to be a Frenchman, sir."

Cathan laughed aloud. "That's high praise, indeed, monsieur, and I thank you. As I say, I have had good teachers."

"You are in the army."

"I've often served as drill instructor. There's little to do in the army on long evenings and for days at a time I would practice with the sword. I love the sport."

Watching carefully, Honor said, "I suppose you are as proficient with a musket and pistol as you are with a sword?"

"There, too, I've had great practice, sir." Cathan's tone was easy, but somehow Honor understood the young man was not being boastful.

"I think that's enough," Honor said. "Suppose we get dressed and go see what that daughter of mine is doing."

Thirty minutes later the two took a carriage back to the inn where Honor had reserved three rooms. "I've never seen such fine swordsmanship. I would like to have you aboard my ship to instruct my men."

"I know little about the navy. Is there a great deal of that sort of work?"

"More than you might think," Honor said as the carriage rolled along the crowded street. "In many cases we batter a ship until she's helpless; then we board her. It's quite close. Usually it comes to swords, more often sabers than foils. I suppose you're trained in the use of the saber also."

"Indeed."

Honor cast a curious glance at Cathan. "I don't suppose you would consider a life at sea? No, that's impossible."

"Is it? And why is that, may I ask?"

"You are too old." Honor saw surprise leap into the young man's eyes and hastened to explain. "It's not a matter of intelligence, strength, or skill, but I think every man who's risen in the navy started when he was very young. Sometimes thirteen as a midshipman; then they learned by coming up through the ranks during many years at sea. You have missed all that and it would be embarrassing to be corrected by a callow midshipman."

"I see your point. No, I think I would not fit in well at all."

"You would do well with the weapons, but there's also a matter of navigation involving mathematics—a science in itself."

When the carriage stopped, they entered the inn and found Shayna ready for dinner. "I suspect you've been out spending your father's money, Miss Shayna," Cathan said, eyeing her new attire.

"Oh, a new dress, is it?" Honor asked.

"Yes, do you like it, Father?" Shayna modeled her high-waisted white gown and short red velvet jacket, waiting for their compliments.

"Come along. We'll discuss your dress over dinner," Honor said, smiling. She took her father's arm as they went downstairs to sit in a private room. Soon the meal arrived: platters of juicy beef and ham, bowls of potato soup, steaming spinach with cream and butter, and fresh-baked bread.

"Better than we get at sea," Honor commented.

"Even for the captain?" Cathan inquired.

"On long voyages almost everything goes bad. But it won't be like that on this one since it's only a couple months."

"I've gone on short voyages with Father," Shayna said. "I loved it."

"You wouldn't if you had to live belowdecks," Honor said wryly. "It's a rough life down there, no mistake."

After the meal, the three went to see a production of *Hamlet*. As they entered, Cathan said, "I've never seen this play."

"It's a strange sort of production," Honor said. "I've never much liked the character of Hamlet."

"Why not?"

"Fellow can't make up his mind. After you see the play, I'll tell you why."

Shayna sat between the two men and more than once Cathan's arm touched hers during the production. She dug her elbow and warned him with a look, but he only winked back at her.

After the play was over, Honor said, "You see why I don't like the fellow? An uncle kills his father and he doesn't do anything."

"Perhaps he had some moral qualm about killing a man, especially one of his own flesh and blood," Cathan put in.

"That's true," Shayna said quickly. "He does wonder whether it's right and he thinks at one time that it might send him to hell."

"Well, I don't argue the philosophy of it. What did you think of the swordplay?" Honor grinned at Cathan.

"Pitiful, sir! I really believe Miss Shayna here could beat either Hamlet or Laertes."

When they reached the inn, they said good night and went to their rooms. But Cathan was restless. It was early for him and he longed to take part in some of the less respectable activities of London life. However, he undressed and went to bed, thinking, *I've got to make a good impression on Wakefield. He's pretty sharp. . . . But he'll be going on a voyage soon. He'll have to leave his little lamb at home without anyone to guard her.* "Well," he said aloud as he lay back, "I'll see to it that she doesn't grow lonely."

❦

"I've got to have fifty pounds for it and not a farthing less."

The ancient bearded man held up the diamond ring that Cathan had placed before him. His shop was small and not at all admirable in any aesthetic sense. The walls were lined with swords, plates, vases, anything of value, and the case he leaned on was filled with watches and jewelry. Taking an eyepiece out of his pocket, he peered through it at the diamond. "Not a clear stone," he said. "Couldn't possibly let you have more than thirty pounds."

"Why, that ring is worth a hundred pounds any day in the week!"

"Not to me! Will you have the thirty?"

Cathan stared at the man, longing with all his heart to reach out and snatch the ring. It had been, for a long time, a rite of passage with him. When he became short of funds, he would take the ring and pawn it; then when he grew flush again, he would redeem it.

He knew thirty pounds would not be enough to see him through. Living in London was expensive and he could not afford to look cheap in front of Sir Honor or Shayna. "Look," he said. "Forty pounds. I'll be back and pay your penalty very soon."

After more dickering he got the cash, stuffed it into his pocket, and warned the jeweler, "You hang on to that ring. I'll be back for it."

"I trust you will, sir."

Leaving the jewelry shop, Cathan's hand went to the bulge that the coins made in his pocket. They seemed light and he bitterly regretted the money he had thrown away earlier.

"It'll have to do," he muttered. "Wakefield will be leaving soon; then I'll invent some story—"

He left the words hanging, but already he knew what he had to do. "I'll have to marry the girl. There's nothing else for it, but that won't be so bad. She's a pretty thing and she wouldn't cramp a man's style of living."

As rain began to fall, he pulled his cloak about him and his hat down over his head. His thoughts ran smoothly. "She's foolish enough about me. All I have to do is ask—but the problem is her father. He doesn't like me. Probably seen fortune hunters before."

Cathan scowled and slapped at a pickpocket who brushed against him. "Keep your hands to yourself or I'll cut them off!"

Cathan Morgan was a man who had known success at almost everything he had tried—except the important things. He was agile, not only with hand and foot, but also with his manners. He could be charming when he chose and was well aware of his good looks. Always in the back of his mind he had known he would have to marry for money. His father had limited resources, so Cathan could not ask him for anything. And now that he had been cashiered from the army, he had no marketable skills.

Entering the inn, he sat down at a table and nodded for a drink. As he slowly sipped it, plans formed. *I'll have to behave myself for a while even after marriage. Sir Honor Wakefield is no man to cross. I know enough about him to know that. But he can afford to keep a son-in-law. . . . It's not what I like to do, but a man has to live. I'll get money out of it, and they'll get good value for it.*

But as he rose, he was depressed that he was being forced to do this thing. Cathan Morgan was a man of almost rabid independence. This was primarily the reason he could not succeed in the army. He had been too free with his criticism of his superior officers and had come within a hairsbreadth of dueling with one of them. He was glad now that he had not or he might be lying in a shallow grave with his neck stretched. He slowly ascended the stairs and shut the door once he was in his room. Leaning against it, he tossed his wet hat on the floor and said aloud, "It won't be bad. She's a pretty thing—and I'll make her a good husband in most ways. . . ."

Four

"There's Nothing like a Woman to Ruin a Man!"

Turning away from the sea, Colonel Ivor Morgan walked toward the house just after dawn had touched the land. He was glad he had begun purchasing this farm when he did. "Land's End," he murmured. "That's a fine name for it. As far south as you can go in England without being out of it entirely."

Only fifteen acres, the land barely merited the title of a working farm at all. Actually it was a piece of a larger property that the landowner had been forced to sell because of financial difficulties. Tired of moving his family from pillar to post, Ivor had scrimped and managed to put down earnest money fifteen years ago. Now at the age of fifty-five, Ivor owned it completely.

As he crested the hill and gazed into the valley where the cottage nestled, he paused, feeling warm as he did every time he looked at his home. "A man needs a place with roots, eh, Jock?" The border collie at his heels looked up and barked sharply, wagging his tail.

"You like it here too, don't you? Well, we'll stay here until both of us are buried in the little cemetery down by the church." He leaned over to tousle the shaggy head of the dog and got his hand licked for his troubles. Straightening up, he said, "Come now. Time for a good breakfast," and followed the path that meandered through a maze of trees. Overhead, blackbirds called harshly and fluttered their wings, rising like a tattered dark cloud in the blue sky.

Ivor approached the house, his eyes approving the thatched roof he had been forced to replace. "Should last forty years," he said with satisfaction, noting the low eaves, two front windows framed with yellow muslin curtains, and sturdy gray stone. He had spent his time between military engagements working on the structure. As he approached the doorway a form appeared and he cried out, "I hope breakfast is ready! I'm starved!"

Lydia Morgan, a petite woman of forty-eight, said with some asperity, "And why would it not be ready? You'd think I never made a breakfast before!" But her brown eyes sparkled as he hugged her and lifted her off her feet. "Don't be foolish! I'm an old woman!"

In answer he kissed her soundly, set her down, and then peeked inside. "Is Cathan up yet?"

"No, sleeping like the dead. I don't think he slept all the way here from London."

"Then he'll have to take for breakfast whatever's left," Ivor said, smiling as he moved inside to the comfort of his home. Having served in the military for thirty-four years, he had lived in barracks, makeshift houses, and inns much of that time. Now this house contained all he needed of a dwelling place on earth. A brick fireplace occupied one wall. On its pine mantle were tins and special plates that Lydia's family had handed down for centuries. In the center of the room on the painted canvas floor was a large oak table with a lamp and six chairs. Between the windows were shelves adorned with cooking utensils, pots and pans, and a pine worktable.

Seating himself at the table, Ivor waited until Lydia set the breakfast on the table: oatmeal, battered eggs, pork chops, scones, and rich milk from their own cow. After she sat down and he asked the blessing, he took a huge mouthful of eggs and then bit into one of the chops.

"You always were heaven's best cook."

Lydia made a good-humored face. "How would you know? You eat so fast you never taste anything!"

It was an old-time argument between them. She ate daintily, taking a long time to finish a meal, while Ivor, used to gulping meals on the run before battles and on the field, bolted his food unless she kept after him.

As they ate, they spoke of the things that make up life. Ivor had retired from the army only six months earlier and still could not believe sometimes that he did not have to get up and see to the needs of five hundred men. When he mentioned this again, Lydia quipped, "Well, if you can take care of five hundred men, you can take care of one wife."

He smiled back. "I can try." He looked around the room. "It's a little lonely with the children married and gone, except for Cathan—and, of course, he's usually gone too."

Seeing the troubled expression on Ivor's face, Lydia replied, "You worry about him, and so do I, but he's all right. He'll find something."

"That's not too easy for a soldier. I wish now he had gone into something like law or business. Can't think what he's to do."

"Perhaps you could get him a commission with another regiment."

Ivor shook his head gloomily, then swallowed some milk from the tumbler. "Not likely. The army's a small world. Everyone in His Majesty's forces knows he was cashiered out."

They had spent long hours worrying about this son of theirs. Their two daughters were married to good men, one a lawyer in Southampton, the other the owner of a large farm on the Scottish border. Their other son, Rees, was doing well with a fine firm in Bristol.

"Why is it that three of our children are doing so well and one is so lost?"

"He's not lost," Lydia said firmly. "He's just slower finding his way than the others."

"He'll have to find something and he's not a steady young man."

"Don't talk that way!"

"Well, he's not! You know how he is. He was always quick to try things and then drop them as soon as he mastered them or got tired of them."

"That was when he was a boy."

"No it wasn't!" Ivor contradicted her. "He's still that way. He was that way in the army. I talked to his officers. He was good at anything he tried, but there was no steadiness in him. I worry about the lad; indeed, I do."

A sound behind them alerted them both and Lydia said, "Hush now! Here he comes!" Then she called, "Good morning! You're up bright and early."

"I smelled the food," Cathan said, clothed simply in wrinkled trousers and an old, too-small shirt that had been his when he was but a boy—it was all he could find to wear. Barefooted, he sat down at the table and grinned sleepily. "You still get up at the crack of dawn, I see."

"Got plenty of breakfast. You must be hungry."

"I am! Didn't eat much on the way back yesterday." In truth Cathan had had no money to buy food. When he left London he had little more than a pound in his pocket after paying his fare on the coach so his stomach had growled all the way. He had gotten in so late that he ate only a meal his mother had thrown together. Now he threw himself zealously into the breakfast.

"Tell us about the Wakefields. Did you have a good visit there?"

"Fine, Mum." He plunged into a description, talking sometimes with his mouth full, waving his fork around. Even with his black hair tousled and his eyes still half closed with fatigue, he still was fine looking—at least so his mother thought. Getting up, she fixed tea, served it to the two men, then poured a cup for herself.

"I hope Honor is becoming as fine a man as his uncle," Ivor said, thinking fondly of the times he and David Wakefield had had together, especially after Ivor's sister, Bethany, had married David. "I always liked David."

"So did I," Lydia said, "and I love the books he writes. It's grand to have a famous author in the family."

"Bethany's been urging us to come and visit them," Ivor continued. "I think we will do that now that I have time."

As the two men talked over tea and Lydia cleaned the dishes, she thought about how different they were. Ivor, with his iron discipline, had been one of the finest officers in His Majesty's forces. Reliable and hardworking, he was unselfish, always thinking first of his family and then of his men. He had been a devoted Christian for as long as she had known him. But Cathan seemed to be living up to the meaning of his name, "battle." Now she wondered if they should have named him something else, like Jonathan, Mark, or some other good Bible name.

After breakfast was over, Ivor took his son out to show him the improvements he had made on the property. He was well aware as he pointed out the fence and the herd of sheep that he was attempting to start that Cathan was not interested, though polite enough to ask a few questions. Finally the two arrived at the stream that bordered one edge of the property. It was only seven or eight feet across in the narrow spots, but at one place it made a crook and filled up a hollow to make a nice pond. Ivor nodded toward it. "A few fish I've caught in there."

"I went fishing at Wakefield," Cathan replied. "Fine pond there. As large as this whole farm, I suppose."

"What is Sir Honor Wakefield like as a marquis?"

"Well, he's a little like you, I would say, Father. Much given to . . . discipline." Cathan almost said *sternness*.

"Of course he would be, him being a captain of a ship. . . . He's never married again. We've all wondered about that."

"It is rather strange. He's a handsome man and he could have married anyone he chose, but he puts his love and attention into his daughter, Shayna. And she lives out the meaning of her Jewish name: "beautiful." She's a very attractive young woman. She had her seventeenth birthday the day I arrived at Wakefield. I got to know her quite well."

Caught by Cathan's tone, Ivor Morgan turned. "You're fond of the lass, are you?"

"Yes, I am."

"You've been fond of young women before."

"I can't deny that. My reputation's in rags, I suppose, where women are concerned."

Cathan said no more about the Wakefields, but late that night after Lydia had gone to bed, father and son sat at the table talking. Ivor understood men very well, but his son less well than he should, although he had tried. Finally he said, "Have you thought about what you'll do now that you're out of the army?" When Cathan hesitated, he continued, "I might be able to find you a place with a regiment. I've got many friends. You'd have to start at the bottom, of course, and you'll have your reputation to live down. But you can overcome it. Men have overcome worse."

Cathan smiled. "Who would have me after being cashiered?"

"I've got a little money put back. We could buy you a commission."

Cathan was touched by the offer, for he understood it was the family's savings that his father would be giving up. "That's like you to offer, Father, but I can't take it." Then he laughed shortly. "I've got a new plan. I'm too old to start in most professions, but

I don't think you'll have to worry about what I'll be doing." He leaned forward. "I'm going to marry a rich wife."

Shocked by this unexpected and cold-blooded statement, Ivor's mouth felt dry. "The young woman—Shayna—you're speaking of her?"

"Yes. She's a sweet girl and she likes me very much."

"What does her father say?"

Suddenly uncertain, Cathan drew back nervously. "Well, I haven't spoken to him, but he loves her very much—and she's got to marry *somebody.*"

"I doubt he'll welcome you. You have no money and no prospects. He'll hope for better things for his daughter. After all, she's the daughter of a marquis. She could marry anybody. Why, there must be a line waiting!"

"I'm not afraid of competition, and as I told you, Father, she loves me. She's very romantic."

It seemed a poor basis for a marriage, that the girl was romantic, and Ivor Morgan knew enough of the Wakefield men to understand that Sir Honor Wakefield would not welcome a bankrupt ex-soldier for his daughter. But he said only, "Well, I'll be happy to meet the girl."

"I will need to borrow a little money from you, Father, just until after the marriage. After that I'll have plenty. I hate to ask, but I have to go back to London and I can't go back like a pauper."

"Of course, Cathan." The two men said no more, but as Ivor lay in bed with his wife that night, he retold the story and ended by saying, "I don't think it's good at all, Lydia."

"Nor do I. It could cause great family problems. We'll just pray for him," she said. "That's all we can do."

Reaching over, Ivor put his arm around his wife and drew her close. "We've prayed for him since he was in your arms the first time. Do you remember?"

"Yes. We prayed that God would use him mightily."

"Is your faith shaken?" he queried anxiously. "We haven't seen that prayer answered."

"We will. God never fails!" Lydia said triumphantly.

⁓⁓⁓⁓⁓⁓

The operating room was crowded, for already the reputation of young Trevor Wakefield was firmly established. The students stood toward the back while several of the hospital's staff physicians stood in a semicircle around the table where the patient lay bound with leather straps, already drugged with laudanum. A bulky man of forty-three, his shaved head gleamed under the gaslights that were mounted in front of large reflectors.

Although he had learned never to show anxiety or uncertainty of any kind, Trevor felt a moment's apprehension. He had done four trephine operations, all successful beyond his teachers' and his own expectations. Now, covered with a white apron, he held up a flat, gleaming piece of metal and said to the students, "This is the plate I will insert. I will ask the metalsmith to make final adjustments on it when we see what we have." He nodded toward a man in working clothes who stood beside an anvil, holding a hammer and watching the surgery activities with interest. "For those of you who have not seen this operation," he continued, holding up a circular saw, "make sure that your trephine is completely sharpened and retempered before each surgery. Now we will begin. I will make my first cut at this point." As he placed his instrument and the steel bit into the man's head, several students grew pale and had to avert their eyes.

"Take this and cut it three centimeters less in diameter. Then expand it three centimeters." Trevor handed the flattened disk over his shoulder to the craftsman who took it. Soon a ringing hammering filled the room.

Trevor somehow had developed the ability to obliterate from

his mind everything in the operating room except the patient and the wound he was tending. Now he raised the piece of skull and peered at the underside with sober triumph. One of the physicians murmured, "You're doing very well, sir," but Trevor did not even hear him. As he fished for splinters with whalebone tongs, a long transverse splinter stirred the depths and the patient muttered, "Don't let me forget my lunch, Molly."

Trevor waited for a moment, then said impatiently, "Let's have the cover! Hurry man!"

"I'm comin', sir. Here it is."

Trevor placed the silver plate on the hole, fastened it down, then restored the patient's scalp to its usual place and sewed it up.

"I congratulate you," Dr. Steinham, a large, heavyset man, said, "on a very delicate maneuver."

"I expect the patient to recover entirely," Trevor said confidently.

As applause burst forth from the students, Steinham raised his voice. "This isn't entertainment, gentlemen! I hope you learned something from Dr. Wakefield's technique."

Pleased by Steinham's praise, Trevor went to wash his hands. He had just finished washing and was going down the hall when Steinham met him. "Come into my office."

"Yes, sir."

The men discussed the surgery for a few minutes; then Steinham leaned back, locked his hands behind his head, and focused on Trevor with shrewd gray eyes. "Something is on your mind these days, Trevor. I can tell. This operation was good, but not as firm as your last one."

Trevor flushed, for he had known this himself but had not thought others had noticed. "You're right, sir. It's strange, isn't it, how little things in a man's mind can come out in his work?"

"What is troubling you, my boy?"

Trevor shook his head. "I don't like to bother you with personal problems."

Steinham had seen Trevor Wakefield's talent from the beginning and was fond of him. "Sometimes it helps to speak of these things. I'll listen if you care to tell me."

"To be truthful, sir, it's not a very original problem."

"A woman?"

Trevor laughed. "You got it the first time. I've fallen very much in love."

"Who is she? Do I know her?"

"Oh no, sir. She's a distant relative of mine. The daughter of Sir Honor Wakefield."

"The sea captain?"

"Indeed. You've heard of him?"

"Oh yes. My brother-in-law served under him. So it's his daughter that you're interested in?"

"Yes, sir. I've known her all of her life."

"But what's the trouble then?" Steinham suddenly smiled. "A little competition?"

"That's it. I have a cousin who's very—dashing. Not at all like me."

"I've seen enough of these "dashing" fellows to know how much they count for. We have a few "dashing" doctors—and they kill about as many as they heal, maybe more. Go on."

They talked for the next fifteen minutes, Trevor grateful at last to share his heart with someone. Finally he spread his hands helplessly. "I don't make much of a show. I'm no dancer and all I can talk about is operations and medicines."

Steinham was quiet for a moment. He knew this young man could be one of the finest doctors who had ever grown up under his tutorship. So he said wisely, "I think you need a vacation, Trevor."

"A vacation, sir?" Trevor asked, startled. "Why, I just got back recently."

"You didn't get the job done. Go back and court this young woman. If you love her, fight for her. There's nothing like a woman to ruin a man," he said, smiling, "or there's nothing like a woman to make him the best that he can be. Go back and throw yourself into it. Cut out this cousin of yours!"

"But as I said, sir, I'm not much on courting."

"Then start and learn. You learned how to do a trephine operation. Now learn how to win a woman. That's an order!"

Trevor Wakefield stared at the older man, a resolve forming within him. "Yes, sir. I will obey your orders at once."

"May the good Lord bless your courtship," Steinham said, slapping Trevor on the shoulder. "You've got a fine career ahead of you. I want to see a good woman standing by your side!"

<hr />

As twilight began to fall over the land, Honor Wakefield stood before the telescope in his observatory. It was one of his favorite hours, when he scanned the heavens picking out the stars he had learned to know as a sailor. "There you are, Arcturus," he murmured. "I would that men were as steady and faithful as you are in your duty." *A man would run out of names, but not God,* he thought, remembering how Scripture said that God named all the stars.

Yet even as he studied the heavens scrolled out before him and the stars that shone like tiny fires against the ebony curtain, he was thinking of other things—mostly of Shayna and her infatuation with Cathan Morgan.

I thought we were rid of him after he went home again. But that very morning, Cathan had returned to Wakefield—to Shayna's delight and Honor's apprehension. So Honor had quickly gone to speak with Bethany and David, who agreed it would be good for Shayna to stay with them while Honor was at sea.

"Keep an eye on her," Honor had told Bethany. "And send for Trevor. Throw them together. I'd like to see something come of that."

Annoyed, he thought of Cathan's arrival speech that morning. "I had business close by and thought I'd drop in to wish you a good voyage, Sir Honor."

His words had not deceived Honor for a moment, for he had seen Shayna's glow at seeing Cathan, and the determination in Cathan's eyes. Having discarded his military uniform, Cathan was now wearing fine new clothes.

Leaving the observatory, Honor started into the house, only to be intercepted in the hall by Cathan, who asked, "May I have a word with you?"

Instantly Honor knew what was in the man's mind. "Come into the library." He led the way and, without sitting down, asked directly, "What is it, Mr. Morgan?"

"I expect you may have guessed, sir. I'm in love with your daughter and would like to ask your permission to marry her."

The two men examined each other almost like duelists across the room. Cathan had prepared himself, for he knew this moment was critical. Shayna had agreed at once when he asked her to marry him, exactly as he had known she would. He had taken her out to the garden and in the midst of the riotous colors he had told her he loved her and wanted to spend his life with her. When he asked her to be his wife, she had thrown herself into his arms and assented—that part had been easy. But Cathan knew from the look in Honor Wakefield's gray blue eyes that this was *not* going to be easy.

"She's very young. I don't think she is ready for marriage at this time."

"With all due respect, sir, she is seventeen and we do love each other greatly. I think she would be devastated, as I would be, if you refused your permission."

Ordinarily Sir Honor Wakefield was cautious with his words. But now he knew there could be no caution. This fellow had come into his house and won his daughter's heart, but he knew deep within his own heart that this was the wrong thing for Shayna.

"I must be frank with you, Morgan," he said. "Your reputation is not good. You have been cashiered from the service, you have no profession—and I assume you have no money. How would you propose to take care of a wife?"

"I do have prospects, sir," Cathan said. This was a lie, and Sir Honor knew this. Nevertheless, Cathan continued, "It's true I was unfortunate with my service, but I am young and strong and, if I may say so, have some talent. And if I set my mind to it, I believe I can be successful."

"Very well. I suggest, Mr. Morgan, that you do so. Go make your way in the world and come back. When you've found your way, we will speak of this matter again."

"But, sir—"

"It would do no good to prolong the argument. Until you have established yourself, I would be a poor father indeed if I did not refuse my permission." He hesitated, then said, "As you say, you have many opportunities. Go prove just one of them and perhaps my answer will be different."

"Sir, I think your answer is not quite just!"

"You cannot care for a wife, that much is true. And I will not keep a son-in-law who has no profession. I will ask you to leave my house and you will be welcomed back when you have proved yourself."

White anger, the temper that had cost him dearly in the past, flared in Cathan Morgan. But with a tremendous effort, he clamped his lips together. "With your permission, I will say good-bye to Shayna."

"Very well, Morgan."

Turning, Cathan left the library and went at once to the drawing room, where he had left Shayna, telling her he was going to ask her father's permission. *I've got to handle it a different way,* he thought. *Shayna will have to turn against her father, but I can't refuse him. She loves him too much for that.*

She came to him, eyes filled with anxiety. "What did Papa say?"

"He said no." As disappointment and hurt leaped into Shayna's eyes, he took her hand. "You mustn't blame him. I have nothing. I am a poor man. He wants you to marry someone rich and influential." Although Honor had not said this, Cathan knew well enough it was true. He also knew those words would not please Shayna, and they did not.

"He doesn't understand! He doesn't know you like I do!"

"That's true, my dear, but such is his answer." He then pulled her in his arms and kissed her, then whispered, "I love you more than all the earth, but I understand your love for your father. You cannot go against him."

"Do you love me, Cathan?" she said softly.

"More than life."

"Then we will find a way." She clung to him, and her body shook as she wept. "We can't be separated! We won't be!"

Pleased, Cathan thought, *If we get married, he'll have to accept me. There may be a rough time for a little while, but he loves her enough and he'll take me for her sake.* Aloud he said, "We'll never be separated! Never!" He pulled away from her, caressing her hands. "I'll be staying at the Lion Inn. Your father has forbidden me the house." He knew this, too, would upset her. "Meet me out by the mound tomorrow night at dusk."

"All right. I will," Shayna said softly. She watched him as he left and then began to tremble. She knew she had to face her father, so she went right to the library.

He stood up as she came in. Seeing she was disturbed, he said without preamble, "I know you're upset, my dear, but I could make no other decision."

"But I love him, Papa!"

"Shayna, you're very young. You don't know men. You must know that next to God I love you more than anything in the world. God has given you to me in trust and I must protect you."

"But I don't need protection!"

The conversation that followed was unpleasant. Shayna was upset; she could not understand why her father would not have Cathan as a son-in-law. He, on the other hand, saw that Shayna was incapable of seeing Cathan for who he really was. Finally, he said, "I'm sorry it's come to this, that we should quarrel. What you need is time. I've arranged for you to stay with David and Bethany while I'm gone."

"You don't trust me!"

"In all truth, I do not," Honor said sadly. "At this time you need good people to help you. You've always loved Bethany and David. Stay with them. Talk with them, Shayna."

"It won't make any difference! I love Cathan and I'll marry him one way or another!"

Sir Honor Wakefield's years of command asserted themselves. "You will not marry him," he said firmly. "I love you and I will not allow you to make this mistake! I will take you to stay with David and Bethany day after tomorrow."

Shayna Wakefield had never asked her father for anything that had not been readily given. Now, however, she saw his set face and discovered, with a start, the iron will that others had seen but that he'd never laid on her. With a sob she ran out of the room and down the hall and threw herself on her bed. It was her first life crisis and she was unprepared. Finally she stood up and wiped her tears away as she determined, "Father's wrong! I love Cathan and he loves me. We'd be miserable apart." Although she was grieved over her and her father's division, Cathan had cast such a spell over her that she could think of no other answer. "I'll marry him and then Father will learn to love him as a son-in-law!"

MOMENT OF VIOLENCE

S hayna had spent two thoroughly miserable weeks at David and Bethany's home. It was not that the two were unkind to her; on the contrary, they showed her more consideration than ever before. Bethany had arranged parties with the young people in the neighborhood, she had ridden to the hounds, and the two had bent over backwards to keep her entertained.

But as Shayna came out of the garden with a basket of flowers that she had just cut, she was aware of a growing discontent. She entered the house and began to arrange the flowers in vases, but her mind was on Cathan Morgan. She thought back to the night they had met secretly after her father had rejected him as a suitor, when Cathan had held her and promised he would love her forever. She had wept.

Her thoughts were interrupted as Bethany entered the room. "Oh, what lovely flowers! They're so beautiful this year!" She picked up one of the snapdragons and admired it.

"They are, aren't they?" Shayna said. She listened as her aunt spoke of the party that was arranged for that evening and finally asked, "Where is Uncle David?"

"He—had some business in the village. He'll be back soon."

Shayna knew her aunt well and the hesitation in Bethany's voice made her curious. "Is anything wrong?"

"Oh no," Bethany assured her, taking the rest of the flowers. "Why don't you get ready and we'll ride over to see the Hendersons today? They have a new mare that Squire Henderson thought you might enjoy riding."

"All right, Aunt Bethany."

As Shayna left, Bethany felt guilty. She knew she could not reveal the business David was on, for he had gone to meet with Cathan Morgan and it was likely to be unpleasant. Cathan had come to the house while Shayna was gone on a visit and David had refused to receive him. He had instead made an engagement to meet him in the village and had left an hour ago. Bethany began to pray, as she always did, for she knew David, mild mannered as he was, would have difficulty dealing with an aggressive young man like Cathan Morgan. *He's as stubborn as all Morgans are,* she thought. *I'm that way myself, but it'll have to be. He can't see Shayna with her father gone after what's happened.*

<hr />

David arrived at the inn early and was directed by the innkeeper to Cathan's room, the second door on the right upstairs. As David stood before the door, he envied his brother, Paul's, ability to handle situations. *I wish I didn't have to do this. I don't think Cathan will take it well. If only Paul were alive, he'd know instantly how to deal with this.* But Paul was gone and there was no recourse, so he knocked.

"How are you, sir?" Cathan said as he opened the door. He shook David's hand.

"I'm very well, and you?" David responded.

"As well as I can be under the circumstances."

"You've been home with your parents. How are they?"

"Settling in. My father's happy in retirement and Mother is glad to have him home."

"I hope to visit them soon and I hope they'll come see us."

"They spoke of that."

Both men knew the talk was merely a screen that shielded them for the moment from the real reason of their meeting. So Cathan plunged in. "I'm glad you came, sir. I've always had confidence in your judgment and my parents think there's no one like you." This was true enough and Cathan was glad to be able to say it, even if his words did embarrass David Wakefield, who was a much more gentle man than Honor Wakefield. "If you would sit down, I would like to tell you my side of the story. I'm sure you heard from Shayna's father."

"Of course we talked," David said hesitantly. "I wish he hadn't had to leave the country at this time, but you understand he had no choice."

"Let me tell you what has happened. Sit down, won't you? Will you have tea?"

"Not just now."

"Very well. Later perhaps." Cathan had prepared his speech well and he began by touching on the matter of his dismissal. "There was no dishonor in my discharge, sir. You may check into that. It wasn't drinking, gambling, or any of those things. Rather it was an altercation I had with a superior officer. I felt he was wrong—I still feel it! He was endangering the lives of the men and when I challenged him, he spoke to me as no officer should speak to another. One thing led to another and I had little chance at the court martial since he was my superior. So I was cashiered for my temper more than a fault of character."

"I'm glad to hear that." As a matter of fact David had already heard this part of the story. Honor had written to a general he knew and had gotten the straight of it. "It's unfortunate," he added, "for a man to lose his profession."

"Indeed it is and I can understand that Sir Wakefield would be apprehensive about a prospective son-in-law with no means of support. All I can say is that I'm young, strong, and reasonably intelligent. I made a success out of my career in the army. I rose more rapidly than any of my juniors and many of my seniors. Those same skills I can put to work in other places."

"Do you have any idea of what those places might be?"

"I think I could go into law, perhaps."

"It takes money to be articled. You would have to apprentice yourself to an attorney and it would take several years."

"I know that, but I'm willing to work hard and Shayna is willing to endure the hardship." Then Cathan played his trump card. "I know Aunt Bethany gave up a lot to marry you. When you lost the title, you had nothing, the same as I have nothing. But she loved you anyway, didn't she?"

"Indeed she did!" David said fervently, his heart going out to the young man. David had never forgotten his own struggle to make a career in writing, nor the way Bethany had stayed at his side during those years.

The two men talked only a short while, for David had little more to say. Before he rose to leave, he said, "I'm sorry I must deny you hospitality, but Sir Honor left strict instructions."

"I understand, Mr. Wakefield. But I feel you do understand me a little." Inwardly Cathan was cheering, for he felt confident that David Wakefield was on his side. "I appreciate any support you can give me—for I do love Shayna dearly."

Although Shayna had been glad to see Trevor, as she always was when he came home from Scotland, their meeting was somewhat of a disaster. Trevor had been amiable enough when he first greeted her and his parents and for a while he was kept busy speaking of his studies and his progress.

But the trouble began as soon as Shayna and Trevor were alone. Trevor had asked her to take a walk with him in the garden and, with some surprise, she agreed. May had come and the flowers were a riot of reds, yellows, and blues. For some time Trevor spoke of how his parents enjoyed their country house. But when they came to the grape arbor that shielded them from the house, he turned to her and said abruptly, "Shayna, I don't know how to say this, but I'm most concerned about you."

Immediately Shayna grew defensive, for intuition told her that Trevor's words had to do with Cathan. "What is it, Trevor?" she said coolly, lifting her chin.

Feeling awkward, Trevor struggled with his words. Although his feelings for her ran deep, he knew she was rather stubborn at times. And now he suspected he was about to intrude on what she considered private ground. "I know I can't say things well, but I'm very concerned about your relationship with Cathan."

"Why should you be interested in that? Have you been hearing things?" Shayna's green eyes flashed and her lips tensed as she stood still, her back straight as a soldier's.

"My parents are concerned and so is your father."

"It's common gossip then. Everyone's talking about me and Cathan."

"Not everyone I'm sure, but your family loves you and—"

"I love Cathan and we're going to be married."

The blunt, defiant statement stunned Trevor. He had not thought the matter had gone this far. As heaviness descended upon him, he shifted his feet. "It's wrong, Shayna. I have nothing against Cathan. Indeed, when we were boys, we were rather close—but he obviously isn't ready for marriage yet."

That was the beginning of the quarrel in which Trevor found himself completely outgunned. While he was not quick with words, Shayna was and she was angry. Although her anger was partially directed at her father, Trevor had no way of knowing that. He stood there miserable and embarrassed as she declared that she loved Cathan, he loved her, and that was all there was to it. When she walked away, he caught up with her. "I should have said this before," he replied, taking her arm and turning her around. As she stared at him defiantly, he said, "I thought, perhaps, it didn't need to be said or that you were too young." He hesitated, then said, "I love you, Shayna, and have for some time."

The words did not catch Shayna completely by surprise. She had known this slow-speaking young man was attracted to her, but she had not realized his feelings ran so deep. She almost said, "Why didn't you tell me?" but she knew this would be useless. Instead, with the problem still struggling in her breast, she spoke again bluntly. "This is no time to speak of that! If you had cared for me, you should have said so. But it's too late now and I ask you not to speak of it again! My mind's made up!"

Then Shayna went to her room, shut the door, and did not come out the rest of the day. Although David and Bethany figured that the talk hadn't gone well, only once did David speak of it. "It's a shame, Son, but we'll hope that it will blow over. These things have a way of burning themselves out quickly."

This was little comfort to Trevor, who considered leaving and going back to Scotland. Instead he went for a long walk and wrestled with the issues, unaware of the beautiful sky or the emerald green of the grassy pathway. Unhappy and uncertain, he finally headed toward home. *I'll have to do something, but I don't know what. She can't marry Cathan!*"

Even as Trevor was speaking to Shayna, she had been aware of the note in her pocket. Delivered secretly to her by a young man from the village, it said, "Meet me tonight after dark. I must see you." Although it was not even signed, she knew Cathan's handwriting.

She did not even struggle with the decision. Instead, she waited impatiently for the sun to go down. It seemed to take forever, and though she went down to dinner to make things look normal, she had almost nothing to say. The other three tried desperately to keep the conversation going, but she excused herself and went to her room, nervous and expectant.

Finally the hour came and she slipped out the back way into the garden, standing breathlessly in the darkness. There was no moon and only a few stars lit the skies. A rustling drew her attention and she whispered, "Cathan?"

Cathan materialized out of the darkness and came to her at once. His teeth gleamed white as he smiled at her. "I had to see you," he said, then kissed her, his lips demanding.

Shayna yielded to him. Then, aware of his impetuous desires, she pushed him back gently, saying, "I can't stay long."

"I know. But this is miserable and we can't go on like this."

"We must! Father's adamant. It will take time."

"He'll never give up because he dislikes me. But there is one way," Cathan said, holding her and stroking her hair. "I love you and I must have you."

"We can't—"

"Listen to me. I've got a carriage waiting. Go inside and get your things. We'll go away together. We'll be married tomorrow." She began to protest, but he said, "Look, sweetheart, once we're married your father will learn to respect me. I'll prove myself to him. I can't live without you and I don't think you can live without me."

Shayna trembled, her mind in a whirl. But as he continued to persuade her, finally she threw her arms around him. "All right, darling. I'll go get my things."

She disappeared into the house, leaving Cathan there in the darkness. What neither of them realized was that Giles Johnson, the gardener, had been out checking his rabbit traps. He had been not ten feet away when Shayna had appeared. He had almost moved, but then it was too late. Hearing everything, his jaw set tightly. He moved stealthily so as not to be heard, entered the house, and went at once upstairs. Knocking at Trevor's door, he waited, and when the door opened and Trevor stared at him with surprise, he said, "Sir, there's trouble going on!"

"What is it, Giles? Predators of some kind?"

"Aye, you might say that. It's Miss Shayna. There's a young man out there. He's come to get her. They're going to run away. I heard him myself."

"Did they see you or hear you?"

"No, but you'd better hurry. She's gone to her room to get her things."

Trevor ran to Shayna's room and knocked. When she opened it, she stared at him almost wildly.

"What do you want, Trevor?"

"You can't do this thing," Trevor spoke at once.

"Stay out of this! It's none of your business!"

"I can't let you do it!"

Shayna, who had her cloak on, did not answer. She reached down and got a small canvas bag, then brushed by him. "I'm leaving!"

She ran down the stairs, with Trevor following. As both emerged out of the door, Shayna called, "Cathan, I'm here!"

Cathan appeared and saw Trevor. Leaning forward, he asked, "What are you doing here, Trevor?"

"I'm here to stop you from doing a wrong thing, Cathan! You can't do this! It's not right!"

"Stay out of it, Trevor!" Shayna insisted.

Cathan took Shayna's arm. "Come along. The carriage is ready."

Trevor grabbed Cathan's arm. "I won't let you do it! You know it's dishonorable!"

Cathan struck out, his fist catching Trevor on the temple. Trevor went down and for a moment the world was nothing but flashing stars. Scrambling to his feet, he stumbled through the darkness. He reached the pair just as Cathan handed Shayna up into the carriage. Filled with anger, Trevor seized Cathan and this time forcefully slung him away.

Without stopping to think, Cathan drew the dagger he always carried. "Get away or you will be hurt, Trevor!"

Shayna began to call out, "Leave him alone, Trevor!"

Trevor, however, knew there were no halfway measures with his cousin. It had always been that way even when they were children since Cathan always could best him physically. Now, with little hope that he would succeed in stopping Cathan, Trevor yelled, "Giles, get your master!"

"Aye!" Giles, who had apparently followed the two, now began to call out, "Mr. David! Mr. David! There's mischief afoot!"

Furious at Trevor for spoiling his plan, Cathan leaped forward and held the dagger up. "Trevor, get away or I'll kill you!"

Trevor threw himself forward, ignoring the knife, and Cathan kept the blade on guard as if it were a sword. He did not really mean to use it, but he felt it enter flesh and then Trevor gasped and fell to the ground. Almost at once the six-foot-two, heavily muscled Giles was there, shouting, "You killed him!" Giles struck out at Cathan, knocking him back against the carriage. When Shayna screamed, Cathan was vaguely aware that she had stumbled out of the carriage. Giles, however, was coming at him with fists flying so he fended him off with the dagger, saying, "Keep away or you're a dead man!"

But Giles pressed forward, taking a dagger slash in his arm as he fought. Finally he caught Cathan in the chest with a mighty blow, knocking him to the ground. As Cathan lay there with his breath knocked out of his body, lights appeared in the house. Giles reached down and wrenched the knife from Cathan's fingers. Panic-stricken, for he did not know whether or not he had killed Trevor, Cathan struggled to his feet. He aimed a solid blow at Giles's mouth, driving him backwards, just as figures ran from the house.

Leaping into the carriage, Cathan picked up the reins and shouted at the horses, who started forward with a tremendous lunge and pounded down the dark road. As the few stars shed their feeble gleam, Cathan Morgan knew despair. All of his plans were over now, for he had wounded and, perhaps, even killed Trevor Wakefield. He cursed, without any idea in his mind about what he would do next.

Six

THE WAY OF THE
TRANSGRESSOR

Cathan sat slumped, his forehead almost touching the gin-soaked table where he had been sitting for almost two hours. The Red Bull Tavern was not known for its delicacy of manners, or its drink either. The liquor was harsh, scraping his throat as it went down to hit his stomach almost like a physical blow. The innkeeper, a burly man with a shock of black hair and a steel hook where his right hand should be, had come over twice, both times demanding payment for the liquor Cathan had been swilling. Cathan had fished up the remains of his money, which consisted of only a few coins. Now his head was swimming and it was difficult to focus his eyes on the innkeeper as he paid for the last bottle.

As he gulped another glass of the potent gin, choking on the fiery liquor and then wiping his eyes from the moisture that sprang there, he tried to think what to do.

A week had passed since he had attempted to elope with Shayna Wakefield. He had fled into the darkness of the night and hidden himself in the worst section of London. As the days passed, he convinced himself that he had not killed Trevor. Such a crime would have been posted, along with a reward for the murderer. Relief had come with this knowledge, but then bitterness at the failure of his master plan. He had already seen himself living at ease as the son-in-law of a rich and powerful man—and now he was a fugitive, for he well knew that charges would probably be brought against him when Sir Honor Wakefield returned from his voyage.

Cathan had spent the money he had and had pawned everything he could get a little cash for. Now he was at the end of his rope. Nothing remained but to slink home and face the accusations in his parents' eyes—even if they did not speak it. For by now, they'd surely heard of the failed elopement.

"Innkeeper, 'nother drink!" he demanded.

The husky innkeeper came over. "Have you got the money to pay for it?"

"Don't worry about it! I'll pay for it!"

The innkeeper shook his head. "No money, no rye!"

Then a voice said, "This one will be on me, Charlie."

The landlord looked around, saw two men sitting at the next table, and scowled. "Don't waste your money," he growled.

"Just give our friend another drink."

Cathan raised his head and blinked, seeing double. "Thanks."

"That's all right, mate. A little down on your luck?"

After Cathan drained the glass, he set it down, shuddering. "That's right," he said, eyeing the two men, who were expensively dressed. One of them was short and fat, with red hair and piggish-looking eyes. The other, seemingly the leader, was tall, with keen black eyes and a clipped black beard.

"My name's Simon," the leader said. "This 'ere's my friend, Bart."

So drunk he could hardly speak, Cathan managed to say, "Glad to meet you. Name's Cathan. Cathan Morgan. But you can call me Cat."

Simon grinned. "Cat. That's a name I go for, mate. Come on over and have another drink."

As Cathan stood up, the room swayed. Bart laughed and said,

"Watch it there! You're liable to fall down and break your skull." As Cathan stumbled and fell into a chair, Bart poured Cathan's glass full, then filled his own glass and that of his companion. "Confusion to the French!" he declared, lifting his glass.

"Confusion!" Cathan muttered, bracing himself against the shock of the alcohol. Then he studied the two, for drunk as he was, he understood they were not treating him out of the generosity of their hearts. He knew they would get to it, so he was not surprised when, after two more drinks, Simon said, "A little shy of cash, I take it?"

"Stone broke."

"I've been there myself many a time, mate. Ain't we, Bart?"

"Right you are," Bart replied. "No sense for a man to stay that way. Not if 'e's clever."

"What have you got on your mind?" Cathan asked, his speech slurred. Although he realized these two had to be up to no good, in his present condition he could think only of an immediate way out of his problems.

"We've got a job on hand. Might be a bit much for the two of us."

"What kind of a job?"

"We're out to liberate some gold and a few jewels," Simon said, lowering his voice. "The way I see it, it ain't right for one man to 'ave so much and some of the rest of us to 'ave so little."

"How do you know I won't turn you in?"

"I don't reckon you'd do that, mate. That way you couldn't 'ave part of the haul," Bart said calmly, pouring himself another drink. "It'll be an easy enough job."

"We've been working on this job a long time," Simon said coolly, but there was cruelty in his dark eyes and twisted lips. "But our mate, 'e got picked up and sent to the hulks. It ain't no two-man job, but three of us could do it neat enough!"

Ordinarily Cathan would have walked away from such a

proposition, but now with his brain fuzzy from alcohol and his future bleak, he knew he could not face going home again a total failure. "Tell me about the job."

"I knew you was a good'un," Simon said, leaning forward. "Now, 'ere's the lay of it. There's this house and we knows the inside of it. We knows where the gold is and it'll be no trick to get it. So two of us goes in, one of us stays outside as a lookout. Soon as we're out with the money, we split three ways. You go your own way with your pocket full of coin."

After more questions and further discussion, Cathan finally responded, "All right, I'm in."

"Good. We'll try to sober you up. Don't drink no more," Simon said.

"I'm as good a man drunk as I am sober," Cathan retorted, waiting for an argument.

But the two merely laughed and said, "Have it your way, but when we go inside you've got to be steady."

"I'll be steady enough."

"Can you use a blade and a pistol?"

"That's my business."

"I sort of thought it were," Simon said slyly. "You got that look about you. We'll have to find you an extra 'orse with no one the wiser. Come on, now. Let's be at it!"

Later that night, the three approached the fortresslike house that loomed high against the dark sky. "Who lives here?" Cathan asked.

"What do you care as long as you get the gold?" Bart hissed.

"They're bound to have some kind of guards, maybe dogs."

"That's all taken care of," Simon said calmly. "We've got the stuff to quiet the dogs down. We've been here three nights in a row. They're lookin' for the meat. Tonight it'll be so drugged they'll drop like they was dead!"

"What about inside?" Cathan queried.

"No guards," Simon whispered, although they were still far enough away that no one could have heard them. "Are you ready with that meat, Bart?"

"Yeah, sure I am."

"Go feed it to the dogs then."

Bart disappeared into the darkness. In fifteen minutes he was back, grinning. "They gobbled it down and was already staggering before I left. They ain't had no meat like that before, you bet!"

"We give 'em fifteen more minutes, then we goes in," Simon said, creeping closer to Cathan. "I want no slipups. No shooting unless we have to. Knives and sword are quieter."

"Ah, you won't need none of 'em. The old man goes to bed early. We got that much out of the gardener," Bart put in.

"Don't worry about me," Cathan said.

The moments ticked off until Simon finally said, "Time to take it. Heads up now."

Stumbling after the two, Cathan had an impulse to turn and run away from this. He well knew what happened to those caught robbing and wanted no part of it, but he was still drunk enough that his natural quick wit was dulled. He followed the two until they came to the edge of a large garden with hedges shaped like animals. It was a ghostly sight, for elephants, camels, and other wild beasts, lit only by the quarter moon, leered at him. He shut his eyes, angry at himself for getting drunk at such a time. "Just let me get out of this," he said under his breath, to no one in particular, "and I'll be out of this country. It'll be Spain for me. Some place where a man can live like a king on a goodly bag of gold."

As they passed the three dogs, Cathan noticed the huge mastiffs were lying on their sides, panting slowly with their eyes shut and chests heaving. "Inside now," Simon insisted. "You come with me, Cat. You stay here, Bart. Come and give the alarm if anybody comes bustin' in."

"Right you are," Bart replied.

Then Simon harshly told Cathan, "Keep your pistol and your blade loose. I don't think we'll need 'em, but that's what you're 'ere for if we have to fight our way out. We're not leaving without that gold if we have to kill everybody in the 'ouse!"

With a start, Cathan realized exactly how rough were his companions and he fervently began to hope no one would interfere with their plans. He followed Simon to a low window that opened at once, being unlocked. Simon stepped inside and then motioned Cathan to throw his leg over the windowsill. Once inside, Cathan swayed, wishing again that he had not drunk so much.

"This way!" As Simon led him out of what apparently was the library and down a hallway, Cathan tried to remember the layout in case he needed a quick retreat. His boots on the stone floor echoed loudly in the silent house. He was perspiring freely and more than once dashed the sweat from his forehead. Sick from all the raw alcohol, he desperately hoped he didn't get the heaves.

Finally Simon halted before a door and put his hand up. It was so dark that Cathan could not see his face, but he felt the man's hand against his chest. "In 'ere," Simon whispered hoarsely. "No noise, mind you!"

Cathan waited while Simon slowly opened the door. Its loud creak seemed like a blast of thunder to Cathan, who started and touched the handle of the sword that hung at his side.

As they slipped through the half-open door into a room that had only a faint glimmer of moonlight, Simon said, "We'll 'ave to do it in the dark."

"Where's the gold?"

"Over 'ere. It's behind a bookcase."

As Cathan's eyes slowly became accustomed to the darkness, Cathan saw the heavy oak bookcase. "It's too 'eavy to move," Simon said, beginning to unload the bookcase. "Good place for a safe, though."

As the men unloaded the books, Cathan dropped one and then another. He was ordinarily sure fingered, but liquor had destroyed his reflexes. Simon cursed, saying, "Clumsy fool! Don't make any more noise!"

So Cathan began to pick them up one at a time. When the books were emptied, Simon hissed, "'Elp me scoot the bookcase over."

Groping in the darkness, Cathan seized one side and Simon the other. They moved it, but it gave a screech as it moved across the bare stone.

"Pick it up!" Simon whispered vehemently. "It's making too much noise!"

But as Cathan picked up his side, his stomach revolted and he vomited. As he stumbled, the bookcase fell over with a resounding crash. He could not stop the vomit that rose to his throat and he lay there gasping and retching.

Afterward he was never able to remember quite what happened. All he knew was that the door opened, a light shone, and the room seemed to be filled with people. He tried to leap to his feet but slipped on his own vomit and went down. He heard Simon shouting, someone cried out, and then as he rose someone struck him on the temple. *Got to get away* was the last thought he had before he slipped into darkness.

❦

Cathan's first confused thought as he came out of the darkness was, *I heard a gunshot, but I didn't fire. It must have been Simon. I didn't even pull the pistol in my belt.*

When he opened his eyes, the room seemed to be moving. But fear came to him when he noticed the steel bars that formed a grate over the high window and then realized he was lying—alone—on the floor of a filthy cell. Looking around wildly, he saw that it contained only a dirty mattress filled with shucks, a table with a bucket, and a chair. His mouth parched and foul tasting, Cathan climbed shakily to his feet. He bent his head, saw that the bucket did contain water, and drank some. Then he scooped out more of it to wash his face. This helped to clear his head a little, so he staggered over to the steel door that had only a peephole. Peering through it, he saw a long corridor and another cell across the way.

Desperate to know his surroundings, Cathan moved the table under the window and climbed on it so he could see outside. He did not recognize the place. He could only see a bare courtyard and a high wall; then from somewhere to his left two armed guards began to walk across the yard. Cathan watched them for a moment, then climbed down from the table to stand in the gloom of the cell.

"What a fool I was!" he said, groaning and holding his head. He leaned against the wall, waiting for the sickness and pain to pass, then sat down on the mattress and tried to think. He must have been there no more than ten minutes when a face appeared in the peephole.

"Well, sleeping beauty's awake!" a rough voice said.

Lurching to his feet, Cathan stumbled across to the door and gasped, "Where is this place?"

"Where is this place!" the guard mocked. "It ain't the Buckingham Palace; you can believe that!"

"Is it the Tower?"

"The Tower? You ain't important enough for the Tower, not unless you got a *sir* before your name. Don't worry, you won't be here long."

"What do you mean by that?"

"I mean you go before the judge within a month. . . . If you got to shoot a man, it ain't smart to shoot a baron."

More fear swept through Cathan. "Is he dead?"

"No, he ain't dead, but he would have been if the medicals hadn't sewed him up. If you had shot another inch or two to the left, he'd a been dead. As it is, I hear he's mad enough to chew nails. Only chance you got is singin' on the chaps that was in it with you."

In despair, Cathan realized that was impossible. He had only two names, which were probably not their real names, and two descriptions. "What will happen?"

"Your best chance is to get sent to prison the rest of your life. Otherwise you might be strung up." Cathan stared at the guard, the words echoing in his aching head. The guard laughed. "Don't make yourself too comfortable," he said and walked away.

Per that prison's stipulations, Cathan was allowed to write one letter. So after a day of hesitation and deep despair, he began to write his father and mother.

⟳⟲

The trial was a joke. His father and mother had come and had hired an advocate with their savings. Even as Cathan stood in the dock, he knew that it was hopeless. There were plenty of witnesses to testify that he had been in the room and, indeed, had remained there, knocked unconscious. When his advocate protested that Cathan had not fired the shot, every one of the baron's servants had sworn that he had held the gun. When Cathan had tried to defend himself, the judge had peered at him and said, "Shut your mouth! Your advocate will speak for you!"

And so, although the barrister had tried to argue and stretch the case out, there had been little he could do.

The jury had not even gone out of the box. They had whispered among themselves and the foreman had stood up and announced, "We find the defendant guilty!"

The judge had wasted no time. "The country would be better off if you were dead, which you would be if Sir Mortimer Wells had been killed. I will therefore show leniency and mercy and sentence you to prison for twenty years. Next case!"

As Cathan stood, listening to the sentence, it was as if a steel door had already clanged shut on his freedom. Twenty years in prison, twenty years of no sunshine, no flowers, no blue skies. It stretched out interminably like doom. As he turned to where his mother and father stood, he saw the pain and grief in their eyes. They came to him, but he stood there stiffly until he was pulled away by the bailiff. As the door slammed, he heard his mother begin to cry. Once back in his cell, he almost wished that the sentence had been hanging. "I can't stand to be shut in!" he cried aloud, struck by an insane desire to bash his head against the stone wall and shatter his brains. Instead he slumped down on the floor, shut his eyes, and hugged his knees as he had done when he was scared as a small boy. Trembling, he saw the future—and knew that what lay ahead was intolerable.

***

Two guards had come for Cathan in the gray dawn. They pulled him to his feet and hustled him out. He had no clothing except that which he had worn on the attempted elopement and an additional warm cloak from his father.

"Where are you taking me?" he demanded.

"It won't be as nice as this!" the guard said, laughing roughly. "You'll be longing for a nice, warm cell like this after you've spent time in the hulks."

"The hulks!" Cathan had heard of the hulks—old ships, not fit for sea duty, that were turned into prison ships. Packed together with rats in the lowest holds of the ship, men lived and died there without ever seeing daylight.

Stripped of hope, Cathan was taken to a closed wagon and thrown inside with three other men. Once the door was shut, it was completely dark. One of the men cursed constantly, but the rest were silent. The ride was long, but finally the wagon stopped and the men were hustled out, the manacles on their hands and feet jangling. As the brightness of the day struck Cathan, he shut his eyes and put his hands up. When he fell headlong because his legs had gone to sleep, he was kicked in the head, then dragged to his feet.

They were at a body of water that had to be the Thames, but evidently it was at the mouth of the channel. A few hundred yards out Cathan saw a ship with its masts removed.

As they traveled by boat to the hulk, somehow the sunshine brought more grief to Cathan than if it had been a miserable, rainy day. *This is what I'll be missing,* he thought, looking up at the blue sky and white clouds.

When they got to the ship, they were driven up a set of stairs that had been fastened to the side. They stood on deck and faced a tall, rawboned man who eyed them coldly. He waited until the guards took the men's chains off and disappeared, then said, "You'll be all right if you cause no trouble. But you try trouble on me and I'll make you know what hell on this earth is like!"

Ten minutes later Cathan had been led down three flights of stairs. He knew that a ship of war normally carried a crew of nearly eight hundred men, but he had heard that hulks carried far more than that. He was right—each deck was packed. And by the dim light that came in through the slots in the side he glimpsed misery.

Finally, at the last deck, which he learned was called the orlop deck, his guard gave him a shove. "No trouble now."

As soon as the guard ascended the ladder, locking the steel door that had no doubt been installed just for a prison ship, a voice said, "Hello, mate. Welcome to the *Courage.*"

Adjusting to the dim light, Cathan Morgan peered in the direction of the voice. He saw a short, muscular man who wore only ragged trousers, cut off at the knees. A patch adorned one eye. "How many did they give you?" the man asked kindly.

"How many what?" Cathan retorted.

"How many years?"

"Twenty!"

A laugh went up, and a coarse voice in the background said, "You won't live more than three or four. Not a dainty thing like you. Ain't he fancy, though?"

"Never you mind them," the first man continued. "My name's Praise God Barebones."

"Your name is what?" Cathan asked, confused and sick at heart.

The man's eye winked in a show of cheerfulness as he explained, "Praise God, that's what they call me. My old man was a Methody preacher, you see. One of John Wesley's men. What do they call you?"

"They call me Cat."

"Cat? That's a funny one."

Cathan stood in the foul hole, overwhelmed with the heat of June and the stench. The air was almost unbreathable. As he glanced around, uncertain what to do next, Praise God said, "Come over. You can have a place by me. We'll get you a mattress and a blanket. You got any money?"

"I did have." Cathan had sense enough not to say anything about the money his father had given him. It was tied to his leg under layers of bandages. He did not know whether to trust the man or not.

Praise God looked him over, then whispered, "You'll learn to trust me."

Cathan followed Praise God as he stepped over the men who

were sitting up and talking in small groups. When they reached the side, Praise God said, "Grub will be comin' pretty soon. I'll show you the ropes. Man needs a friend in a place like this. He needs the good Lord too."

"Don't talk to me about God!" Cathan said, his voice lethal. "I can't believe in a God of love!" Then, staring around at his new world, he made a quiet vow: "I'll never have anything to do with God!"

The

1 8 0 0   Part ── TWO   1 8 0 1

Dauntless

Seven

A Pair of Miracles

The grass was so green that it almost hurt the eyes to look upon it. As Cathan Morgan stood barefoot on its tender blades, he inhaled the intoxicating morning air, feeling it tingle all the way down to his fingertips. Then, out of sheer exultation at the beautiful day, he began to run. The warm breeze whipped through his black hair as his heart began to pound with the exercise.

Overhead the azure sky was ornamented with clouds that moved across the arch of the horizon like obedient sheep. As Cathan ran, he absorbed the smells, the sounds, and the colors that lay around him. Never had he felt such joy!

"Come on, boy, you can do better than that!" Cathan cried to the huge red hound with floppy ears who loped easily beside him, barking or uttering a contented growl from time to time.

With a burst of speed the hound took off, disappearing over a small rise covered with red, purple, and white wildflowers.

"Come back, Bob!" Cathan called, beginning to gasp, his chest suddenly on fire with the lack of oxygen. Then he felt himself falling as the blue sky turned a leprous gray and the green grass shriveled to a crisp brown under his feet.

"Bob! Come back, Bob!" he whispered, his voice raspy. "Don't leave me—"

When Cathan opened his eyes, for an instant he couldn't reconcile the gloomy space that surrounded him with the beauty that had fled so abruptly. Then the shapes, odors, and noise of the prison rushed back in on him.

The dream had been so real, especially since he had not seen the open sky or a blade of grass for the seven months he'd been on the *Courage*. Indeed he had not seen the dog, Bob, since he was a child, for Bob had long been buried.

As the stench of unwashed bodies and open buckets filled with waste assaulted his nostrils, he gagged. He thought he had gotten used to it months ago, but now it was as if he had come in from a summer field to this hell afloat that was called a hulk. Closing his eyes as a spasm of coughing wracked him, he felt pain in his chest. When a hand touched his brow, he flinched and opened his eyes.

"Lie easy, Cat."

Looking into the gloom, Cathan saw the familiar features of Praise God Barebones. He was wearing a rag tied around his forehead to hold his graying hair back. His body was emaciated, but so was every other man's in the hulk.

"Praise, I had a dream." Cathan had to gasp the words out. He was muffled up in greasy black pants and his feet were wrapped with rags, but he was still blue with cold. His heavy cloak, patched many times, was tucked closely around him.

Praise God leaned over, smiled, and said, "Lie easy, Brother. You'll weather this lee shore yet."

Having spent so many months with Praise God Barebones, Cathan had come to understand the man's language, which was tinged with expressions taken from his life aboard a man-of-war in the Royal Navy. A lee shore was a danger to mariners, for vessels carried ashore by the wind often crashed on the rocks. Now Cathan blinked his eyes and licked his dry lips. He shivered and at the same time felt himself raging with fever. He had seen it before, for few days or weeks passed without one of their number being hauled upward—dead from the gaol fever. He had never thought he could become so accustomed to death. In the army he had seen death—indeed, at close range—but never for an extended period of time. Here death was a daily companion that wandered through the bowels of the ship, a gray specter that stopped to peer at its victims from time to time. Cathan had had dreams of such a one and now thought he saw him standing just beyond Praise God's shoulder.

He tried to speak, but his lungs were so filled that he could not. He coughed and spat up a nauseous mix. Since he could not even raise his head, the spittle ran down his cheeks. As Praise wiped it off gently, Cathan managed to croak, "He's got me this time—Old Man Death."

"Never you think of it. God's not through with you yet, laddie," Praise said gently.

For the first time since he was a child, Cathan Morgan felt his eyes fill with tears. In the first few months when he had come into the hulk, he had been hard, had cursed his fate, and had wanted no friendship with any man. Nor had he found it, except for Praise God Darebones. The ex-sailor simply refused to be put off and had said on more than one occasion, "Every man needs a friend. Two are better than one, Cat, for if one falls down alone, who will lift him up?" Now Praise dipped a tattered rag into a bucket of icy cold water and began to bathe Cathan. "We're goin' to weather this together. Never you fear."

Ordinarily Cathan would have been mortified by the tears running down his cheeks. He had always been a proud young man, but life in the hulks was enough to break the pride of the sternest and strongest. Since there was no sun to mark the beginning or ending of each day, time had passed so slowly and tediously the first month that he had grown afraid he would lose his mind. He had raged at God, at Praise, at his captors, so that he won no prizes for being a good prisoner. It did not matter, however, for even good behavior would have won him no merit with his cruel jailers. Most of them were little more than criminals themselves and robbed their starving charges whenever possible.

Inside it was cold, but outside Cathan could hear the bitter wind howling like a wolf, rising in intensity and clawing at the gun ports. Praise had told him that, while at sea, this lower deck had been filled with cannons and hundreds of men sleeping on hammocks. "It's not so bad belowdecks when all the gun ports are open," Praise had said. "The fresh air and God's good sunlight come in."

But on a hulk ship, the gun ports were screwed tight, never to be opened again. Everything that came in—food, clothing, medicine—had to come from above, down a dark and murky ladder way. And everything that went up—the waste, the prisoners who finally served their sentence, or the corpses who did not live to do so—had to go up the same way.

Cathan lay there a long time, his mind coming and going with fever. When he was awake, he was aware of the misery around him: the sounds of coughing, listless conversations, pitiful cries, fiery curses, or the angry yell of a guard. Sometimes a fight would break out, although most of the prisoners were too weak to waste their strength on such activities. Whenever he looked down the long line in the murky light cast by a few glassed-in candles, it was like a scene out of Dante's *Inferno*. Men huddled together for warmth, their faces pale and eyes sunken.

After that, Cathan did not know how long he had the fever, but one thing seemed constant: Praise's voice reading from the portion of the Bible that he possessed. Whenever Praise could see by the light of a feeble candle, he would read from the book of John, Acts, or one of the Epistles. It was not really that Praise needed the light, for Cathan had long ago learned that the seaman had memorized what Scripture he had, including the entire New Testament. As time passed and Praise read verses such as, "For the Father loveth the Son, and sheweth him all things that himself doeth: and he will shew him greater works than these, that ye may marvel," the words sank into Cathan's soul.

Then one day as Cathan drifted between reality and a comalike state, he had whispered to Praise, "Grandfather, read some more." In his weakened, confused condition, it was as if his evangelist grandfather, Gareth Morgan, were reading. Some of Cathan's earliest memories were of lying beside his grandfather on a large bed and listening to him as he read the Old Testament stories of David defeating Goliath and Jonah being belched up by a whale. They had thrilled him and had sunk into his mind and being. Now they comforted his soul.

Praise had looked down with surprise. Seeing the glittering feverish eyes, he knew the young man was close to death. He carefully wrapped the section of Bible into a piece of worn oilskin to protect it, concealed it in a wooden box that he had managed to obtain, and said to a large man who sat with his back against the bulkhead, "I think we'd better get him up to the doctor, Jim."

The big man stirred. "It won't do no good, mate. You know that Doc Graves is nothin' but a drunk and cares for nothin' but himself."

Praise and Jim Starnes had become good friends, Praise having led the big man to the Lord nearly a year earlier. Although he knew Jim was right, Praise said urgently, "We got to try!"

"All right," Starnes said.

It was a herculean struggle. First they had to convince the armed guard at the doorway that Cathan was sick enough to go to the doctor. That had to be *very* sick, but finally they convinced him, or rather bribed him with the promise of tobacco that Starnes had but no longer used. The two staggered up the ladderlike steps two decks with Cathan and then down the hallway to the doctor's quarters. When they entered, they found, as expected, that Dr. Graves was drunk. Wearing a travesty of a uniform, he was sprawled in a chair, his enormous bulk overflowing it. In a slurred voice, he said, "What's this? No more patients!"

"Dr. Graves, I think he's dyin'," Praise said.

Graves scowled and reached over to pick up a bottle. He did not bother to pour it into a glass but simply tilted it up, letting the liquid run down his throat. Wiping his mouth with his filthy sleeve, he lurched over to where the two had laid Cathan down. Graves felt his pulse, then pulled his eyelids up and stared into the whites. Stepping back, he said, "He won't see Christmas. He's a dead man."

"Can't you do somethin' for him?" Praise pleaded. "If he had some blankets and could stay in the hospital here—"

"There ain't no room in the hospital, Barebones! Get him out of here!"

However, after some argument Praise was able to convince the doctor that he would somehow pay for the space. "Put him down there," Graves said. "You'll have to move a corpse out of the bed first."

Jim and Praise struggled with their burden, for any physical effort was difficult for them or any of the prisoners because they got so little nourishing food. Panting with the effort, they finally got Morgan into the bunk.

As Praise drew up a blanket over the wasted form of his friend, Cathan suddenly opened his eyes. "The hospital," he whispered, his reason momentarily returning. "It won't do any good, Praise. I'm going to die."

"Now, don't you be talkin' like that, lad," Praise said, putting all the encouragement he could in his voice. "You're going to be a well man. But you've got to give your heart to the good Lord Jesus, Cat. Will you do it now?"

"No, I won't," Cat insisted weakly.

Praise and Jim exchanged hopeless glances. They both had prayed for this young man for months and now Jim whispered, "He's going to meet God and he ain't saved. He'll go right straight to hell."

"No, he won't. God's given me a promise," Barebones said, eyes determined. "We'll just have to pray him through. It ain't never too late if a man will only look to Jesus."

<hr />

Time ceased to exist for Cathan Morgan as he drifted in and out of consciousness. He was aware of voices around him, then was in a hole so deep that no noise penetrated. When he would pass almost beyond all human help, somehow, almost as if the voice and hands of Praise God Barebones were keeping him alive, reason would return.

The strongest thing in his poor, battered consciousness was Praise's voice, singing the old songs of Zion. One in particular reminded him of his boyhood, for both his grandfather and father had loved the song and had sung it well.

Now as he surfaced from the dark pit of his own mind, the words of the song sank into him almost like stones falling into deep water:

There is a fountain filled with blood,
Drawn from Emmanuel's veins;
And sinners, plunged beneath that flood,
Lose all their guilty stains.

The dying thief rejoiced to see
That fountain in his day;
And there may I, though vile as he,
Wash all my sins away.

Dear dying Lamb, thy precious blood
Shall never lose its power,
Till all the ransomed church of God
Be saved, to sin no more.

As the song went on, Cathan's mind wandered. Sometimes he felt that he had already died and that the darkness surrounding him was the blackness of the pit itself. He lost awareness of the hulk, of Praise God, who had been hovering over him, and finally, with a startling clarity, he heard the voice of his beloved grandfather Gareth Morgan. Cathan remembered when, as a twelve-year-old, he had accompanied his grandfather to a chapel not far from his home. And now he seemed to see his grandfather, holding his arms out and pleading with the congregation. Then, by some miracle of memory, his grandfather's words about the dying thief floated back to him:

See that thief hanging upon the cross. Behold the fiends at the foot with their open mouths, charming themselves with the sweet thought that another soul shall give them meat in hell. Behold the death bird, fluttering his wings over the poor wretch's head. Vengeance passes by and stamps him for her own as "a condemned sinner." On his brow is the agony of upcoming death. Look in his heart: It is filthy with the crust of years of sin and the smoke of lust hangs within.

Look at him. He is dying. One foot seems to be in hell; the other hangs tottering in life—only kept by a nail. But there is a power in Jesus' eye. That thief looks; he whispers, "Lord, remember me." And what happens to that thief? Where is the hard anguish? It is not there. Instead there is a smile upon his lips. The fiends of hell, where are they? There are none, but a bright seraph is present with his wings outstretched, his hands ready to snatch that soul,

now a precious jewel, and bear it aloft to the palace of the
great King. Look at his breast, now white with purity, and
see not the word *condemned* but *justified*. Look in the
Book of Life, where his name is already engraved. That is
the power of Jesus, and that power shall endure forever.
He who saved the thief can save the worst man who ever
lived, for his powerful name shall endure forever.

As the voice faded away, Cathan realized he was totally conscious—indeed more conscious than he had ever been in his life. The
vision of his grandfather had been keen. His heart crushed with grief,
Cathan realized what a godless life he had led. And yet, in spite of this,
he kept hearing the phrase *The name of Jesus shall live forever!*

For a long time he lay there thinking of his sins, of his parents,
who had wept over him, and of his grandparents, especially his
Grandfather Gareth, who had enfolded him in his arms once when
he had been but a child and said, "One day, my boy, you will belong
to the Lord Jesus." That vision came so sharply that Cathan knew
these dormant memories had risen at the behest of God. In that
dank prison of the *Courage,* God suddenly had become more real
to Cathan than he ever had been in Cathan's days of freedom.

Cathan had not prayed since he had grown to full manhood,
so the words of sorrow came haltingly to his lips. "Oh, God, it's
too late for me, perhaps. But the dying thief took one look at Jesus
and that, Lord, is all I know to do." As the fever burned his body,
Cathan had a sense that someone had entered the hole of the
hulk. He saw no lights; he heard nothing except the groans of his
fellow prisoners, but somehow he knew he was in the presence
of God. "Jesus," Cathan said, "I want to know you—even if it's
only for one hour before I die. Forgive my sins and trespasses,
O Lord, for they are blacker than hell itself. I look to you, Lord
Jesus, and to your blood on the cross and I can do nothing else
except cry out to you for mercy."

Praise awakened suddenly from a sound sleep and rolled over on the hard boards next to Cathan, stretching his shoulders. He straightened up, then turned to look at his friend. Praise was surprised to see that Cathan's eyes were open and that he regarded Praise with a peculiar expression.

"How is it with you, Cat?" Praise asked, leaning over to touch the young man's face. Astonished, he shook his head in wonder. "Your fever—Praise God, your fever's gone, my boy!"

Cathan looked up at the kind older man and smiled, then said slowly, "Something has happened, Praise. I have met the Lord. He has saved my soul."

Praise gave a cry of joy and Jim Starnes, who was sleeping next to him on the hospital floor, awoke with a start. When he saw the smile and the tears running down Praise God Barebones's face, Jim cried, "Glory to God! Glory to God!" He jumped to his feet and asked Cathan, "And have you found the Lord Jesus?"

"Yes, Jim," Cathan said in wonder. "He came to me and took all my sins away."

Praise God and Jim Starnes got up, joined hands, and awkwardly danced around the deck, then knelt over Cathan Morgan. Tears ran down all three faces. Finally it was Praise God Barebones who managed to say in a choking tone, "Today is Christmas, Cathan—and God has done two miracles! He's healed your body and saved your soul! Blessed be his holy name forever!"

"Amen," Cathan whispered, marveling at what had happened. "This peace I feel—does it last? Will it go away, Praise?"

"No, it's forever," Praise God responded, impulsively throwing his arms around his young friend. Then with a broken voice, Praise continued, "You've come home, Cathan Morgan—home where God lives and you'll never leave there!"

TREVOR GETS
AN OFFER

As Trevor Wakefield rode the chestnut mare down the lane toward his destination, he felt a sense of freedom.

"It's good to be here, out of Scotland and in England again." His words came involuntarily and he smiled at his habit of speaking aloud. "Someday someone will hear me," he muttered, nudging the mare to a faster gait, "and have me locked up in Bedlam." The mare twitched her ears, broke into a gallop and Trevor, who was much better at setting a broken limb than at riding, held on.

As the mare crested a rise, Trevor pulled awkwardly on the bridle and the mare came to a shuddering stop. She sidled to one side trying to pull the lines from his hands and he firmly pulled them back, saying, "You're the most impudent and rebellious female I've ever seen, Rosie." Finally he got the mare still and looked down into the valley where Wakefield Manor lay. Although Trevor was not the marquis, still he was of Wakefield blood and knew that this place had roots that went far back into history. Now he soaked up the scene, his mind going back over the long period he had spent in Scotland training as a physician. He had learned much and had made some friends, but he was glad to be home. The new century had begun clicking off the months, and it was now May—almost a full year after he'd been injured in Cathan and Shayna's attempted elopement.

"Let's go, girl," he said and the mare began taking the downhill road that led past the outlying fields surrounding the manor. As they came closer to Wakefield Manor, he thought of how unhappy the conclusion of his training had been because he had been unable to put Shayna out of his mind. He had seen her only twice since Cathan's imprisonment and both times had been brief, unsatisfying encounters. She had seemed different to him, more subdued. She had lost some of the lightness and vivaciousness he had always admired.

I should have pressed my case, he thought. *But I still don't know how she feels about Cathan! I hope she's got the scoundrel out of her mind by now.* It was not a very firm hope, yet Trevor clung to it. In the many letters he had written her from Edinburgh, he had hinted that she might like to confide in him about her feelings for him—and for Cathan. She had answered his notes briefly and impersonally, as if out of duty, and she did not mention Cathan at all.

"Hello, Master Trevor! Or is it Dr. Trevor now?"

Trevor pulled up the mare and stepped down from the saddle as Michael Devon came running to take the reins. When she tried to jerk away, he held her with a practiced hand. "Well now, sir," Michael said smiling, "it's good to see you back at Wakefield. And how is your good family?"

"Very well, Michael. I saw my grandfather. He told me to be sure and give you his best regards."

Michael's face showed great pleasure. "And how is the good man doing?"

"Still hearty at eighty-four. I wish I may have his strength when I am that age."

"Ah, the good Lord does it for him! I'll never forget it was Rev. Gareth Morgan that first led me to know the Lord Jesus. I was a sinner in the very pits of hell and I well remember how that man preached the glories of the cross. It went through my heart like an arrow, it did! Ah, many years ago, but still fresh as if it were yesterday."

"He's a fine minister. I'll be seeing him soon, so I'll give him your blessings."

"Do that. And if he can come by and preach, there's a few working here now that could use a burning gospel sermon."

"I'll put that in his ear. I'm sure he'd love to see you again. Is Sir Honor at home?"

"That he is. Let me take the mare and you go right in."

Leaving Michael, who slapped the mare on the jaw as a way of showing he was not to be tampered with, Trevor walked up the steps that led to the stately house. His knock at the door echoed loudly.

"Hello, Mary," he said, when it opened. "Is your master in?"

"Yes, sir! You wait in the drawing room and I'll fetch him for you, Doctor."

Trevor followed the maid down the hallway. Turning to his left, he stepped inside the room and walked over to the pianoforte. Sitting down, he picked out a melody on it, remembering with sorrow that it was a song he and Shayna had practiced together on his visits before Cathan had entered the picture. He was a better-than-average musician and she had a splendid soprano voice. He had enjoyed playing the evenings she sang and now he missed them.

"Well, Trevor, my boy, I'm glad to see you," a voice said, interrupting his reverie. Sir Honor Wakefield came into the room swiftly, a smile on his face.

"I'm happy to see you, Sir Honor."

"Mary, bring tea. India for me and China for my guest. Am I right?"

"Exactly right."

"Sit down. I want to hear about your latest triumphs at the university and the hospital," Honor said.

"I didn't bring home many medals."

"Now, now, I want no false modesty. I have a letter from Dr. Steinham. As a matter of fact, I wrote to him, checking up on you."

"Well, you couldn't have picked a better one to ask. That man has been a godsend to me. I don't think I could have made it if it weren't for him."

"He says you're going to be one of the finest physicians and surgeons in England. Gratifying, indeed, very gratifying! Your parents must be very proud."

"Yes, sir, they seem to be."

"What now? Ready to begin a rich practice in London?"

Trevor hesitated. That was exactly his plan until recently, when he had begun to feel restless. He had spoken to no one about his immediate future, except to tell his parents that he had had one offer to join an eminent physician as an assistant. "I'm . . . not quite certain," he said.

The faltering reply caught Honor Wakefield's attention. Although he said no more about it as the maid brought the tea in, he filed Trevor's hesitation in his mind. Finally, Honor shot a question at his guest. "Has Shayna written you lately?"

"Her replies have been irregular." Trevor shifted uneasily, then touched the cleft in his chin—a sign of nervousness that Honor had come to recognize. "I've written her many times, but I haven't been able to say what I've wanted to say."

"I'm worried about her, Trevor."

"Are you?" Trevor looked up quickly. "She's not ill, is she?"

"Oh no, not physically! It might be better if she were."

"Surely it's not mental," Trevor said with some surprise.

"More emotional I would say. She hasn't been the same since that dreadful affair with Cathan Morgan." Honor's brow clouded over with anger. "I wish the fellow had never come here! He turned her whole world upside down."

Trevor had expected something like this, but he was a little shocked at the severity of Shayna's condition. He knew that Honor Wakefield was not a man to overstate or exaggerate, so he asked, "How is she different?"

"She's moody, Trevor, and she never was before. She's always been like a bird, flitting around cheerfully, singing. But the house has been quiet since all that happened." Then Honor continued, "She makes no new friends and doesn't go out much. I've tried to take her to London and she goes reluctantly. You know she's never been like that before."

"She hasn't spoken of Cathan?"

"Not a word, and to be truthful, I haven't known whether to mention it or not." He cocked his head to the side. "Perhaps she'll talk to you. You two were always great friends—and you would like to be more, of course."

"Yes, I would. I love Shayna and would like to marry her, but I'm a rather dull fellow. No dash at all."

Honor Wakefield leaped out of his chair impulsively, as he sometimes did when something moved or disturbed him, and said, "We've had enough dashing fellows, Trevor. That's where it all started."

"Do you think she really loved him?"

"I don't think she really knows what love is. She's got her head so stuffed full of notions that she's confused. But now that you're here it will be better. Time will improve things, I'm sure." Honor clenched his fists, then let them fall at his side. "I don't know whether she really loved him or not," he said heavily, "but I hope, for her sake, that she didn't. She's got to get over this thing—there's no other way!"

⌐⌐⌐

Shayna brushed her hair listlessly. She had always taken great pride in her hair, but now she looked in the mirror with indifference. Then, tossing the brush down, she walked over to the desk, sat down, and began to write. She had begun a letter to Trevor three

97

days earlier and had thrown away several drafts. Now she began again, wrote several lines, then tossed the quill down and again crumpled the sheet in her hands. Throwing it on the floor, she sat there in silence until a knock came. Lucy, her maid, stepped inside, her eyes sparkling. "Miss Shayna, you have a caller."

"Who is it, Lucy?"

"It's Mr. Trevor. He's just come and he's asking for you."

With a wave of distaste, Shayna looked at the wadded-up ball of paper and knew that if she could not say what she wanted in a letter, she would have little success face-to-face with Trevor. So she said, "All right. I'll be right down."

"Let me fix your hair—"

"No, it's fine."

"Well, put on that new dress we bought in London. The green one that matches your eyes."

"This dress will do."

As Shayna swept out of the room, Lucy stood there, a dissatisfied expression in her eyes. "Well, la-di-da. What a change this is. I've seen the time when you spent half a day changing dresses and driving me crazy about your hair, and now this!" Spotting the wadded paper, she glanced toward the door, then picked up the paper. Smoothing it out, she ran her eyes across the lines and shook her head. "It's a fool you are, turning away from a fine man like Mr. Trevor Wakefield!" Deep in thought, Lucy stood there for a moment. "She'll have to get that no-account jailbird out of her mind! He was not for her and she was too foolish to see it!"

Meanwhile, Shayna had descended the stairs and entered the study, where her father and Trevor were drinking tea.

Both rose and Trevor came toward her, smiling. "Shayna, it's good to see you."

"It's good to see you, too, Trevor," she said, without expression. "Did you just get in?"

"Yes, last Thursday. I spent some time with my parents. My grandfather was there. It was good to see them all again."

"Sit down and have tea, Daughter."

Obeying her father's request, Shayna sat down and steeled herself for what she feared might be an ordeal. She had never been able, since Cathan's arrest, to identify what was going on in her own heart. She had wept herself to sleep for days and lost weight, for she had lost her appetite as well. As the months passed, she had gained the weight back and was now looking physically as well as ever. But she still thought of Cathan Morgan every day. She remembered the pressure of his arms around her and the touch of his lips on hers. But she also had come to understand that Cathan had used her badly—that he had been after her for her money and position. Though she had never admitted it to anyone, she had grown ashamed of her behavior. Now as she looked at Trevor, she realized she still held rancor toward him for the part he had played in Cathan's arrest. She had never voiced this to anyone, knowing that it was unfair, and yet she could not help it.

Trevor's voice broke into her thoughts. "I'm all through with my medical studies now."

"Congratulations," Honor said jovially. "I'll have to call you Dr. Wakefield now!"

Trevor laughed lightly. "I don't think that will be necessary. Let me get a little bit of experience first and be sure that I don't kill more than I cure."

As Trevor related his experiences at the hospital over the past months, Honor searched his daughter's face for some clue as to how she felt about the man. *I believe she's resentful of Trevor and of me,* he finally realized. *If she had been a boy, I could have talked to her. But what man can talk to a young girl about love? It's hopeless.*

Finally Trevor said to Shayna, "I'd like to see what you've been doing in your garden."

"Yes," Honor said quickly, "show him that new breed of rose you've been so proud of."

"A new breed of rose? What's that about?"

"Oh, I have been experimenting a little. It's nothing much." Although Shayna usually loved gardening, this spring she had paid less attention to it than ever before in her life. But she said kindly, "If you'd like to see it, I'll show you."

The two left Honor in the drawing room and soon were out in the rose garden. It was a large area adjoining the house, decorated with statuary and a high hedge. "Why, this is beautiful! It always is!" Trevor inhaled the fragrance around him. "The best smell of anything I've ever encountered."

"They do smell nice, don't they?" Shayna led the way to a single plant and touched one of the large blossoms. "This is the one the gardener and I have been working on." The flower she indicated was a large rose, primarily yellow but with a slight orange tint. "I'd like someday to breed an all-orange rose."

"I've never seen one of those. Is there such a thing?"

"No, but there will be." Shayna smiled and turned to him. "The gardener is really the head of this project. He just lets me pretend that I know what I'm talking about."

"It's very beautiful. Think what a dozen of these would look like all together."

"I think they would be like the evening sunset—mostly orange but with glints of crimson and yellow."

They talked for some time about the garden, then sat down on a bench and chatted about mutual friends. Trevor tried to get her to speak of Cathan, but she was reticent. Because he loved this girl with all his heart, it pained him that there was little he could do to break through her reserve.

Finally, almost in desperation, Trevor cleared his throat. "Have you thought much about what happened—with Cathan, I mean?"

Shayna reacted quickly, as if he had touched a sore spot. "I have heard from his mother several times, never from him."

"It was unfortunate. I pity the fellow." This was not exactly true, but Trevor felt he had to say something. He had been filled with a fury that he had not known himself capable of when he discovered what his cousin had tried to do. Ever since, he had been convinced that Cathan was nothing but a fortune hunter and would have brought ruin to Shayna's life, not to speak of his own. Now he said, "I wish you could forget him, Shayna."

"Forget him? How can I do that?"

Her words were so sharp that Trevor blinked. "Well, after all, he's out of your life."

Shayna did not reply. She thought of how eagerly she had received Cathan's mother's letters and more than once had written back to her. There was little she could say except to express her sorrow for the whole affair. She felt somewhat guilty, but she could not fathom why. More than once she had said to herself, *If Trevor and Father hadn't interfered, I'd be married to Cathan now and we'd be happy.* It was a struggle for her to put this resentment aside. No matter how much she tried to bury it with both men, she was always conscious of it.

Rising, Shayna switched the subject. "You'll be practicing in London, I suppose."

"It's what I had planned, but now I'm not certain." As he took her hand and held it, she looked at him, startled, for he was not a man given to sudden gestures. "I'm sorry about what happened. Really I am. I only want the best for you. We've been friends a long time."

Then Shayna knew that being a good friend was not what was on Trevor Wakefield's mind. She knew that he loved her, wanted to marry her, and would be a faithful husband in every way. Still, even as she thought of this, she saw Cathan's face, black hair, and rash grin. She thought of him being in a dank prison, unshaven.

101

So with a coldness she could not help, she said, "I must go in now."

Trevor sighed and followed her inside, his heart heavy, wondering what it would take to change the things that stood between them.

The sun had risen like a huge crimson wafer over the moors, throwing its ruddy beams on the faces of the two men who walked ten feet apart across the broken ground. A speckled spaniel ranged to and fro, head down, all morning while Sir Honor Wakefield called out, "Find those birds, Toby. You can do it!"

"That's a fine dog, sir," Trevor said. He held the fowling piece awkwardly, for he had spent little time hunting. He had come at Sir Honor's invitation, more from a desire to spend time with his host than to kill game. Now, as the two men trudged homeward, Honor spoke of making Wakefield into a profitable farming organization.

"You seem to know every field and every tree," Trevor said with admiration. "I don't see how you do it—being gone as much as you are aboard ship."

"I love this place," Honor admitted. "My father and mother loved it too."

"Do you ever think about the days when you were growing up in America with the Indians?"

"Very often. It was a simple life, Trevor. That was the best thing about it. You got food to eat for the day, you worked, you slept at night. A young man would find a woman and they would marry and have children. There were hard times as well—death, disease, and no cures, but it was not a bad life."

"There's a lot to be said for simplicity. It's a rare commodity in our world, isn't it?"

"Indeed it is. It's a little bit simpler at sea—especially for the captain," Honor said, grinning.

"I suppose so. That's probably the closest thing to an absolute monarchy we have left."

"You know, you're right about that," Honor replied. "I've often thought of it."

"What about this new command of yours? What sort of ship is she?" Trevor queried.

"The *Dauntless*. She's getting a little old for one thing. Twenty-five years is old for a frigate. You have no idea, Trevor, how the sea—the tides and winds—wracks a ship. Then in battle an eighteen-pound ball comes crashing through and breaks into the hull. Well, the *Dauntless* has had a bad history."

"How is that, sir?"

"Her crew was involved with the mutiny of the *Noir.*"

"At Spitshead, where the sailors mutinied for better conditions?"

"Exactly. If that had happened in Antigua or outside England, I think every man would have been hanged. But I sympathize with the lower decks. A seaman's life is hard. Poor pay, and even that's withheld from him for six months, lest he run away. And they stay at sea for years with terrible food and a chance to become crippled or get their head blown off. So I'm not totally out of sympathy with the mutiny. It wasn't like they were at sea. We couldn't have stood for it there, of course."

"And you have the same crew? That sounds dangerous."

"Well, I have a few good men from other commands. I'll just have to take the crew as it is," Honor said, then stopped walking. With his eyes fixed on Trevor, he said, "I have a proposition for you."

"A proposition?"

"I wish you would come with me on this voyage as my surgeon."

"Me, sir? I'm no sailor."

"That won't be difficult. I can get you qualified before I sail."
He hastened to say, "There's not much money, of course—nothing like what you would make in a regular practice. But it would be good experience for you, especially if we see action." Honor's face darkened. "You'd get more experience on amputations and wounds after one battle at sea than you would in ten years ashore."

Taken completely by surprise, Trevor was almost speechless.
Finally he said, "I appreciate your offer, but I'm afraid I just wouldn't be qualified."

"As you will," Honor said, a rueful smile on his face. "We can impress men by force for deck hands, but there's no way to force a doctor. We need one badly."

The two men returned to the house and all afternoon Trevor thought of what Honor Wakefield had said. He had no interest in becoming a seagoing doctor, at least not as a long-term project.
He knew now that he could never win Shayna by fine manners but wondered if he could wear her down with kindness. *Perhaps if I tell her I love her often enough, she'll come to believe it.*

The dinner that night was excellent. It consisted of roasted duck, corn-bread stuffing, potatoes and onions in a heavy cream, corn pudding, green beans, fresh bread, and berry cobbler. But Shayna ate very little, merely listening as her father described one of his naval battles.

"First voyage will be simply to carry dispatches," Honor said.
"That's an excuse to get the crew in shape. It takes time to make a fighting ship."

"You mean there won't be any action on this voyage, Father?"
Shayna queried.

"No, highly unlikely. We won't be anyplace close to the French fleet. No, it will be simply a training voyage."

Shayna put her fork down. "Let me go with you,"

Honor was taken aback. "Go with me? Why, my dear, you don't—"

"I know. You've told me often how uncomfortable it is on a ship, but I get to see so little of you. Please take me."

It was the first request Shayna had made of her father in a long time. Struck by the insistence in her eyes, he was in a quandary. On one hand, he knew she was lonely at Wakefield. But he had doubts as to whether a frigate would be a suitable place for her. Still, on the whole, he thought quickly, *At least it would be a change—it would break the routine here. She won't be bored. I'll see to that.*

"Well, if you would really like to go, I think that can be arranged."

"Really, Father?" Shayna's eyes grew warm. "That would be so nice. We could have so much time together."

As Trevor listened, he made a quick decision. "Do you know, Shayna, your father has invited me to come on board as physician. I've decided to do it."

Shayna blinked with surprise. "That will be nice."

"Too bad we can't take a pianoforte along so we could have music," Trevor said teasingly.

"No pianos on a fighting ship," Honor said, amused and pleased at Trevor's decision. He knew exactly what was on the young man's mind. As he looked at the couple, he thought, *Maybe it will work out. Nothing like a long cruise to bring two young people together.*

THE HAND OF GOD

The pale light that outlined the sealed gun ports cast a feeble glow in the lower deck of the hulk, where a sodden air of despondency hung over the majority of the men.

But Cathan Morgan had grown stronger in the months since he had recovered from his fever. Now it was almost summer in the year 1801 and, although he was thin, still he was much healthier than many of his deck mates. Since he had turned his life over to God, he had been shocked at how peace could come even in the most squalid of circumstances day after day, week after week, and month after month. Now he remarked to Praise, who sat across from him rereading lines from the Bible, "I know God is in me because I would have lost my mind long before this if he weren't."

Praise God looked up and smiled. He had lost several teeth from disease, but still his eyes were clear. "Right you are, my boy. The peace of God passeth all understandin's. That's what the Book says."

"I give God the glory," Cathan said fondly, "but you were a good helper. I couldn't have made it without you."

"I'm glad I was here for you. It was your time, you know. Some men find God easily and some like you and me have to be put through torment before we will accept the grace of the good Lord."

Cathan thought about the twist of fate that had brought him to this terrible place and then he remembered Shayna Wakefield. He could almost see her green eyes and smell the perfume she always wore. She seemed to him a creature from another world, another life, and he could not but feel shame as he thought of how he had attempted to misuse her. "Praise," he said suddenly, "I think about the wicked things I did before I became a believer."

"Don't think about them. They are under the blood," Praise said sharply. "When you were saved, God took all your sins, my boy, and carried them to the deepest hole in the ocean. Then he threw them in and put up a sign that says 'no fishin.'"

Cathan laughed, loving the language his friend used to explain biblical truths. "What if they do come to me? What do I do then?"

"Just tell that old devil, 'You'll have to go talk to the Lord Jesus about it. None of my business anymore. He took them from me. Just go see Jesus.'" Praise chortled and slapped his thigh. "Then that old devil won't tarry long, I'll tell you that."

Talking to Praise, as he commented on the Scripture, was much like a Bible course. The two had nothing to do all day long since there was no entertainment, no walks out on deck, nothing except the eternal gloom and stench of their prison. Some of their time was spent in thinking of the past, which could be rather painful, but more of it came to be spent reading the Scriptures and talking about the meaning of it. Cathan had watched Praise carefully and had seen how he showed kindness to new prisoners and tried to protect them from the rougher elements of their prison. He also knew that many of them had responded—and that at least seven had come to know Jesus as Savior through the ministry of Praise God Barebones. These had gathered themselves together and stayed in one particular area with Praise, Cathan, and Jim. So during the interminable hours, Barebones spoke powerfully of redemption and heaven and warned solemnly about the fires of hell.

One day, Praise had been commenting on the nature of the Christian, how the flesh warred against the spirit, when he said, "Well, that's enough sermonizin' for one day."

Praise God was near the end of his sentence, lacking only a month, and Cathan was sad to think of losing his friend. Nevertheless, he was glad that Praise would at last be in the open air, free again. "What will you do when you are out?" Cathan asked.

"Do? I'll take another ship. That's all I know."

"I'll miss you when you're gone."

"I'll miss you, too. You know, Jesus says where two or three of us are gathered in his name, he is there in the midst of them. So you'll have these dear brothers here and it'll be up to you to support the weak. The older, stronger Christians must bear the burdens of those who are not so strong."

"I don't know as I could be much help."

"You have the power of your testimony—how Jesus came into your life and changed your heart. That's all the gospel is, Cat. God changin' men's hearts through the blood of Christ. Repentance and faith in Jesus, that's it! Don't get me started again!"

All the same, Cathan thought, *I will miss him.* And that night as they lay down to sleep, he grew more sad still, realizing he himself had little hope of ever getting out of his prison.

But the next morning after their meager breakfast, Praise God said, "You know, I had a dream last night. The most real I ever had. The Scripture says that old men will dream dreams and young men will have visions."

"What did you dream about? Something good to eat, I bet!" Cathan said eagerly.

"Not a bit of it!" Praise snorted. "I dreamed about you."

"About me?"

"Yes. I could see you standin' in the wind. You were shaved, you had on clean clothes, and your hair was blowin'. It looked like the sea. It seemed like the Lord was sayin' to me, 'I'm going to set my servant Cathan free.'" Upon seeing Cathan's quizzical stare, Praise continued, "The good Lord sometimes uses dreams to speak to people. Look at the Scripture. Joseph was instructed in a dream to take Mary as his wife and later to take his family and flee to Egypt." Praise squeezed Cathan's arm. "Look in the Word of God for your miracle—the one you need, my boy. And then don't cast away your confidence. Always believe that God is able to do more than you think."

"That would be more than I could think, all right. I've got almost twenty years to serve in this place."

But Praise God said, "No, I don't think so. I believe God is going to do a mighty miracle!"

For four days after Praise God shared his dream with Cathan, neither man spoke of it. Cathan, however, could not help remembering the certainty in Praise God's voice, the prophetic ring. So quietly Cathan began to pray that God would reveal something to him. "Let me hear your voice, O Lord," he prayed when the others were sleeping fitfully.

His prayer was not answered in the way he expected. The days passed until only a week was left before Praise's sentence was up. The two were speaking quietly when they heard the tramping of boots and the rattle of the barred door being swung back. Looking up, they saw a marine, armed with a musket, and beside him an officer who called out, "Morgan! Cathan Morgan!"

Cathan stared wildly at Praise. He had never been singled out for anything. Most men were singled out for punishment, but he could think of nothing he had done to offend.

Praise slapped him on the shoulder. "Go see what it is. It may be the hand of God workin'."

Cathan rose, stepping over men to get to the stairway. "I'm Morgan!"

"This way."

Cathan mounted the steps and the door slammed behind him. "What is it?" he asked.

"You'll find out. Come along."

The officer, whose name Morgan did not know, led him up several more flights of steps and then into the sunlight. Instantly blinded, Cathan stopped, putting his hand over his eyes and blinking furiously.

"Come along, man!" the officer said, wrinkling his nose. "You stink like the grave! Hurry up with you now!"

Prodded along by the butt of the marine's musket, Cathan stumbled forward. He could barely see another door open and when he stepped inside, the glare lessened and he lowered his hand.

"This is Morgan, sir," the officer said.

Cathan soon realized that he was in what used to be the captain's quarters. It was crowded with a desk and several beds. The open windows of the stern let in the light. As his eyes adjusted, Cathan realized that there was a short, round civilian sitting behind the desk.

"You're Cathan Morgan?" the man asked.

"Yes, sir, that's my name," Cathan replied courteously.

"Here, come and sit down. I have something to say to you."

Cathan shuffled forward, taking the chair the man offered. His mind was reeling and he could not imagine what he had been called here for. "Am I in some kind of trouble?"

The civilian smiled and stood up, a calculating look in his light blue eyes. "Quite the contrary." Straightening the ill-fitting wig that perched on his head, he said, "My name is Jerome Tyson. That means nothing to you, of course, but I think it will mean a great deal shortly." Tyson held on to his words as if they were precious, as if he were enjoying the sound of his own voice. "I am sure you are wondering why I'm here and why I've called you for an audience."

"Yes, sir, of course I am."

"Your father hired me some time ago to do what I could to clear you from the charges. I assure you, sir, I have been working assiduously, most assiduously in your case."

"My father's a poor man. I would guess, sir, you don't take the cases of poor men too often."

"And how do you figure that?"

"Men who wear diamonds on their finger and gold chains around their neck didn't get them defending poor people."

"Ah," Tyson said, looking like a fat shark. Then he laughed, jiggling his triple chins and shaking his round belly. "You're a sharp one," he said, wagging his finger. "I can see that, Cathan Morgan! Perhaps a bit too sharp for your own good."

"Why do you say that, Mr. Tyson?"

"It's either the ones who are too stupid or too smart for their own good who wind up in the hulks. You're not stupid and, therefore, you're a little too clever. But I admire your father. My father was in the same regiment and they were good friends. He came to me and asked me to see what I could do for you and I agreed."

"So you're not getting paid for this."

"I assure you I *am* being remunerated—to some degree. The laborer is worthy of his hire and you must not muzzle the ox that treadeth out the corn."

Although Cathan did not know what was coming, he grinned. He liked this roly-poly lawyer, realizing that the flabby outside cloaked a mind as sharp as any rapier. "Have you made any progress, Mr. Tyson?"

"I may say that, yes, I have. I most certainly have made progress."

Cathan waited for him to speak, then grew impatient. "For heaven's sake, don't torment me, Mr. Tyson! What progress?"

"I will not be hurried, sir! This case is going to be one of my favorites. Little enough money in it, of course, but I will have done my fellow man good. That is what we are put here for. To serve our fellow man." Tyson moved a chair around the desk by Cathan, then planted himself on the seat of it. "Now, you are familiar with the name Sir Mortimer Wells?"

"I should be. He's the reason I'm here."

"Exactly. You were accused of having shot Sir Mortimer Wells, is that not the case?"

"I think you may say so, Mr. Tyson."

"Let me put a case to you then, young man. We will suppose that there were others involved in the robbery. Yes, there were accomplices. Perhaps more than one accomplice."

Cathan stiffened and sat straight up, his eyes glowing. He gripped his knees to quell their trembling. "You found out who the accomplices were?"

Tyson caressed his gold necklace. "Please, I will not be hurried." He waited to see if Cathan would protest, then, seeing he would not, continued, "Now then, we will suppose that these two accomplices were apprehended and that they were tried for murder and sentenced."

He waited to see the effect this had on Cathan. "Ah, that touches you, I see."

"They were caught and convicted? Are they dead?"

"Indeed, they have gone to that undiscovered country from whence no traveler returns. Yes, Mr. Cathan Morgan, I may say they are deceased."

Questions burst from Cathan's lips, but they were stopped by Tyson's pudgy hand. "Please, you shall know all. Let us suppose that these two hardened criminals, murderers though they were, saw that they were doomed to hang by the neck until they were dead. Let us suppose then that a certain lawyer retained by a certain gentleman to defend his son interviewed these two and found that they were totally, absolutely, and irrevocably unrepentant. But they still had a few weeks of life and wanted to live well." Then Tyson leaned forward, his eyes gleaming. "Let us suppose that said lawyer supplied them with a certain amount of cash. How does that strike you?"

Having learned that Tyson would not be hurried, Cathan said, "It sounds fine, Mr. Tyson. There is more, I assume?"

"Indeed there is. And the more consists of this, my dear sir. These two confessed to the robbery of the house of Sir Mortimer Wells; one of them confessed to having fired the shot that wounded him, and this confession was put into print. They both signed their names," Tyson said, excitedly. "Now, let us suppose that this certain lawyer took this document to Sir Mortimer Wells."

The raucous cries of seagulls broke the silence of the cabin as Cathan sat frozen to his chair, scarcely daring to breathe. "You took the confession to Sir Mortimer Wells?"

"Indeed I did, sir. Indeed I did, and you may depend upon it. Sir Mortimer Wells is a hard man—but he is also an eminently fair man."

"What did he say?"

"He said in effect that an injustice had been done and he would use his influence to see that it was rectified. And, indeed, Sir Mortimer's influence is great with the courts."

"How long have you known this?"

"For nearly a month."

"Then why didn't you come to me with it?"

"And what would you have done? Suppose I had come back today and said nothing had changed. You still must serve your sentence. It would have been cruel and inhuman and humanity is my business, sir."

Still not knowing what the visit meant, Cathan watched as if hypnotized as Jerome Tyson pulled a paper from his breast and held it dramatically in the air. "What I have here, sir, is the verdict of the court. It is—"

"May I see it?"

"Allow me to give you the substance of it. It simply says that since you were not guilty of attempted murder, but from all intents were merely a drunken fool, your sentence of twenty years has been remitted."

"Thank God!" Cathan burst out. He stood to his feet, trembling, with tears in his eyes.

"Yes, indeed!" Tyson said, also standing. "Thank God, but you have not heard the rest."

"The rest? Is there more?"

"You were, after all, guilty of robbery, and the sentence for that in England can be quite severe."

The joy that had welled up in Cathan dissipated. "Then I can't leave this place? Did they cut it in half? Ten years?" Even that seemed interminable to him, as if he had been sentenced for the first time.

"It's not so bad as that, my dear Cathan. But even Sir Mortimer was not able to get you off scot free, but he was able to influence the judge to offer you a choice."

"A choice? What sort of choice?"

"You can either serve two more years in this place—or you can join those from the prison who are being pressed into naval service."

"Serve on a ship? But I'm not a sailor."

"The press is indiscriminatory. Yes, indeed, indiscriminatory," Tyson said, shrugging. "These days, with Napoléon threatening the shores, the Royal Navy takes any man who can haul on a rope. Never fear, they will be glad to get a young man such as yourself." He paused, then said, "There is your choice, Cathan. Either stay here two more years or serve as a sailor in His Majesty's Royal Navy."

"I'll take the navy," Cathan said instantly.

"I should think so! Here's the chance to serve your country and to get out of this foul hole."

"When can I leave?"

"I stopped by the Admiralty and discovered that the press will be coming in three days to get those who are eligible. You'll be leaving with them."

"Who are eligible?" Cathan demanded.

"Those finishing their sentences or those convicted of minor crimes."

Cathan got up and walked to the window, where he could see the green of the water and the blue sky if he squinted. Turning, he said, "Thank you, Mr. Tyson, for all you have done. You have, indeed, been the servant of one piece of humanity and I can only offer you my humble thanks."

"Excellent! Now then, I regret you must spend three more days, but it will not be long. Shall I tell your father anything?"

"Could I write him a letter?" Cathan asked.

"Indeed you could. I have paper, a pen, and ink. Sit here."

Cathan sat down at the table and took the writing equipment. Dipping the quill in the ink, he began to write:

> My dear father and mother,
> I can never thank you enough for your confidence in
> me. It is only through your help that it has been possible
> for me to leave this place.
> I am a believer in Jesus now, and my dear friend, Praise
> God Barebones, has told me many times that God's hand
> is always on us. I realize that I was brought to this place
> by my own foolishness, but perhaps it was for this
> reason—to arrest my wild career and bring me into the

family of God. Now I thank God that whatever happens I know Jesus Christ. . . .

When he had finished he gave the letter to the lawyer, who folded it and stuck it in his pocket. Then Tyson picked up his hat and cane and shook Cathan's hand. "I rejoice to see you released. Your father and mother are fine people and you have shamed them. I pray you will not do so again."

"I will attempt never to give offense again. Good-bye, sir."

Ten minutes later, back in the hole, Cathan told this story to Praise God. The older man began to weep. "It's the hand of God and no other."

Jeremiah Peters, the muscular twenty-six-year-old second lieutenant of the *Dauntless,* stared with distaste at the miserable specimens who stood blinking like owls in the sunlight. He grunted to the coxswain, "And *this* is what we're supposed to fight the Frenchies with? Don't think we'll ever make sailors out of them."

His thickset coxswain, Max Kolb, pulled on his fierce-looking mustache. "They'll do to pull a rope or stop a ball."

A tall man in a disreputable uniform showed up. "Lieutenant, here is the muster."

"Are they all here?"

"Yes, and one more has been added." The man marked a name with his skinny finger. "This one. He volunteered."

Peters's eyes opened wide. "What's that name?" he demanded, then called, "Praise God Barebones?"

"Aye, sir, that's me."

Peters turned to see a thin man with a patch over one eye and scars on his face from old fights.

"You're a volunteer, are you?"

"Yes, sir. On my last ship I served the center starboard gun on the lower deck."

"What were you doing in prison?"

"I attacked an officer when I was drunk," Praise said regretfully, "but I'll make you a good hand, sir."

"We'll see to that. Any of the rest of you men had service?" Peters's eyes ran up and down the line and got no response.

"Well," he said to Kolb, "it'll fill the muster out."

"Yes, sir. Shall we load 'em and take 'em to the ship?"

"Yes." Peters watched as the fourteen skeleton-like men dressed in rags stumbled toward the ship. *Some of them will probably die before we're out of sight of land,* he thought, but then shrugged. This was the press and you took the dregs in order to get the ship underway. After all, some might well turn into passable hands, especially the one with the odd name of Praise God Barebones.

⚬⚬⚬

"There she is. What do you think of her, Cat?"

Cathan looked up at the ship. "She's big," he said.

"Not that big. Why, she's only a frigate," Praise replied.

Cathan shuffled along in line, gasping when they were hosed down with water warmed by the sun. Kolb, the coxswain, grinned as the water hit the new hands, who jumped up and down and howled. But Cathan welcomed the water, holding his hands out and his head back, rejoicing as the water sloshed through the dirt and filth of the *Courage.*

When they were deloused with a foul-smelling concoction, they dressed hurriedly again in their old rags—something Cathan hated to do. He had no idea where they were being taken next, but Lt. Peters and Kolb were there to prod them. Kolb had a knotted rope that he used to "encourage" any stragglers.

"Are these the pressed hands from the hulk, Lt. Peters?"

"Yes, sir."

Capt. Honor Wakefield looked down from the quarterdeck at the men who stared back at him with fear and apprehension—all except one.

Cathan Morgan could not believe his eyes! There was Honor Wakefield, dressed in the full uniform of a captain in His Majesty's navy, with an epaulet on one shoulder of his blue coat. *If Praise is right and God is engineering this, he's certainly doing it in a bizarre manner!* Cathan thought wildly.

On his part, Honor Wakefield was calmly eyeing the pressed hands, who all looked alike—with long beards, matted hair, and rags. "You men are now members of the crew of His Majesty's frigate, the *Dauntless*. I am Capt. Wakefield and welcome you aboard. If you mind your duties, you will find me fair. If you neglect them, there will be punishment. . . ."

Capt. Wakefield had spoken these words many times and they came to his lips almost without thought. As he walked down the line, looking each man in the face, he knew he would not know them later, when they were shaved and in their uniforms. Still, he liked to give the men a personal welcome.

"You will be taught your duties by—" The words cut off sharply as the captain looked into Cathan Morgan's eyes. *I've got to be wrong! It can't be!* Honor thought. But there was no mistaking Cathan, despite the beard and the long hair. For all his poise, Capt. Honor Wakefield could not think of a thing to say. Finally, he turned and walked away, disappearing back on the quarterdeck and then into the door leading to his quarters.

"All right, take them below and get them fitted out," Lt. Peters said.

"Come along," Kolb said roughly. "We'll make sailors out of you or kill you. One of the two."

⁘

Both Trevor and Shayna noticed that Honor was strangely silent. He had been in good spirits for the past two days since all three of them had moved aboard the *Dauntless,* taking pleasure in showing them about the ship. It had been an enjoyable time for Shayna, new and different, although she had been on ships before. Her cabin was very small, but it contained the necessary elements of life and she had even begun to be more pleasant to Trevor.

"Something troubling you, Father?" Shayna finally asked.

"I'm afraid there is."

"Is it something to do with the ship? Bad news?" Trevor asked.

"No, not really." Honor folded his white napkin and put it down. He'd eaten practically nothing. Now he looked at Shayna. "I hardly know how to tell you this, either of you. Something occurred this afternoon that I wouldn't have thought possible. . . . As you may have heard, we took on a group of pressed men out of the hulks. It's a common enough practice. We get a few good hands out of it." He paused, trying to find a way to make his news less shocking. "One of the hands is Cathan Morgan."

"Cathan!" Shayna's hands flew to her lips. "You can't mean it, Father!"

"I'm afraid I do. I had no idea, of course. I can't imagine how it happened."

Shaken, Trevor said, "But his sentence was twenty years. Is it common to let men with a sentence like that out?"

"It depends. When the need is great enough, they let out murderers. We usually don't investigate. Just take what we can get."

"He should be transferred to another ship," Trevor said, seeing the expression on Shayna's face. "It would be most uncomfortable to have him aboard the *Dauntless.*"

"I agree, but we're weighing anchor right now. I've already given the orders." Watching his daughter's face, Honor asked, "Does this disturb you, Shayna?"

Finding herself unable to speak, Shayna Wakefield rose and left the table.

As the door shut, Trevor said, "This is bad, sir, very bad!"

"I'll get rid of the fellow. We'll be passing other ships. I'll simply transfer him."

Honor had been more shaken by the experience than he had ever been by battle. Seeing Cathan Morgan there was like seeing a ghost rise from the grave. Honor had hoped more than anything else that that young man would never be seen or heard from again, especially in Shayna's life. And now that they were all on board one small ship of war, contact was inevitable.

Resolution tightened Honor's jaw. "We'll see to it that they have nothing to do with one another," he said as Trevor took his leave. Then Honor slumped in his chair. "Why did he have to show up on this one ship of all the ships in His Majesty's navy?" he said, groaning. He could see no good coming out of it. Finally he stood up and waved the sailor to take away the food. Then he stared out the stern windows of his cabin, wondering if he could handle the days that were to come with wisdom.

T e n

CRUISING

Any individual who is plucked out of his normal routine and thrown into one that is entirely different must, as a matter of course, suffer a measure of confusion. One who is thrown into prison must, for the first few days—or even weeks or months—acclimate himself to the loss of familiar things and somehow find his way through the maze of customs, surroundings, and regulations of his new life. For some this takes place rapidly, while others never adjust.

For Cathan Morgan, the adjustment from prison to life as a seaman on board the *Dauntless* was relatively simple—at least less traumatic than it was for others who had never known military service. Cathan, having lived among men under rigid discipline, quickly learned that the cosmos that constituted the fighting ship differed little from a regiment on land.

"You'll find the way of it," Praise said confidently as he guided Cathan through the motions of sea life that first day. "It's a might confusin', all those sails, ropes, and different decks, but mind your manners, stay on the good side of the officers, and you'll find it's a good life."

So Cathan threw himself into learning his duties as quickly as he could. He was issued a seaman's kit, which consisted of two blue jackets, one pea jacket, two pairs of blue trousers, two pairs of shoes, six shirts, four pairs of stockings, two Guernsey frocks, two hats, two handkerchiefs, a comforter, several pairs of flannel drawers, one pillow, two blankets, and two hammocks. In addition to this, for warm weather he drew four duck frocks, four pairs of duck trousers, a straw hat, and a canvas hat for squalls.

"You'll pay for all that—or it'll be taken out of your pay, I should say," Praise said, grinning at Cathan as they loaded supplies from the upper deck down to the hold.

Seeing Cathan's amazement about how much food had to come on board, Praise said, "You got to remember that we might not be touchin' land for six months. So for every man on the ship we'll have to have seven pounds of biscuits a week, seven gallons of beer, four pounds of beef, two pounds of pork, a quart of peas, a pint and a half of oatmeal, six ounces of sugar, and the same of butter. Each of us will get twelve ounces of cheese and a half pint of vinegar, not to mention the lime juice and two pounds of tobacco. Multiply all that by a few hundred men and you got quite a load. And that doesn't include all the barrels of water."

"I don't guess we'll starve," Cathan murmured.

At mealtime, Cathan found himself assigned to a mess where seven other men ate between two of the cannons on the lower deck. A board was lowered on ropes and the men gathered to put their food on it. When a plate was set before him by the leader of the mess, Cathan looked at Praise, wondering what the amorphous mass was.

"That's figgy-dowdey," Praise said. "Eat hearty."

Eat hearty was exactly what Cathan did. No matter how repulsive it looked, to him it tasted better than anything he had had since his imprisonment.

"You make figgy-dowdey by takin' biscuit, puttin' it in a stout canvas bag, and poundin' it for about half an hour," Praise explained. "Then you add bits of pork fat, plums, figs, rum, and currants. Not bad after what we've been livin' on, eh my boy?"

"I'm thankful to God for figgy-dowdey," Cathan said.

"That's the spirit, my boy," Praise responded.

As Cathan looked around the crowded deck, which had beams so low that he could not straighten up and great guns facing outward on both sides, he was satisfied. The ports were open so that the sunlight streamed in and men were eating, talking, and laughing. "You read me that Scripture," Cathan said, "where Paul said he'd learned to be content. Well, I'm content. I believe God's put me here."

"Amen to that!" Praise said, resting his chin in his hands, his eyes thoughtful. "As I've told you before, God's hand is on everything. He sees the fall of the sparrow. It's good to know that God cares about all we do."

For the next two days Cathan managed to soak up a great deal of sea life. Each day began with cleaning the upper decks with "holy stone," so named because it was approximately the size of a Bible. Part of the crew pumped the bilges, which was hard work. Then the hammocks were carried upstairs and stowed in nets around the side of the vessel.

Bells were a part of every sailor's life. Cathan learned that he had to come from his hammock before eight bells in the middle watch—or an officer with a starter would encourage him. Eight bells in the forenoon watch was the signal for dinner. He even learned that the days could be measured by what the one-legged cook, Francis Goforth, served: Cheese and duff on Monday, salt beef on Tuesday, dried peas and duff on Wednesday, salt pork on Thursday, dried peas and cheese on Friday, salt beef again on Saturday, and salt pork and figgy-dowdey on Sunday, always accompanied by biscuits.

The days went by with the beat of drums and the sound of the pipe. Cathan never slept more than four hours at a time, for that was the length of a watch. This perpetual movement on the deck with nothing in sight but the endless sea and the sky made Cathan feel as if he had entered another world.

Cathan saw Honor Wakefield often. As he learned to work the sails and haul the ropes, his eyes often went to the quarterdeck, where Capt. Wakefield paced back and forth, sometimes talking with his other officers. He was also certain that the captain had his eye on him, although he never got close enough to speak to him. During that time he did not see Shayna, although he'd heard she was on the ship. He did catch one glimpse of Trevor, but he was certain Trevor did not recognize him.

During these first days an event transpired that made several of the ship's officers notice Cathan. One bright Thursday afternoon a cry came from Lt. Peters. "Gunnery practice! Every man to his station!"

"Come along, lad," Praise said. "Now you'll see what these big ships are all about. If it weren't for the guns, they'd be nothing but transports."

The ship became a beehive of activity. The lower decks were filled with running men and Praise jerked Cathan's arm, saying, "We'll be in Karl's crew." Karl Steinmetz, a huge German with blond hair in the usual pigtail and mild blue eyes, was the strongest man on the ship. As he gathered his men around him, his eyes fell on Cathan. "Have you ever fired a gun, Morgan?"

Cathan thought of the hundreds or, perhaps, the thousands of times that he had fired or directed artillery. It was the thing he did best, but, not wanting to give up his secret, he replied, "Not one like this, Karl."

"Well, it can kill a man, so watch out."

The gun practice began. The crew included Karl, who was the captain of the gun, the second captain, as well as a sponger, a fireman, a powder boy, and several men like himself to muscle the monstrous gun into place. The only difference Cathan could see between the eighteen pounder and a piece of field artillery was that the gun had to be run out and run in. It was heavy, dangerous work, but Cathan soon learned that a well-trained crew could carry out the whole operation in less than two minutes.

By the end of the drill, the deck was filled with smoke and Cathan's ears were almost deafened. But his experience had been noticed.

Karl eyed Cathan. "You've fired guns before."

"Field artillery. Quite a bit."

"You done well," Steinmetz said as he walked away. Then, when he saw Napoléon Devere, a short muscular Frenchman, he called, "Hey, Nappy, we got one good'un out of the hulks."

"Which one's that?" Devere asked. As a Frenchman, he was a rarity in the English navy. But he hated Napoléon and the new government of France, for his family had died on the guillotine.

"The black-haired one named Morgan," Steinmetz said, explaining Cathan's expert touch with the guns.

"We'll be needing him," Nappy replied. "We don't have many good hands on this ship, not with the guns anyway."

Later in the day Gunner Devere was giving his report of the gun practice to Capt. Wakefield. The first lieutenant, Lewis Stillitoe, a strongly built man of thirty with brown hair, was also there.

"They're all thumbs right now, sir," Devere said. "But there's a few bright spots. One of the new hands out of the hulks has had a lot of experience with guns."

"What's his name?" Capt. Wakefield demanded.

"Morgan I think, sir."

As the gunner spoke the name, Capt. Wakefield started. When Stillitoe saw the response, he wondered if Capt. Wakefield knew the man—or something about him. Although he did not dare ask such a personal question of his captain, he filed the information in his memory. But the question lingered: *What could a captain in His Majesty's navy have to do with a prisoner out of the hulks?*

"I would like to invite you to dinner, Lt. Stillitoe," Honor said, "along with the other officers."

"It would be my privilege, sir."

Leaving the deck, Honor went to his cabin and sat at the desk, thinking of what he had heard. He regretted that he had not turned Cathan off even before the ship left England. Now it was too late—unless they encountered another ship to which Morgan could be transferred, Honor would have to learn to live with his presence.

⌒⌒⌒⌒⌒

The captain's day cabin had been set for dinner. It was the most ornate spot on the ship, with its mahogany dining table, green leather chairs, and red carpet. The company consisted of Honor's three lieutenants, the three midshipmen, Trevor, and Honor's daughter, who sat at his right hand.

The meal had been pleasant enough, though stilted. The lieutenants had not learned the habits of their new captain and so waited for him to make comments. On his part, Honor Wakefield was analyzing the three officers. If he had to work with them, he needed to know their strengths and weaknesses.

First Lieutenant Lewis Stillitoe was the man who would command the *Dauntless* if Wakefield himself fell in battle. Already Honor was pleased with this man. He had discovered that Stillitoe had risen from the lower deck, which was unusual. He was tough as Wang leather, but fair.

The second lieutenant, Jeremiah Peters, was a more complicated man. Honor had already discovered that he had a streak of arrogance, that he took no thought for the comfort of the crew. He also watched carefully as Peters spoke to Shayna, who sat next to him. *A ladies' man,* he thought as Peters smiled and kept up a running conversation that Shayna seemed to find interesting.

The hazel-eyed third lieutenant, Eben Roxby, was thirty-five. A bulky redhead, well over six feet, Roxby had a continual sunburn. He was also free with his starter and seemed to take pleasure in it. That, and the fact that he was a very poor navigator, made Wakefield rather nervous. Still, he was strong and worked hard, so Wakefield resolved to get the most out of him.

The three midshipmen, rather uncomfortable being in the same room with their officers, said nothing unless spoken to. Midshipman Clarence Hyde, at fifteen, was confident, audacious, and tough. Maurice Dockstetter, on the other hand, two years Hyde's junior, was frail and sickly. He had little business being on a ship at all.

The black-haired third midshipman, William Flynt, was nineteen, but he looked older than his actual age. It was true, of course, that some men remained midshipmen even into their thirties or forties, but this was not usual. Flynt had failed the lieutenant's test twice, Wakefield had discovered. He also suspected that Flynt was a bully.

Tobias Cain, the marine officer, was a trim man of thirty with direct brown eyes. He was equally at home on land or sea, and his red uniform seemed to have been painted on his body. It was he who lifted his glass for the first toast. "To our new captain. May he be victorious in all that he undertakes."

Wakefield grinned and proposed his own toast. "To you, Major, and to your good men."

Several toasts took place and then Stillitoe, still thinking of the odd look in his captain's eye at the mention of Morgan, boldly said, "I understand from Gunner Devere that we finally managed to get some good hands out of the hulks."

"Nothing good that I can see," Lt. Roxby said. "Nothing but jailbirds! They'll do for cannon fodder, I suppose!"

"Not according to Nappy," Stillitoe said, raising his eyebrows. "Two of them are going to be fine hands. One of them has a strange name—Praise God Barebones."

Peters agreed. "Yes, he served before. I think he might be a good man."

"The other served in the army, I understand. Devere says he's the best new hand he's ever seen at gun practice. His name is Cathan Morgan," Stillitoe said, watching the captain. But he was startled when the captain's daughter and Trevor Wakefield both gasped. Although the silence lasted only an instant, Stillitoe knew then that there was more to the captain's relationship with Cathan Morgan. *So Miss Shayna knows Morgan—and the doctor does too. He looks pale as a ghost,* Stillitoe thought, eyeing the captain, who was drumming his fingers nervously on the white tablecloth.

After that, neither the captain, his daughter, nor Trevor had anything to say, so the meal was quiet.

When they left the room, Peters said to Stillitoe, "What about that girl? She's a beauty, isn't she?" He grinned broadly. "I think Miss Shayna Wakefield and I are going to be good friends."

Lt. Stillitoe, who did not believe in mixing business with pleasure, said, "You'd better stay away from her, Lieutenant. The captain may not like officers romancing his daughter."

But Peters, whose uncle was an admiral and used his influence shamefully, just said, "Well, she's a pippin and I intend to see more of her."

"What do you know about Morgan?" Stillitoe queried.

"Morgan? Nothing. Just some kind of criminal."

Satisfied that Peters knew no more than himself, Stillitoe went to his own cabin. For a time, he lay on his bed thinking about the reactions of the captain, the woman, and the doctor to hearing Cathan Morgan's name. *I'll find out about it,* Stillitoe pledged. *We'll see what Morgan himself has to say.*

❦

Shayna's tiny cabin had been created for her from part of her father's quarters. It was only large enough for a narrow bed, a small chest, and a dressing table, where she now sat writing in her journal. The quill moved slowly at first, then more rapidly as thoughts came to her.

> We have been at sea now for two weeks and I have seen Cathan only twice, both times at a distance. But I have thought of little else. I cannot speak to Trevor of this, but I know he is angry that Father didn't put him off the ship before the voyage started. Father, too, is angry. I know he dislikes Cathan, and what happened between us is a painful memory.

As the ship slowly dipped and rose, Shayna thought dreamily back to the days when she had fallen in love with Cathan. She could still remember his kisses and how she had longed to be completely his. Ashamed, she impulsively wrote:

> Do I still love him? No, I cannot. How could I? As Father said, he's nothing but a fortune hunter. He got what he deserved and I wish he had never been released. I wish he were not on this ship!

But even as she penned the words, she knew she was not speaking her heart. She sprinkled sand on the damp ink, blew it off, closed the journal, and finally lay down on the bed. She wanted to go on deck, but she feared seeing Cathan. *Why do I care what he thinks? He's nothing but a criminal who tried to use me!* As these thoughts rolled uncontrollably through her mind, she wanted to cry. Instead, she blinked back the tears, forcing herself to think of other things.

⚜

A few hours later Shayna was making her way from the quarterdeck toward the prow, where she had spent many hours watching the ship nose down into the green waters. She loved the wind as it whistled across the deck, the flapping of the sails, the creaking of the masts, and the sibilant whispering of the water as the *Dauntless* forged ahead. As she walked the gangway, suddenly she found herself face-to-face with Cathan Morgan, who had stepped from a ladder that led down to the lower deck. Seeing her, he stopped as if he had run into a stone wall. She stared at him, her throat tightening.

Cathan was wearing the seaman's uniform—duck pants, and a shirt that outlined his strong upper body. He was thinner than she remembered, of course, as a result of prison life. But his eyes were the same and they held hers.

Cathan was also silent. He had wondered if he would ever see this woman again and now she stood not ten feet away. He took in the trim form, the richness of her hair, the smoothness of her cheeks. Of all the things in his life that he had been ashamed of, he was most ashamed of his treatment of this girl. He wanted to ask her forgiveness, but saw pain and anger in her eyes. He could not blame her, so impulsively he turned and hurried back down the ladder.

As Cathan disappeared, Shayna Wakefield emitted a sob. Then a voice behind her asked, "Are you all right, Miss Shayna?"

Turning quickly, Shayna saw Lt. Stillitoe. She knew he must have seen the brief encounter between her and Morgan, so she swallowed hard and said firmly, "I'm fine, Lieutenant."

But as Shayna turned toward the prow of the ship, Stillitoe was not convinced. He was, in fact, more determined than ever to find out about Morgan's relationship to the Wakefields.

Eleven

A CALL TO
PUNISHMENT

D r. Trevor Wakefield had quickly discovered that the medical care on board a fighting ship left a great deal to be desired. Indeed, it was almost nonexistent. Lt. Stillitoe had given Trevor a tour of the ship, including the lowest part, called the hold, which was stuffed with powder, shot, and supplies. The orlop deck above the hold was crowded with the tiers where the huge cables that held the anchor were kept, as well as many of the other supplies. At the forward part of the orlop deck, where the midshipmen lived, was also the cockpit, where those wounded in battle were treated. Forward of the cockpit were dark, airless cabins for the junior officers.

Now as Trevor looked around his little kingdom, running his eyes over the saws, retractors, artery hooks, and other surgical tools, he realized how inadequate they were. He thought of other items, such as plaster of paris for setting broken limbs, and knew he should have ordered them in more sufficient quantities.

"Patient's all ready, sir." Trevor's assistant, a short, fat young man named Simon Lawler, interrupted his thoughts.

"I'll be right there."

Quickly Trevor stepped out of the cockpit into a larger room. On the table a patient was already held down by padded leather straps. Trevor placed his hand lightly on the seaman's pale forehead and, looking into his eyes, decided that the drops of laudanum he had administered earlier had taken effect. Seeing that the man's belly had been shaved and washed, he glanced at seaman Johnson, who stood next to his friend Danny's head. Trevor had found it was comforting for patients to have one of their friends near and Danny had particularly asked for Johnson.

"It'll be over soon. I'm going to pour some wine over your belly. At first you may feel a little stab, but you must be as still as possible."

"Yes, Danny," Johnson encouraged. "Be still for the doctor."

"Right," Danny said, the drug slurring his words. "Have right at it, Doctor!"

The surgery went well and soon Trevor was tying off the last suture.

"He's a tough one," Trevor said to Johnson.

"Yes, he is, Doctor. A good man." Johnson's face was pale, for he had never seen an operation before.

Trevor gave instructions to Lawler, then said, "Keep him here for a while. I don't want him tearing those stitches out, so if he starts tossing, give him ten more drops of laudanum."

"Aye, sir, I'll do that."

Leaving the surgery, Trevor ascended to his own cabin, where he washed his hands and put on a clean shirt. Then he made his way to the captain's cabin and knocked. When the captain invited him in, he said, "I've just finished the surgery."

Honor looked up curiously. "How did it go?"

"It was a simple enough operation. I've always had success with it. I expect the man to be fine."

"Sit down. I want to talk to you, Trevor. Here, have some of this tea. It's very good."

"Thank you, Captain."

Trevor relaxed, sipping the tea. He was not unhappy in his choice to come on board ship, for the seamen seemed grateful to have a real physician with them. After the busyness of his years of study, he had also enjoyed the long hours of quietness that he had spent on deck watching the sea and sky change colors.

But what he had thought about since the ship departed from England still nagged at him. Finally he spoke his question aloud. "Do you still intend to transfer Cathan?"

Startled by Trevor's abruptness, Wakefield rubbed his chin thoughtfully. "I suppose so." He had pondered this same question almost every day. Now he asked, "Does his presence on board bother you?"

"Yes, it does."

"Do you hate him then, Trevor?"

"I'd not like to say that!"

"I think, perhaps, you do. If another man steals a woman's love from you, I hardly see how you could refrain from hating him."

"It's what he did to Shayna," Trevor said slowly, "that disturbs me most. More than what he did to me."

"I've wondered how she feels about him. We're not as close as we used to be, so she no longer talks with me about matters of the heart." Troubled, Honor stared at Trevor. "I think the wise thing to do would be to get rid of Cathan."

Trevor arose at once, relieved. "I think so, sir."

Honor watched him leave, then dropped to his knees. *Lord,* he prayed fervently, *how can I help this child of mine? I fear for her.*

<hr />

Roxby, the third lieutenant, picked up a heavy saber from the armory's rack of weapons, then nodded to Midshipman Hyde. "We'll do some sword drill this morning."

"Yes, sir!" Hyde said, his blue eyes lighting up. Gathering an armload of sabers and cutlasses, he followed Roxby up on deck where a dozen of the new crew members waited.

"It's time to make men out of you," Roxby said. "Here, Roberts, let's see what you've got."

The crewman he addressed had a pale, thin face, since he had only recently conquered the seasickness that had plagued him ever since leaving land. As a mild-mannered tailor who had been pressed into military duty, Roberts took the sword awkwardly.

Lt. Roxby advanced, saying, "All right. When you board a ship, you're liable to see someone coming at you with the intent of cutting your throat. Roberts, see if you can stop me."

What happened, of course, was a farce. Roberts lifted his sword ineffectually and with one blow Lt. Roxby struck it from him. Instantly he pressed the blade against Robert's throat and said, "Now you're a dead man!" He slapped the ex-tailor on the shoulder with the flat of his cutlass.

"All right, you next. Let's see what you got. . . ."

Up on the quarterdeck Capt. Wakefield stood with his first and second lieutenants, watching the sword drill.

"They're not much, are they, sir?" Peters said.

"When you consider where they've come from, I suppose they're just average," Honor replied.

When Roxby called out, "All right, Morgan, let's see if you got anything in you!" Honor began to watch intensely.

At once Cathan stepped forward, taking the sword offered to him by Midshipman Hyde. The tow-haired young man winked at him, but Cathan let nothing show on his face.

As the two men faced each other in the small open space. Cathan turned his body to the right, waiting for the lieutenant to begin.

"Let's see you cut me down!" Lt. Roxby called.

Cathan simply lifted his sword and waited. He was aware that Capt. Wakefield and his other officers were watching, but he gave his full attention to Roxby. He knew that the third lieutenant was a bully, using his starter far more than was necessary on the confused landsmen and he had heard Lt. Stillitoe warn Roxby about this more than once. Cathan also knew that Roxby, for some reason, had taken a dislike to him, although he had never given any offense.

Roxby advanced. "See if you can stop me then!" He stepped forward and came down with an overhead blow, crying out, "Get your sword up!"

What transpired next shocked Stillitoe, who knew that Roxby, for all his faults, was the best swordsman on the ship. When Roxby brought the sword down, Morgan simply lifted his saber, engaged the blade of the other, and deflected it to the side in a lightning movement.

"Well done! Morgan is quick!" Peters exclaimed.

Roxby, angered at his failure, began a series of blows, which were parried expertly by Cathan. As Roxby's face reddened, his blows grew harder. But no matter how quickly he swung his blade, he found it parried. He also saw that Morgan's face was totally calm and his eyes almost amused.

"Look how easily he handles Roxby," Peters said.

"He was in the army. That's where he learned to use a cutlass," Capt. Wakefield responded.

Stillitoe glanced at the captain. "I've never seen a better man with a sword. I'd hate to cross blades with him."

"I wouldn't mind going a round," Lt. Peters said.

Roxby, who was gasping for breath, was aware that Morgan was toying with him. When the captain said, "That's enough, Lieutenant! Dismiss the men!" Roxby dropped his sword point, hatred on his face.

"All right, dismissed!" Roxby yelled hoarsely, but his eyes followed Morgan as he handed the sword back to Midshipman Hyde. Hyde took the swords and then grinned at the lieutenant. "Not a bad man to have on your side, is he, Lieutenant?"

"Shut your mouth, Hyde!" Roxby grunted and stalked away.

Moving to where Cathan was standing, Hyde said, "I'd stay away from the lieutenant if I was you, Morgan. He's got it in for you."

"Thanks, Mr. Hyde, but I don't know of any place where I could go that he couldn't find me."

"Well, he's a hard man. Just watch yourself."

Sunset had come and gone, leaving a pale afterglow on the ocean. Shayna had always found this hour of the day fascinating, so she often came to the bow to watch the orb as it dropped beneath the waters. Somehow it was a symbol to her of inexplicable loss, such as she felt. Restlessly she glanced down at the figurehead below the bowsprit. Although the carving of the woman was poorly done, still the sculptor had caught a smile on her face and a sense of exultation in the flowing garments that seemed to catch the wind.

Shayna leaned forward on the rail, watching as the waters turned gray and then black. Then she looked up at the faint moon and the stars that glittered against the horizon. Impressed by the majesty of creation, she realized that she and the whole ship were merely specks on a limitless ocean.

Then a sound interrupted her and she turned to see a man's figure.

"Who is it?" she said quickly, thinking it was perhaps Lt. Stillitoe, who often passed by her when she came to stand in the bow.

"Hello, Shayna."

It was Cathan's voice. Shayna held her breath, willing him to go away, but instead he stepped closer. The moon's light fell upon his face, revealing the dark pools of his eyes. "I've been wanting to speak to you."

"I don't want to speak to you!" she retorted.

"I should not blame you." To her surprise, Cathan began to walk away. His action surprised her, for she remembered him as a determined man.

"Wait," she said.

As he turned, feelings warred within her. Since the night of their attempted elopement, she had thought of him and now he stood before her. It was impossible for her to calm herself.

"Yes?" he asked, balancing himself against the roll of the ship.

"What do you want?" she said harshly.

"I wanted to ask you to forgive me."

They were the last words Shayna had expected and for a moment she thought she had misheard him. "Forgive you?" she demanded.

"Yes. Ever since I've known you were on the ship I had hoped I could speak to you." He hesitated, knowing his time was short but seeing that she was frozen into immobility. "I behaved very badly, very wrongly toward you, Shayna. It was not honorable and I ask your pardon."

Shayna could not believe the humility in his quiet words. To her, this was not Cathan Morgan! Words came tumbling out of her mouth almost incoherently. "Forgive you? After what you did? Do you deny that you courted me simply for money?"

"No, I can't deny that."

"What a fool I was to listen to you, to think of you! Trevor was right, but I wouldn't listen to him. . . ."

Cathan listened without moving a muscle. He had never seen Shayna angry, but now he realized that this proud woman would never be able to forgive him for the way he'd deceived her. As Shayna stepped closer, all the memory of her weakness in ever loving him exploded within her. Almost without volition, her hand flashed out and she slapped him on the cheek. "You stay away from me, you jailbird!"

At that moment, another voice spoke immediately behind Cathan. "What's this? Is this man annoying you, Miss Wakefield?"

Both Cathan and Shayna were startled. In the intensity of their meeting they had not realized that anyone else was on deck. Then Roxby had materialized out of the murky darkness and grabbed Cathan's arm. "I can see he's giving you trouble, miss."

Unable to speak, Shayna took one look at Cathan's face, then ran blindly into the darkness.

"Well now, you've been asking for trouble and you're going to get it. You're under arrest, Morgan."

"On what charge?"

"Assaulting the captain's daughter."

"I didn't lay a hand on her."

"She laid a hand on you, didn't she?"

From the gleam in Roxby's eyes, Cathan knew there was no way out, so he stood silently. "If I had my way, you'd hang from the yardarm for this. The least you'll get will be a taste of the cat."

<hr />

"I'll have to take action, of course. Lt. Roxby's bringing charges of insubordination."

Trevor stood beside the captain as the two faced aft. It was early morning and word had gotten around the ship, even before Trevor awoke, that Cathan Morgan had been arrested by Lt. Roxby for annoying the captain's daughter.

"I haven't seen Shayna," Trevor said. "Did the fellow put his hands on her?"

"She won't say anything about it. I think she's ashamed of the whole thing." Honor slapped his hands together in disgust. "Why did this have to happen?"

"What does Roxby say?"

"He says Morgan was insolent to Shayna and then to him."

"Do you believe him?"

"It doesn't matter whether I do or not. When one of my officers brings a charge against one of the crew, I can't take sides. That's the way it is on a ship."

"What will happen to Cathan?"

"I will have to see that punishment is administered."

"What sort of punishment?" Trevor asked.

"He'll be flogged."

Trevor did not answer for a time. He had never seen a flogging, for there had been none on board the *Dauntless* since the ship had left port. He had heard, however, of the harshness of it. "I have no sympathy for the fellow, but wouldn't it be better simply to transfer him as you'd planned, Captain?"

"It's too late for that now," Wakefield said heavily. "Every man on the crew knows he's been charged by one of the officers. If I let him go, it would breed trouble. You must understand that, Trevor. . . . I should never have taken him on board, but now I have to do my duty."

<hr />

"I'll have to ask you to remain belowdecks this morning, Shayna."

Looking up quickly, Shayna studied her father's face. She had hardly said a word to him since the incident occurred, but now she asked, "What is it?"

Honor hesitated, then said, "It's a call for punishment. I don't want you to witness it. It's a very brutal thing."

Shayna immediately dropped her gaze, for she knew enough about life in the navy to know that any crewman who challenged an officer could not be ignored. "I wish that the lieutenant had not come on deck," she said, her voice unsteady. "It's none of his business."

"Roxby's accusation is that Morgan was insolent and even lifted his hand against him."

"Do you believe that?"

"It doesn't matter whether I believe it or not. He's made the charge and the crew knows it. Stay downstairs, Daughter."

Leaving Shayna's cabin, the captain stepped out on the deck where the men had gathered to witness the punishment. As the master of arms read the charges, Honor's and Cathan's eyes met. Honor Wakefield hoped desperately that he could find some trace of shame or guilt there, but Morgan's eyes were calm, impassive.

"Seaman Morgan is accused of insolence to his officers! The sentence is twenty lashes!"

"Do any of this man's officers care to put in a word for him?" Capt. Wakefield asked.

He had no hope that they would, for neither Peters nor Stillitoe would interfere. For just one moment silence fell, then Capt. Wakefield commanded, "Seize him up!"

Morgan took off his shirt, facing a grate that had been rigged upright against the brake of the quarterdeck. His hands were made fast as Capt. Wakefield read the articles of war that covered the offense. Then Wakefield said sharply, "Do your duty!"

The bosun's mate took the cat-o'-nine-tails out of a red baize bag. He ran the strands through his hands, then took position just to the left of the restrained Morgan. Drawing back the cat, he brought it down with all his force along the naked back. Immediately Morgan's back was lined with blue stripes. Again the cat drew back and by the time half a dozen strokes had fallen, blood streamed down the back of the offender.

Honor Wakefield forced himself to keep his eyes on the scene. It would not do for the captain to refuse to watch, for he was sure that some of the men would be watching for a sign of weakness. Honor waited for Morgan's cries of pain, but none came.

Finally the bosun's mate stepped back and looked up at Honor. "Punishment completed, sir."

"Take him down."

Praise God Barebones hurried to cut Cathan down. He caught the sagging body and whispered, "We'll fix you right, lad." He and Job, the foretopman, dragged Cathan away from the grate and dashed his back with saltwater to cleanse the wound.

"You took it well," Job said, his eyes approving. He glanced up at the officers who were still watching and his lips tightened. "Don't give 'em the satisfaction of hearing you cry out. That's what I say."

For his part, Trevor had watched the scene with horror. It was brutal, unlike anything he had ever witnessed. And even from where he stood, just behind the captain and the lieutenants, he could see Morgan's torn flesh. Sickened, he turned away and made his way to the cockpit, where he sat down and covered his face with trembling hands. "I don't like the fellow—but that shouldn't happen to any man!"

Twelve

A MATTER OF DUTY

I don't think he'll come to see you on his own, sir, but I'm really worried about him."

Trevor Wakefield had expected the seaman who appeared before him to have one of the usual complaints. He had never spoken with Praise God Barebones before, but he was automatically suspicious, for he knew Barebones had been in prison with Morgan. So he asked brusquely what his trouble was and Barebones answered quickly, "It's my mate, Morgan."

"What's wrong with him?"

"Well, I can't wake him up, sir."

"Can't wake him up? What do you mean by that?"

Praise God shifted his weight uncomfortably, for he could see the antagonism in the physician's eyes. "Well, sir, it's his back. It ain't ever healed proper since he got flogged. He went back on duty, but he started gettin' fever two days ago. I tried to get him to come in and see you, but he wouldn't do it."

"Have him come in. I'll take a look at him."

"Yes, sir, but—"

"Don't argue with me, Barebones, just do as I say!"

"Yes, sir!"

As soon as Barebones was gone, Trevor tried to take stock of his feelings. It had been a week since Morgan's flogging and he

145

had not gotten over the sight of it yet. Neither he, Shayna, nor Honor Wakefield had mentioned the affair. But now as he stood there, he wondered what sort of scheme Morgan was concocting now. "I have no trust in the man," he muttered angrily, pacing the floor while he waited.

When the door opened, Trevor was shocked to see Praise God and Karl Steinmetz carrying a limp form.

"Put him over there," Trevor said.

The two men moved carefully and Praise God said, "Lay him on his face, Karl. "

When Trevor stepped forward to remove the shirt that was draped around Morgan's shoulders, he blinked with shock to see the infected flesh. "How long has it been like this?" he demanded.

"I don't know, sir. I didn't know nothin' was wrong with him until he just collapsed. Then he went into a fever and we couldn't wake him up to go on deck," Praise God said.

"He shouldn't have had to go back on duty with a back like that. I've never seen such a bad one," Steinmetz said.

"All right, I'll take care of him."

"If I can help you, Doctor, just call on me," Praise God said. Then the two men left the room.

Trevor Wakefield moved quickly, for one touch of Morgan's flesh told him the fever had to come down. He cleaned the back, applied ointment, and bound it with clean bandages. He turned suddenly at a sound and saw that Morgan's eyes were open but showed no sign of recognition. "You're going to be all right," he said grimly, but Morgan did not answer. Trevor sat beside Morgan's still form for over an hour, knowing he was delirious.

When Simon Lawler came in, he asked with surprise, "What's wrong with him?"

"He's got an infected back. Sit beside him."

"Yes, sir. Did you know there's a ship alongside?"

"No. An enemy ship?"

"Nah, sir, one of ours."

Trevor went up on deck and saw that the *Dauntless* was being paced by a smaller ship. As the captain of the other ship put out a boat, Capt. Wakefield watched eagerly from the quarterdeck.

An hour later, Lt. Peters brought Trevor a message. "Captain would like to see you, please, Dr. Wakefield."

"Thank you, Lieutenant."

Going quickly to the captain's cabin, Trevor found Honor standing in front of the stern windows, looking at some documents on his desk.

"Ah, Doctor. I suppose you saw the ship?"

"Yes, sir, I did."

"It's one of ours, a sloop called the *Cutlass*. I think it may answer."

"Answer what, Captain?"

"I have spoken with the captain. He's agreed to take Morgan aboard."

For a moment Trevor was tempted to agree. Then he knew that would be impossible. "I'm afraid that won't answer, Capt. Wakefield."

"What? What are you talking about?"

"Cathan's mates brought him in a short while ago. His back has become infected and he's got a high fever."

"I didn't know he was ill."

"Well, neither did his mates."

"Is it serious?" Honor asked.

"With a high fever like that it could be. If they don't have a physician on board, he could die."

"Well, sloops don't carry physicians." Honor stared hard at the doctor. "Are you certain about this?"

"I couldn't answer for his life if he's moved. He'll need constant care."

"That settles it," Honor said angrily. "I thought we'd solved that problem! Now we have another one!"

"What's that, sir?"

"Capt. Simms gave me something to worry about. He says there's a French third rater called the *Montrose* in these waters."

"An enemy ship?"

"Of course. And from all I hear of her, and all that Captain Simms has heard, she's a killer. Already sunk two of our frigates in single-ship actions. We're not prepared to meet a larger ship like that, especially one so well gunned and so well commanded. This crew's not ready and neither is the ship."

"What will you do?"

"I'll pray we don't encounter her," Honor said grimly. "If we do, we'll just have to trust in our speed to get away."

Such plans were beyond Trevor's knowledge so he simply said, "Well, I'll keep Cathan under my care."

"Let me know what happens."

"I'll do that."

❦

Shayna had watched the captain of the *Cutlass* board the *Dauntless* and then return to his own ship. She waited until it had disappeared, then went to see her father.

"Were there any letters on that ship?" she asked.

"No, she did not come from England." He stopped, eyed her, then asked, "Have you talked to Trevor lately?"

"No."

"Then you don't know about Cathan."

"Cathan? What about him?" Shayna had not seen Cathan since the night she slapped him, because she had stayed in her cabin to avoid him. Now she looked up quickly. "What's he done now?"

"He's in rather bad condition, Trevor tells me."

"What's wrong with him?"

"His back got infected and he didn't report it. He collapsed and his mates took him to Trevor. He hasn't recovered consciousness yet, I don't think."

Shayna stared at her father, eyes stricken by the news. "What will happen to him?"

"You'll have to ask Trevor about that. I'm sure he'll take care of him." Then he said gently, "Shayna, how do you feel about this man?"

"I don't know. . . . But I wouldn't like to see any man die, especially when it was partly my fault."

"I've never asked you what happened that night on deck, but if you'd care to tell me, I'll listen," Honor said kindly.

"I—told him I hated him and I slapped him. And that's when Lt. Roxby stepped out."

"Did Morgan assault you?"

"No, he—he told me he was sorry for what he had done to me."

"And that's all?"

"Yes, that's all," she said angrily. "I think Roxby lied! I don't think Cathan said anything to him!"

"No? Well, we can't prove that. . . . I was going to transfer him to the *Cutlass,* but he was too sick to go. Maybe he'll recover. I promise to get rid of him as soon as possible." To his surprise, she said nothing and left the cabin.

All afternoon Shayna kept to herself. When she and her father had dinner together, neither of them spoke of Cathan. Finally she said, "I'm going to bed. I'm a little tired."

"Good night, Shayna. I hope you sleep well."

Shayna went to her cabin but did not undress. Her mind was troubled and she knew she could not sleep. As the hours wore on, she heard the piping of the bosun's whistle at the eight o'clock watch and the movement of the men from the lower deck to the upper deck.

Finally an idea came to her. *I've got to know how he is.* As she left her cabin and walked down the corridor to the ladder, she did not pass anyone. When she stepped inside the room, she expected to find Trevor, but he was not there. By the light of the lantern she saw Cathan Morgan lying on a low bunk. She did not go to him straightaway, for she did not know what to say. But now as she moved forward, she saw that he was lying on his stomach, his face turned toward her. She crept forward and whispered, "Cathan—?"

When he did not move, she paused uncertainly. His face was flushed and he spoke, but she could not understand what he was saying. Leaning closer, she asked, "Cathan, can you hear me?"

Again he muttered and she knew he was delirious. Curious, she lifted the sheet, catching her breath when she saw the oozing bandages. She lowered the sheet, a shudder running through her body, and knelt beside the low bunk. His hand was on the floor and she picked it up and held it. She was fearful that someone would come in, mostly Trevor, but she also felt pity for this man who had been so brutally and undeservedly mistreated. Not knowing what else to do, she leaned forward over him. Once she thought he said her name, but she could not be sure. Finally she rose, put his hand down gently, and said quietly, "I'm sorry. . . ."

Shayna managed to get back to her room without seeing anyone. Closing the door, she stood still with her back against it. The sight of Cathan's torn flesh had affected her terribly and her hands were trembling. Pressing her fist hard against her lips, she sat there in silence.

<hr />

From time to time a voice Cathan couldn't understand came out of the darkness. Hands, sometimes hard and harsh, touched him, bringing cool relief to his warm body. He did not know where he was. Just when he began to rise from the darkness, the room would sway and he would plunge down again with fever.

He did not know how long he lay there until he finally regained consciousness. Lying on his stomach, he was suddenly aware of movement and his eyes opened to focus on a man who sat on a chair next to his bed. He tried to speak, but his lips were dry and the sound was more like a croak.

"Are you awake?" Trevor Wakefield asked, seeing that Cathan's eyes were clear. Despite his dislike of Cathan, Trevor felt a surge of victory. He hated to lose any medical case and he had been concerned that his patient would die. The fever had raged dangerously high. As Cathan struggled to sit up, Trevor said, "Here, let me help you. How do you feel?"

"Thirsty!"

Trevor had tried to give the patient water, but it had been difficult. Now he quickly poured water into a tin cup and held it to Cathan's lips. "Easy there. That's enough at one time."

"What . . . ?"

"Your back got infected. You're very weak, but you're going to be all right." Trevor held his hand on Cathan's forehead. "Your fever's broken. I don't think it will come back. Here, take some more water. Just a little."

Cathan sipped at the water gratefully, savoring it, and then licked his lips. "How long have I been here?"

"Three days."

Cathan stared at Trevor. It was like coming out of a dream, but memories kept nagging at him. "Have you been here—all the time?"

"Some of it. Lawler took care of you too."

Cathan Morgan had also dreamed that Shayna Wakefield had come, taken his hand, and spoken to him. But he knew that could not be, so he did not mention it. He stretched his arms carefully and instantly the pain came.

"You should have turned yourself in. Why did you have to be such a fool?"

"I guess I was born a fool."

"Well, it nearly killed you this time," Trevor said. "You need to eat something. Do you want to sit up in a chair?" Cathan nodded, accepting the doctor's help. Then Trevor said, "I'll get you some broth."

When Trevor returned from the galley, he saw that Cathan was still awake. After Cathan ate the soup eagerly, Trevor said, "You've got to rest up. The infection ought to be gone in a few days, but you won't be doing much work for a while."

"Thanks," Cathan said softly.

"Don't thank me, that's my job!" was what Trevor wanted to say, for he was still angry. But the expression in Cathan's dark eyes stopped him. "You can have some more soup in a couple of hours. I want you to eat small meals, very nutritious food. Are you feeling nauseated?"

"No," Cathan replied.

"I'll have to treat your back regularly to be sure the infection doesn't start again." Trevor left the room and went directly to the captain, who was with Shayna. Watching them carefully, Trevor said, "He's not going to die."

"He's awake?" Shayna asked quickly.

"Yes, the infection's gone and I don't think the fever will come back."

"Will you keep him in the sick bay, Trevor?"

"For a couple of days anyway. A hammock wouldn't be much good for his back in that condition." Trevor hesitated, wanting to ask if Shayna wanted to see Cathan, but he dared not. Finally, with a slight shrug, he asked, "Any sign of that French ship?"

"No, and I'm hoping we don't see any," Honor said.

When Trevor left, Shayna said, "I'm glad he's better. I felt responsible for him."

"I'll try to get him off the ship as soon as I can. I had hoped to send him with the *Cutlass,* but Trevor said he was too ill." Although Honor wanted to discuss the matter with Shayna further, she merely turned and left the room. As her footsteps receded, Honor once again felt hopeless, wishing his wife had lived. She would have known what to do or say to Shayna.

When the *Dauntless* had at last touched land and transferred some cargo and dispatches, Capt. Wakefield ordered her to refit and start back for England. They had not seen any sign of the *Montrose* or any other French ships of war, for which he was profoundly grateful.

Honor Wakefield had not asked directly after Cathan, but as the weeks passed Trevor had informed him that Cathan had healed miraculously. "I never saw anything like it," Trevor had said. "The flesh just seemed to knit together after the infection was gone."

Shayna had not inquired either, but one day she had seen Cathan on deck, moving easily with no sign of discomfort. He did not see her and she had ducked behind the mizzenmast to avoid his gaze, for she wanted no more confrontation with him.

"We'll go around the ship tomorrow, Lt. Stillitoe," Capt. Wakefield said. The next morning hammocks were piped up half an hour earlier than usual.

At the end of breakfast, Cathan threw himself into the habitual activity, grateful that his back no longer pained him. Praise had prayed for him to heal quickly and Cathan felt God had answered that prayer.

Now all hands shaved, including Cathan, and those with pigtails sought out their tie mates for a mutual combing and replaiting. It had been amusing to Cathan how much attention the seamen paid to their hair. Often, when the weather was fair, they would sprawl on the forecastle and comb out their long hair, some of them plaiting it up again for one another.

Although Cathan himself kept his hair relatively short, he helped Praise God put *his* pigtails in a proper state.

The marines polished, pipe-clayed, and brushed all morning until Lt. Peters called out, "Beat to quarters!" and drum strokes echoed. The marines filed across the deck to form ranks. The seamen ran to their appointed stations in single rows along the rest of the quarterdeck, the gangways, and the forecastle. The midshipmen and the officers called out, "Toe the line!" until the men were reduced to some sort of order. Then Lt. Stillitoe stepped across the deck to speak to the captain. "All officers have reported, sir."

"Very well, Lt. Stillitoe, we will go around the ship."

This was the time when the captain looked into every part of the ship, from the mast down to the hold. At each division the officers saluted, the men whipped off their hats, smoothed their hair, and stood straight. Only once during that inspection did Capt. Wakefield hesitate and that was when he came to Cathan Morgan. He had not intended to speak, but found himself staring into the eyes of his young kinsman. "Are you fit for duty, Morgan?"

"Aye, sir."

"See that you do your duty then."

"Aye, sir."

After the inspection Cathan went off watch and sat beside Oren, one of his mess mates, who always longed to be ashore.

"Oren, what will you do if you ever get off this ship?"

"Me, I'm going to take an oar and start walkin' inland."

"You hate the sea that bad?"

"Don't you?"

"No, I don't really hate it."

"I don't see why you shouldn't after the beating you took."

The coxswain loudly interrupted them. "Don't plan on no sleep tonight. The glass is fallin'."

"A storm?" Morgan asked.

"Yes, and a bad 'un from the looks of it."

In the months that he had been on the sea, Cathan had seen many storms. But there had been none as terrible as the one that began tossing the *Dauntless* around as if it were a toy. On land there was someplace to hide, a hole to get into, but at sea where was a man to go?

It was not the worst storm that the regular hands had experienced, but it was bad enough. Capt. Wakefield ordered the ship to have a closed-reef foresail and a mizzen storm staysail and the ship was driven before the mighty blast of the wind even with that small amount of canvas.

Lt. Stillitoe and the captain were still on duty past three in the morning when the rain began sweeping in solid sheets across the deck. Lt. Peters put on his oilskins and crept up the ladder, followed by Lt. Roxby. All officers were worried, although they did not like to say so.

Capt. Wakefield gripped the helm, waiting for the ship to come around after a heavy wave had knocked her head to leeward. A series of prolonged lightning flashes lit up the sky as an enormous thundercloud rolled almost within arm's reach. The *Dauntless* pitched and then went down, sending her entire forecastle deep under green water. Belowdecks, Cathan Morgan was thrown off his feet, rolling out of control past the cannons.

Cathan wondered if the ship would ever rise again, but slowly the ship righted itself. Then Cathan heard a horrified cry, "Loose cannon! Loose cannon!" as water surged through the ship.

Grabbing at the cannon he stood beside to keep his balance as the ship lurched again, Cathan saw Nappy, the gunner, leap toward one of the huge guns that had broken loose. It rolled backwards, crashed into the gun on the starboard side, and then shot forward again.

Men screamed in fear as Nappy made a leap. He caught one of the wheels, but was tossed aside as the eighteen pounder careered into the mast that came down from the top and extended to the keel.

"Loose cannon! Loose cannon!" the men cried.

Cathan Morgan had no experience with such a thing as this. A cannon on shore might roll downhill, but when the deck was first tilting forward, then rearing backward, there was no defense.

Beside him, Praise screamed, "It'll crash through the side and sink us if we don't stop it!"

But the men were more concerned about staying out of the monster's path than stopping it.

The cannon continued to wheel quickly, as if it had a mind of its own.

"What can I do, Nappy?" Cathan jumped to stand beside the gunner and saw fear on the man's face.

"We got to stop the wheels. Shove somethin' between them."

Cathan looked around, grabbed one of the long poles used to sponge down the gun, and ran toward the cannon. When it turned suddenly and lunged at him, he stepped to one side, his feet almost slipping on the wet deck. The bone-crushing wheel passed within an inch of his foot.

"That's it!" Nappy said, picking up a rammer himself as he and Cathan chased the runaway cannon.

But when Nappy almost had it, his feet slipped. The muzzle of the cannon smashed against his arm and drove him through the air.

Cathan heard the gunner's cry and saw him lying on the deck, holding his arm. Because it was twisted at an impossible angle, Cathan knew it was broken.

Running forward, he dodged the cannon that banged again against the mast and even against his ribs, knowing it would be sudden death if he lost his balance. Finally Cathan saw his opportunity. He stepped in front of the gun as it rushed toward him, then stepped aside as it passed, ramming the pole in between the spokes. It caught, jerking the rammer out of his hand. The cannon barrel whizzed by, narrowly missing his head, and spun in a circle since only one wheel was secure. Grabbing up another rammer, Morgan waited his chance, then jabbed at the right wheel. It caught, and then the cannon was still.

"Help me tie it down," he called to the men. Now that the cannon was secure, men streamed out to manhandle it back to its position, shove it into place, and fasten it down.

Morgan ran over to where Devere was lying. "Is it bad, Nappy?"

Devere glanced down at his broken arm and shrugged. "Not as bad as it could have been. I'm glad you were here, Cathan."

When the storm blew itself out, Capt. Wakefield could at last draw a sigh of relief. He had not taken his clothes off for over sixty hours, afraid that the ship would founder. "Well, Stillitoe, that was a close one," he said.

Stillitoe was as weary as his captain. "I wouldn't care to go through that again." He looked up at the rigging that had been torn by the fierce wind. "It'll take awhile to patch this together."

"Yes, it will."

Stillitoe cocked his head. "Have you talked to Devere?"

"Yes. That cannon nearly sunk us."

"He says it was Morgan who stopped it. If it hadn't been for him, that gun might have gone right through the side of the ship. Then we'd all be at the bottom of the sea feeding the sharks."

"Yes, that's what Devere told me."

"I think Morgan deserves a little commendation."

"What did you have in mind?"

"I don't want to pry into your business, Captain. I have felt somehow that you didn't like Morgan. True enough, he doesn't have any experience, but I've been keeping up with him," Stillitoe said, keeping his balance easily now that the heavy waves had calmed down. "We don't have a gunner now. Dr. Wakefield tells me that was such a bad break that he can't let Devere come back to duty again."

"What do you suggest?"

"We need a gunner—and you won't like what I'm going to say."

"Say your mind, Lieutenant."

"There's no man on this ship who can lay a gun like Morgan. I guess it was his experience in the artillery."

"Are you suggesting we make him gunner on this ship?"

"He's the best fitted for the job," Stillitoe countered.

Wakefield stared at his lieutenant. "I do have something against the man. But I won't let it stand in my way. I've talked to Devere myself. He says the same as you. Let's give him a temporary warrant. He has to have some authority. I don't know how the other men will take it. Some of them have long years of service."

"But they can't aim guns like Morgan can. I say give him a chance."

"So be it."

It was not a popular decision, especially with Eben Roxby. Although a warrant officer was not a regular officer, still it meant that Cathan would be lifted from the usual run of deckhands. Roxby had argued furiously against it, but the captain had finally said, "That's my decision, Roxby. I advise you to live with it."

───────

Trevor and Shayna were talking in the captain's day cabin when Trevor said finally, "I've tried not to say anything about this, Shayna, but I can't keep quiet any longer—"

"Please," Shayna interrupted, "don't say it, Trevor."

"I have to. You must know how much I love you. I haven't changed, but I have to know how you feel."

Disturbed, Shayna said, "I don't know how I feel."

"Are you still in love with Cathan?" Trevor demanded.

Her eyes pleaded with him. "Please, don't ask me! I don't know anything anymore! I know he's not a good man."

"Well, he has courage. He proved that when he saved the ship. Every man on the crew was running from that cannon except him and Devere. . . ." When Shayna said nothing more, Trevor said abruptly, "I think you're still in love with him," and left the room. He went at once to find Cathan, who was scrubbing the deck, and said, "Morgan, come with me."

"Yes, Doctor." Cathan rose and followed the doctor down to the cockpit. As soon as they were alone, Trevor said, "I think you're a counterfeit, Morgan. You're pretending to be a Christian, but I have no confidence in you. I think you're the same man you always were."

"I'm sorry you think that, Dr. Wakefield."

"I want you to stay away from Shayna," Trevor blurted out.

"I think I can safely promise that," Morgan said dryly.

"I mean it! I've heard your story about how you were converted, but you'll never convince me."

"No, I don't suppose I ever will. Is that all, sir?"

"That's all," Trevor said, dissatisfied with the interview. For the next few days he kept away from Shayna and Cathan Morgan.

⁂

Honor Wakefield knew something was troubling his daughter and the doctor, but he did not feel comfortable asking. And the trouble was taken out of his mind suddenly when the watch up on the mast said, "Deck there! Ship off the port bow!"

Honor put out his glass at once but could see nothing. "What do you make of her?"

"Ship of war, sir!"

"Is she English?"

"No, sir, not English!"

"Well, tell me what she is, man!"

The lookout peered again. "She's a ship of the line, maybe a third rater! French by the color of her sails!"

Soon Honor was joined by Peters, Roxby, and Stillitoe.

"It has to be the *Montrose,* I'm afraid," Capt. Wakefield said, eyeing the tattered sails that still had not been repaired. "I doubt if we can outrun unless we can get more canvas up. Get to it, all of you! We've got to have more sail!"

"Can't we fight her, sir?" Lt. Peters said eagerly. "She'd be quite a prize."

"A frigate fight a ship of the line in a single action? No!" Honor replied vehemently.

The ship became a beehive of activity, but as the *Montrose* drew closer it became evident that the *Dauntless* could not mount enough fresh canvas to outrun her.

"It'll have to be a fight, sir," Stillitoe said. "We'd better get ready."

"I think you're right, Lieutenant," Honor said grimly. "It's going to be a hard one."

"We can do it, sir."

"I'm glad to see you're so confident. See that the men are fed and that they get all the rest they can. We'll run before her until she catches us, then we'll turn and rend her as best we can."

Going back to his cabin, Honor Wakefield found his daughter sitting at his desk writing. When she saw his face, she asked, "What is it? Something wrong?"

"It's the *Montrose.* We're going to have to fight her."

Shayna hurried to him. "Will we win?" she asked.

"No man can say about a thing like that. She outguns us and we were badly hurt in that storm. Most of the crew have never seen action." After a pause, he said, "But it's you I'm worried about, Shayna." He groaned and hugged her tightly. "I wish I'd never let you get on board this ship!"

Comforted by her father's arms, Shayna said, "It will be all right."

"I trust God it will. . . . You can't fight," he said gently, "but you can pray."

Seeing the love in her father's eyes, Shayna squeezed his hands. "I will," she said and ran from the cabin.

Then Honor began to pray. *Oh, God, you know there's no way we can win a fight with that ship. She's too big and has too many guns. We're not able, but you're able, O God, and I ask you to help us. And I especially ask that you let my daughter endure this coming fight in safety.*

Heat

Part THREE

1 8 0 1

of Battle

Thirteen

DAY OF DISCOVERY

With creaking timbers and the wind singing through her rigging, the *Dauntless* rode the waves easily under shortened sail. But as the men manned the sails, the wind on her beam grew stronger and Capt. Wakefield nodded with approval to Lt. Stillitoe, who stood beside him.

"I think you may instruct my daughter to go below, Lieutenant."

"Aye, Captain!"

Stillitoe made his way to where Shayna stood, one hand on the rail. The wind pulled at her skirt, tossing her auburn hair and turning her cheeks pink under their tan. Touching his hat in a salute, the lieutenant said, "Ma'am, I'm ordered to escort you below."

"But I want to stay on deck and watch the action."

Shocked, Stillitoe responded, "Oh no, ma'am, that would not be possible!" Realizing she had no concept of what a battle at sea was like, he quickly said, "It's the captain's orders, ma'am. I must obey—and so must you."

"Very well, Lieutenant, I will be obedient."

"We'll put you down in the hold, where you'll be safe."

The hold proved to be a stinking, frightening dungeon. For a moment Shayna considered protesting but, by the light of the candle, she saw that the lieutenant's face was tense.

"I'm sorry there are no better provisions, but really, ma'am, this is the safest part of the whole ship."

"I will be fine, Lieutenant," Shayna said, smiling. "You may go back to your duties now."

Returning to the deck, Stillitoe heard the cry from the mast-head. "Sail hold! Deck there, sail right ahead! I believe it's the *Montrose,* sir!"

Capt. Wakefield and Stillitoe looked up to where the lookout was clinging to his perch, swinging around in dizzy circles as the ship pitched and swooped over the waves. "She is the *Montrose,* sir!" the loud cry came. "She's headed on the starboard tack, same course as us!" Then he added, "She must have seen us!"

"Man the braces!" Honor shouted. "Portray helm! Stillitoe, beat the quarters, if you please, and clear for action!"

Immediately Stillitoe cried out an order and drums began rolling. The hands began pouring up on deck. Honor watched as the men went through the well-learned drill. The guns were run out, the deck sanded, the hoses rigged to the pumps, the bulk-heads torn down. Then, seeing the *Montrose* sailing on the oppo-site tack towards her, Honor growled at the quartermaster, "Steer small!"

"Aye, sir!"

As waves crashed loudly around the ship, Stillitoe came back and peered at the enemy ship. "The *Montrose* won't be able to lower her deck ports."

"No, she will not. That will be to our advantage. Still, we're heavily outgunned."

"Lieutenant, see that the matches in the tubs are alight."

"Aye, sir."

The flintlock trigger mechanism was much simpler, but with spray breaking aboard it could not be relied upon until the guns grew hot. Honor watched as the old-fashioned method of igni-tion—through coils of slow match—was prepared. Looking up he saw that the *Montrose* had reached her top sails now and was staggering along, close hauled under storm canvas. Even as he watched, a puff of enemy smoke was blown by the wind. But it was still far enough away that the sound of the shot was muffled.

"We'll be passing mighty close, Captain," Stillitoe remarked. He was calm and Honor was glad, for if he fell, Stillitoe would assume command of the *Dauntless*. Stillitoe was a fine lieutenant, but he had never seen action. Honor knew that when the balls began flying and men began dying, even the steadiest of men might turn coward.

The *Montrose* emitted another puff of smoke and this time both men heard the sound of the shot as it passed overhead. Another taunt and a crash from the waist told them that the shot had struck.

The two ships approached each other rapidly. Taking a last look up at the weather vane and topsails, Honor called out, "Stand by! Fire as your guns bear!" From the corner of his mouth he said to the men at the wheel, "Put your helm aweather. Hold her so!" The starboard guns of the *Dauntless* exploded shot into the *Montrose's* side and Honor flinched as he heard the screams of the wounded.

"Well done, sir!" cried Stillitoe.

"Stand by to go about!"

The men stood ready at the sheets and braces as the ship whipped about. The guns were already loaded on the starboard side, and on the port side the gun crews were thrusting wet swabs down the bore to extinguish any fragments of cartridges. They rammed in the charges, the shot, and then heaved the guns back into the firing position.

Quickly they approached the large ship, managing to put in another broadside. "That's about the best we can do," Stillitoe said regretfully.

"I'm afraid so. We're going to have to receive some heavy iron."

Now the two ships met again and Stillitoe ran down the deck screaming, "Fire as you will, men, let them have it!" The deck's broadside crashed out raggedly as the more expert gun crews got their shots off more quickly than the others. The lower decks opened like clockwork and the big guns vomited flame and smoke.

In the madness of battle Honor noted that, as usual, he was calm. Something about battle did this to him. He might be excited in a drill, but when the actual fighting started, it was as though a curtain fell over him. He stood watching as the iron hail from the enemy ship swept the *Dauntless*'s deck. Dead men were piled around the mast where they had been dragged so as not to encumber the gun crews. His eyes ran over the wounded men, some of them certain to die. From time to time they were dragged down the hatchways to where Trevor Wakefield awaited them in the cockpit. But in a time of war, Honor had no time for pity, so he blocked all this out.

So far the *Dauntless* had done well, for she had caught the *Montrose* by surprise. But now the heavier guns and the greater number of them began to tell and as Honor put the *Dauntless* about again, he saw that they were going to pass the *Montrose* to leeward. "I hope to hit her in the stern, Stillitoe, to knock her rudder off."

As the two ships approached, seconds seemed like minutes. They were passing so close that Honor could see every detail on the enemy's deck, including the captain as he screamed orders at his men. Then the *Montrose* lifted out of the sea as she fired a broadside. A shot whistled close to Honor's ear, making an eerie sound as part of the *Dauntless*'s rigging fell. He managed to throw his hand up, but the rigging knocked him to the deck. He wallowed there for a moment, then freed himself and as he got to his feet, he saw ruin all around him. The mizzenmast was gone, snapped off nine feet from the deck, taking the main topgallant with it. The mast, yards, sails, and rigging trailed alongside the unparted shrouds. Then he saw the *Montrose* crossing his stern and felt sick with defeat.

He began to cry out orders. "Lt. Stillitoe, have Lt. Peters clear the deck!"

"Aye, sir. He's wounded, but still able to work the ship."

<hr />

On the lower gun deck, the gun ports were all open. But the light that came in only served to show the havoc that had been wrought by the heavy balls that had pierced the sides of the ship. At least five gun crews had died by the enemy cannon and the living wounded were constantly being carried down to the cockpit.

"A hot work, ain't it, Cat?" Praise God said as the men grunted over the big gun, wheeling it back for loading. Cathan had wondered how he would stand in action. It had been one thing to fight on land, where a man could move about and take cover from enemy fire, but on the *Dauntless* there was nowhere to run. Men were dying on every side of him.

Despite the horror of the scene, Cathan felt a sense of satisfaction, for he was able to keep his fear under control. Ramming the powder charge down, he stepped back while the shot was rammed in. "How are we doing, Praise?" he yelled.

"I reckon we're holdin' our own, but she's a big 'un! It'll take the good Lord to get us out of this!"

At that instant, Lt. Eben Roxby, who was running down the line screaming commands, was struck in the back by an eighteen-pound shot. With no officer to direct the general firing, some of the raw hands began to panic. One of them yelled, "We got to get out of here!"

"Be still, you fool!" Clarence Hyde screamed. Although this was his first battle, Hyde had courage that went beyond his fifteen years. He threw himself in front of several of the men who were scrambling to leave the gun deck, but they simply shoved him aside, ignoring his protest.

"We've got to stop 'em!" Praise cried. "If we don't fire the guns, we'll wind up in a prison for the rest of the war!"

Conscious of Praise's words, Cathan ran over to Roxby's mangled body. Pulling out the dead man's sword, he leaped over the bodies and, fighting and shoving, made his way to the ladder.

"Back to your guns!" he screamed.

"Get out of the way, Morgan!" said Franklin, a poor sailor and a bully. But he was big enough to bull his way forward so that now he stood in front of his mates, challenging Cathan.

Although Cathan was a much smaller man, he lifted the sword, shouting, "Franklin, the enemy may not kill you, but I certainly will if you don't get back to your gun!"

Franklin, filled with fear and panic, lunged forward.

With a movement quicker than thought, Cathan struck out, catching the big man across the temple with the flat of his sword. When Franklin staggered, the tip of Cathan's blade was at his throat. "Back to your guns or I'll slit your throat, you swine!" Cathan screamed. "Fight like a man!"

It was one of those moments in battle on which the action turned. If the men succeeded in leaving their guns, the *Dauntless* would have no teeth on the lower gun deck and would certainly lose. For an instant, Cathan wondered whether Franklin would take up his challenge—and if so, if Cathan could do what he had threatened. To kill a man was not what he desired and he knew he could not do it. Still, Cathan carried out his bluff convincingly. Pressing the blade so that it drew blood, he said, "What'll it be? Are you ready to die, Franklin?"

Franklin gulped, his face pale under the black powder stains. He turned and pushed his way backward. A thrill went through Cathan as Franklin yelled, "All of you, get back to your guns!

We'll whip this fellow! Let's see some pride in you! We're Englishmen and we can blow that Frenchy out of the water!"

Midshipman Hyde stepped closer and whispered, "I'm glad you came, Morgan."

"I think we can handle it, sir," was all Cathan said.

"Maybe you'd better go up and down the line and encourage the men. I think they'll listen to you."

"I'll take the port and you take the starboard, sir."

"Good! Now, let's give that Frenchy some of its own!"

Down in the cockpit Trevor Wakefield had more than he could handle. The wounded had been brought down in such numbers that it was all he could do to find room to work. The floors were growing slippery with blood, so he called out harshly, "Sand under our feet here! Quick now!"

Man after man came to him. Some Trevor knew were dead, for all practical purposes, but he would say to his assistant, "Give this one enough laudanum to put him out."

"He won't never wake up, sir."

"I know that," Trevor snapped, "but there's no sense in his suffering!"

As the guns overhead crashed, shaking the very deck under his feet, Trevor worked on, blocking out the horror so that his hands were swift and sure.

Not far from where Trevor was working, Shayna crouched in the hold. The sounds of the guns, muffled as they were by the decks above, still came with reverberating crashes. Suddenly something ran over her foot. Letting a scream escape, she jumped backward, peering down at the huge gray rat that had appeared. "Go away—go away!" she cried, holding the candle high. As she stared at the animal's red eyes, the ship trembled again.

"I'm going to die!" Shayna said the words aloud in terror. Although she had thought of death, somehow she had pictured it as a far-off event that would happen in a clean bed with physicians, family, and friends around. Now she thought of what it would be like as the ship went down into the cold green water.

Despite herself she began to weep. She had wept before over romance novels, but those had been people who existed only in ink on the pages of a book. This was *real*.

She thought of her father and how he had tried his best to be a good father, sometimes substituting giving her things for giving her himself. Scenes from her childhood, in which she had been granted everything she wanted, passed before her. Now she might die in this dreadful place. She would never be married and have children, and then grandchildren.

Then, without willing it, in the midst of the din and stench, she had a clear vision of Cathan Morgan. Closing her eyes, she thought of how he had first come into her life, held her, and kissed her. She had never admitted to herself that she had been in error in receiving his courtship. But now that she was faced with the ultimate reality of death itself, she knew the feelings she had had for him had been more because of his good looks and charm than from anything deeper. Still, despite that, it was Cathan she thought of with regret as she cried out, "Oh, God, I've been so wrong! Spare me from this death and give me a chance to serve you in a way that you deserve!"

It was the first sincere prayer Shayna Wakefield had ever prayed. And as she knelt in the darkness of that hold, she began to sense the presence of God.

⌦⌫⌦

"We can't keep this up, Captain!" Stillitoe yelled, as he saw the *Montrose* preparing to come about again. Stillitoe's face was marked with black powder, for he had stopped to help one of the gun crews get off a broadside. His hands were smeared with blood from moving the dead gunner.

"I believe you're right, Lieutenant. We don't have enough officers to continue the battle. Do you think we can get enough sail to outrun her?"

"I think so. We've taken down most of her courses and we still have our mainsail and the forward sails untouched."

"Put her about then and head for that fog bank over there," Honor said. "I hate to be whipped!"

"She's just too big for us, Captain."

"I know. You're right. Put her about!"

As the *Dauntless* turned responsively despite the loss of sail, it became obvious she would be able to run away from the *Montrose*.

Honor Wakefield walked around the ship, encouraging the men. "You've done well. She's too heavily gunned for us, but she knows she's been in a battle."

"Right, Captain!" came the reply from an elderly gunner who had lost most of his front teeth. "We'll get her the next time!"

Pleased at the man's spirit, Honor moved down the line, speaking cheerfully to the men and urging them to clear the battle damage. Then he went downstairs to the cockpit, where Trevor was finishing an operation. "How is it going, Doctor?"

Under the lantern that swayed with the motion of the ship, Trevor looked sallow. "I'm doing the best I can, sir."

"I'm sure of that. How many have we lost?"

"I'll give you a full report after I've finished surgery," Trevor said, his lips pinched into a tight line.

"Very good. I'll see that you have some men down here to clean up and to offer what help they can."

Moving on to the gun deck, the captain was greeted with a cheer as he stepped down the ladder. Hyde, his tow hair wild and blue eyes electric with excitement, saluted briskly. "Captain, have we defeated the enemy?"

"Not quite. We'll live to fight another day, Mr. Hyde."

Hyde looked down the line of guns. "Sir, Mr. Roxby's dead."

"I'm sorry to hear of it."

"It was very bad, sir. If it hadn't been for Seaman Morgan, I think it would have been a disaster."

"What happened, Hyde?"

The young man spoke with great animation and finished his narration by saying, "And it was Cathan Morgan who stopped them from leaving their guns. Otherwise every man jack of them would have fled."

"That's good to hear. I'll have a word with the men."

As Honor expressed his gratitude and commendation to the men, he was thinking, *What am I going to say to Morgan? What can I say?* For in spite of Cathan's good work, Honor was still troubled by his hard feelings for the man. Still, if the lower gun decks had stopped firing, he well knew that the ship would have been lost.

Coming to where Morgan stood with the rest of his gun crew, Honor stopped. He studied the younger man's face, reading nothing there except respectful attention.

"You did well, I understand, Morgan."

"All the men did well, sir."

"Yes, I must admit that. Still, Mr. Hyde said if it had not been for your quick action, we might have lost the fire of our guns. I'm very gratified you showed such initiative."

"He did that, sir," Praise said quickly. "It was a bit of panic. I seen it once before and Morgan here was the only thing that kept us from losing our guns."

Honor hesitated, wanting to say something personal, but he knew the men were listening. So instead he said, "I'll keep this in mind, Morgan. It was a fine bit of action and your captain is grateful."

"I only did my duty, Captain, as all the men did."

It was a good answer and as Wakefield moved back up the ladder and climbed to the poop deck, he watched as the men repaired the ship. Looking back, he saw the *Montrose* attempting a pursuit, but with most of her rigging shot away he knew there was no danger.

"Father, are you all right?" Shayna said, directly behind him.

Turning, Honor saw that her face was white and her eyes wide. Hugging her, he said, "Yes, I'm fine, and you?"

"I was frightened for a while," Shayna said, unsure of how much she wanted to tell her father about what had happened to her in the dark hold. "I thought I was going to die." Her green eyes thoughtful, Shayna chose each word carefully. "Then I began realizing how frivolous my life has been . . . how I've spent so much time living in a world that's not real."

This was exactly what Honor Wakefield had always thought, so he said gently, "It makes a difference when you're facing reality like a battle at sea."

"Yes, and do you know what? For the first time in my life, Papa," she said, "I thought about God. When I prayed, it was like Jesus came down into that dark hold. I didn't see him, of course, and I didn't hear anything but the guns, but inside I had a peace that I've never known before." A wonderful smile lit up her face.

"I think he was, my dear," Honor said, feeling a surge of pride and relief. *She's grown up,* Honor thought, *and she'll never be the same again.* As the two stood there, oblivious to the covert stares of the crew, Shayna said, "All I ever knew about Jesus was what I read in a book about him, but now I know him for myself!"

Fourteen

"LOVE NEVER CHANGES"

C athan had to stoop, ducking his head under the low beams as he groped his way through the the semidark-ness of the lower deck. Here, deep in the *Dauntless's* hull, there was little ventilation and his stomach rebelled against the mingled stenches of bilge, tar, and blood. As the ship plunged, the lanterns kept up a haphazard motion, forming dancing shadows over the wounded. Trevor Wakefield stood around a heavily scrubbed table.

"What do you want?" Trevor demanded when he saw Cathan.

"I thought I might help with my mate."

"Who is he?"

"Miller, sir."

Weary with the long hours of work under terrific strain, Trevor had an impulse to curtly send Cathan away. But help was scarce, so he said simply, "All right," then turned back to his surgery. When it was over, Trevor asked, "Which one is Miller?"

Knowing that Trevor Wakefield despised him, Cathan answered quickly. "Over here."

"Put him on the table."

Miller, no more than eighteen, was lifted up. Fright shone in his eyes as he grabbed at Morgan's arm.

"It'll be all right, John," Cathan said gently.

"Don't let him take my foot off!" Miller pleaded.

"The doctor will do the best for you. Don't worry; I'll be right here," Cathan said soothingly. Gritting his teeth, Cathan helped hold Miller, watching as Trevor did the operation.

Then when Miller had been moved off the table, Cathan asked, "Do you need me to help any more, Doctor?"

"I need all the help I can get. This next operation is more difficult."

"I'll help all I can."

"We'll do Midshipman Dockstetter."

The young boy who soon lay on the table had already been heavily sedated with laudanum so that he was unconscious. Again, Cathan did his part to assist Trevor as the doctor probed for the metal object in Dockstetter's ribs. After finding it, he closed the wound and applied a bandage. "I'm obliged to you, Morgan."

"Certainly, Doctor, anytime."

As Cathan left the room, Trevor Wakefield watched him go, wondering, *How can a man be such an utter villain with an innocent girl and be a hero to these men and the ship too? It's like he's two men and I'll never understand either one of them.*

❧

"I don't know how we're going to get the ship ready, but we'll have to."

The dead on deck outnumbered the living and every man who could walk was used for handling the ship and plugging the shot holes. Some of the crew had simply collapsed and lay sprawled on the main deck.

Looking over the ship carefully, Capt. Wakefield saw other signs of battle apart from the sheeted corpses and the dark stains not yet washed away. Jagged splinters stood up here and there and the ship's sides were pierced with shot holes, covered only roughly by canvas. The port sills were stained black with powder and an eighteen pounder was half buried in the tough oak. But the ship was afloat and it was only a matter of repair to get her ready again.

"Orders, sir?" Stillitoe asked quietly.

"Today is Sunday."

"Shall I pipe the church?"

"I think we will do so." Despite the wreckage on deck, Honor felt he was doing the right thing.

The coxswain's whistle soon sounded the call to church service. As Honor read from the Psalms, the sound of the old words calmed the men. Taking off his hat, Honor ignored the printed prayer that was available for all captains. His clear voice echoed over the waters that surrounded the *Dauntless:* "Oh, God our Father, you are merciful above all that we can know. From everlasting to everlasting thou art God. We thank you for preserving the ship and those of us who have survived. We grieve for those who have gone and pray for them and for their families. We know that your hand is on us and we ask that you keep us safe in the days to come. We ask it in the name of Jesus Christ, our Lord."

As amens rang around the deck, Capt. Wakefield lifted his head. He spotted Cathan Morgan, who had removed his hat, an odd expression in his eyes.

As Lt. Stillitoe dismissed the men, Shayna came to stand beside her father. "That was a fine choice of Scripture and a good prayer, Papa."

"Thank you, my dear. The men need all the comfort they can get."

"How many were—killed?"

"Fourteen, and a great many more wounded. Trevor's done a magnificent job."

"I'm sure he has," Shayna said abruptly, for she had caught sight of Cathan Morgan who, with his mates, was still standing on deck. As their glances met for a moment, Shayna could not help but remember their times together. Ever since her time in the hold, many memories had come flooding back to her. But unable to read what was in his dark eyes, she turned and walked away.

As the *Dauntless* crept between two headlands into a channel, the cutter Capt. Wakefield had sent out with Stillitoe to sound the depths moved slowly. As the ship dropped anchor inside a hidden natural harbor surrounded by mountains, Honor sighed with relief. They had limped along, expecting at any moment to encounter the *Montrose* again or another enemy ship. Now he would have time to refit the ship.

Soon the men were on land. Judging by the pathlessness of the closely packed vegetation, there was no human life around. Strange birds flitted through the twilight of the branches as Honor examined their setting and said to Stillitoe, "We'll have to work hard, Stillitoe, to get the ship fitted out."

It was terribly hard work. As the ship lay defenseless on her side, the carpenter and his men working on the bottom, the officers knew well that they were helpless if a ship did appear. Soon toiling gangs were set to work and the men were driven from earliest dawn as long as daylight lasted. Many of the ship's company picked oakum to stuff as caulking in the sides between the planks. The shot holes were plugged, the strained seams were caulked and pitched, and missing sheets of copper were replaced by the last few sheets the ship carried.

For four days the tiny bay was filled with the sounds of hammers, mallets, and axes. Then the seventy-five-foot main yard had to be swayed up and hung vertical. It was lowered down, coaxed through the main deck and then through the orlop until it rested solidly on the keelson.

Finally Capt. Wakefield said to his officers, "Well, we have a ship again."

"Yes, sir!" Lt. Peters said. Although he was an aristocrat, he had worked hard as a manual laborer, winning the respect of his captain.

"I think we'll be ready for duty again when we can get the sails fitted," Stillitoe said, eyes gleaming.

"I hardly expected to be in action," Honor said, "but the men have done well, and so have you gentlemen."

"Thank you, sir," both responded. Then Stillitoe said, "We're short a lieutenant and we lost our gunner."

"I know it will be difficult."

"If there were a capable midshipman, I think it would be a good time to give him a temporary assignment as acting lieutenant."

"I don't think any of our midshipmen are capable," Honor said regretfully. "Hyde will be one day, but he's not now."

As they talked further, Stillitoe said, "Have you considered making Morgan the permanent gunner, sir? We could give him a full warrant. I think he could handle the lower deck."

"Do you think such an appointment would be successful?"

"Oh yes!" Stillitoe responded instantly. "I've questioned the men very carefully. He has a natural flare for leadership."

"Well, he was an officer in the army, for whatever that's worth," Peters said. "I think we'll have to do something. The two of us can't handle the upper deck and the lower deck."

"Speak to him, will you, Stillitoe?" Honor said reluctantly.

"Yes, sir."

That very day Stillitoe called Cathan aside. "You did well during the action, Morgan. The captain has instructed me to make you the gunner, if you are agreeable."

"I'm not a naval man, as you know, Lieutenant."

"You know how to command the men and that's all that's necessary. You won't be an officer, you understand?"

"Yes, I understand. I'll be happy to do whatever I can."

"I'm sure you'll do very well," Stillitoe said and went on to outline the duties, although Cathan had observed the gunner's duties many times.

Finally Cathan said, "I'm not sure the men will look favorably on this. Some of them have much more experience on a fighting ship than I have."

"You'll have a mate to help, an old hand," Stillitoe said, grinning. "Praise God Barebones. What a name, but he's a good man. He'll be your assistant."

So Cathan Morgan, with Praise beside him, began his command of the big guns on the lower deck. He found that the men did not resent him—or at least did not say so. They had seen him face down Franklin with a sword.

Who would have thought I'd ever command any part of a ship? Cathan thought, amused by God's working. *Well, I may be an officer or an admiral before this is over. Who knows?*

It was two days after Cathan was appointed gunner that he had an encounter with Shayna Wakefield. He had gone down to the hospital, such as it was, to see his young friend John Miller. To his surprise, he saw that John had a visitor. Since there was only one woman on the ship, Cathan knew at once who it was and would have left, but she had already turned.

Shayna said, "I just came to visit some of the wounded men."

"That she did," John said with a smile. "Cheered me up, too. I don't mind losin' the foot so much now. Miss Wakefield tells me I can get a peg and stay in the navy. That's what her father says. Maybe as a cook."

"That's fine, John." Relieved to see John feeling better, Cathan talked with him for a few minutes. But as Shayna got up to leave, he said hurriedly, "I'll be back. I need to speak with Miss Wakefield."

When they were outside, he caught up with her. As she faced him, a strange expression on her face, she looked beautiful.

Cathan could not help but think of how he had appeared the last time he had courted her.

"I wanted to thank you for coming to see John. He's been very worried about the loss of his foot."

"He's a fine young man. It's dreadful that he's had such misfortune."

"Did your father really say that about making him a cook?"

"Yes, he did, after I explained that John doesn't have any family or anywhere to go."

"That's very kind of you, Shayna—I mean, Miss Wakefield."

Stirred by his use of her first name, Shayna said, "It's very awkward talking with you, Cathan."

"It is, isn't it?"

"What happened seems like another world. I don't think I was ever as shocked as when I saw you aboard the *Dauntless.*"

"Well, the hand of God must be in it. That's all I can say," Cathan said confidently.

"The hand of God? Do you mean that or is it just an expression?"

"God's in all things, although we don't realize it."

"You never said anything about God before," Shayna said, surprised.

"I didn't know God before."

"And you do now?"

Cathan hesitated, then said. "A lot of things happened to me in prison and one of them was that I met a man who knew God. I was about to die and he never gave up on me. That made an impact on me."

"You seem—different."

"I hope I am." Shifting his weight, Cathan said, "I wanted to ask your forgiveness again for the way I treated you after we first met. I was utterly wrong and I am deeply sorry for it. I hope you will forgive me."

Shayna's eyes opened wide, for now she knew this was not the same man she had known before. There was a new spirit in him. "Of course I will."

"Thank you."

He turned to go, but Shayna said, "Wait! I've had some things happen in my life, too. I don't suppose I knew what love was in those days." She bit her lip. "And I'm not sure I know now."

Cathan leaned toward her, watching her green eyes in the lantern light. "I don't know much about love either," he said. "The only thing I'm sure of is that it lasts forever."

"Do you really believe that, in spite of seeing people in love break away and almost hate each other?" Shayna queried.

"I believe there's real love. I'm not sure I've seen that too often." He grinned, increasing his attractiveness in the flickering light. "I'm having to start all over, Shayna. All my ideas have to be changed. Praise is working with me, but I'm a pretty slow disciple, I'm afraid."

At that moment someone stepped on the stairs and Shayna knew she had to leave. "Good-bye," she said softly.

When Cathan could no longer see her, he thought bitterly about the way he had treated her. *I should have been shot.* Then he remembered what Praise had said so often. *Don't be moanin' over old sins. God's forgiven them. Christ has nailed them to the cross. Go on from here.*

As Cathan thought of Shayna, realizing whatever he had felt for her earlier was not real love, he was filled with something he could not explain. "She's a fine woman," he whispered aloud, then turned to go back and sit with John.

Fifteen

THE COST OF DUTY

It was now December. Oren, perhaps the most delicate man on board the *Dauntless,* had succumbed to an injury that had brought on complications. Ever since a fall from the mizzenmast he had been unconscious and as Trevor Wakefield prepared to do the trephine, he looked around at those he had drafted to help him with the operation. Karl Steinmetz, the strongest man on the ship, was a close friend of Oren's. As he stood at his mate's right, he asked nervously, "Will he be all right, Doctor?"

"We will see. He seems to be unconscious so I will now perform the operation." Trevor had already sharpened and retempered his largest trephine and now held up the circular saw. The small group, which included Karl, Cathan, and the foretopman, Job, grew uneasily silent as they looked at Oren, strapped firmly to the table. It was one thing to fight a battle, another to deliberately cut into a man's skull.

"We will begin," Trevor murmured. "Karl, you and your strength will prove invaluable. You must be absolutely steady. Do you understand?"

"Aye, Doctor."

"If you'll support steadily, I'll begin my first cut."

The three men watched with horror in their eyes and soon they were peering into Oren's skull as Trevor fished with a long instrument.

Cathan felt himself growing sick, but he gritted his teeth and took his eyes away from the sight before him. He did not look back until the surgeon had restored Oren's scalp to its usual place and sewed it up.

"I believe it was successful," Trevor said, sweat dripping from his brow.

"The Lord be thanked!" Steinmetz gasped, then suddenly left the orlop deck, with Job following quickly. As Trevor's helpers cleaned up the patient, Cathan also started for the door. Then he heard his name called.

Trevor Wakefield had followed him. "A word with you, Morgan."

"Yes, Doctor?"

"I want to give you a warning," Trevor said, his voice expressionless but his eyes hard. "Stay away from the captain's daughter. I've warned you about this before."

"Why, Doctor—"

"I don't want to talk about it. You've done enough damage to that poor girl and her family. You mind what I say!"

"Aye, sir."

As Cathan left the lower deck, Trevor thought about what he had done. It had been on his mind for some time to speak to Cathan about Shayna, but now that he had done it, he felt somewhat uneasy. *If it was anybody's place,* he thought, *to speak to the man, I suppose it was Capt. Wakefield's.* Shaking off his indecision, he washed his hands and returned to check the supplies. One of his assistants stood beside him, checking off the items with a pen.

"We have eight yards of Welsh linen bandage, twelve yards of the fire linen, barn tourniquets. We have enough mercury, but we're short on laudanum," Trevor said.

"That we are, Doctor. If we have another battle at sea, it'll have to be rum for the wounded men."

Leaving the cockpit, Trevor moved up on the deck and toward

the stern of the vessel. Leaning on the rail, he watched the water churn in the wake of the *Dauntless* and thought of Shayna. Ever since he had been on board the *Dauntless,* he had felt awkward around her, perhaps partly because of his antagonism toward Cathan Morgan. Trevor was not a harsh man by any means. On the contrary, most people noticed his gentleness. As he watched a group of dolphins pace the ship, he tried to ascertain why he hated Cathan so much. Was it the harm he had brought to Shayna or Trevor's own chagrin at losing the young woman he professed to love? He tried to put the matter out of his mind but could not.

Then he heard a sound and turned to see Shayna, dressed in a brown wool dress and jacket.

"A beautiful day, isn't it?" he said, nodding toward the azure sky almost free of clouds.

Shayna stood beside Trevor, saying little but smiling from time to time at his remarks. Her hair was tied back and the pale sun brought out the auburn tints. A lock of it had escaped and curled down over her forehead. Trevor resisted the impulse to reach out and replace it. Instead, he asked, "Are you glad you came on the voyage?"

Shayna did not answer at once; then finally she sighed. "I don't think so."

Instantly Trevor thought he understood her feelings. "It's Cathan, isn't it?"

"Yes, it is. I feel somehow . . . ," Shayna began. But she could not complete her sentence, for she was uncertain about her feelings. "I don't know, Trevor. I just wish I hadn't come."

Reaching over, Trevor took her hand. Surprise leaped to her eyes at this unusual gesture. "I was never very demonstrative, was I? Perhaps I was unsure of myself."

"Why, Trevor!"

"I've got to know, Shayna. I can't keep on as I have been." As the wind blew his reddish hair, Trevor's face grew tense. He still held her hand and she made no attempt to withdraw it. "Is there any chance at all for me?"

Shayna knew the time had come to be totally honest. "You're the finest man I know, Trevor," she said gently and then looked up into his eyes. "But I'm not the woman who could make you happy."

Trevor drew a deep breath, filling his lungs with the salty air, then released it slowly. "I thought that was the way it would be."

"Don't be angry with me, Trevor. I couldn't bear that."

"Angry with you? Why, of course not." He released her hands then and the two turned to lean upon the rail together. Neither spoke for a time; then Trevor said, "I'll accept that you can't love me, but I have a warning for you."

"It's about Cathan, isn't it?"

"Yes."

"I can't understand him. He seems to be a wholly different man now."

"You haven't had time to know him!" Trevor said sharply. "Be very careful. You're very impressionable, Shayna. You always were."

"Yes, I was, wasn't I?" She faced him then. "I will be careful, and thank you for your warning." Then, putting her hand on his chest, she let it rest there for a brief moment. "I'm sorry it can't be the way you'd like."

After she left, Trevor looked back at the wake. As he stood outside of himself, analyzing his feelings and motives, he discovered, to his surprise, that although there was sadness at losing the girl, he felt relief. "There was never any real chance for me," he murmured aloud. When a gull sailed past his head, Trevor grinned wryly. "I wish I didn't have any more problems than you have, old boy. All you need is a fish to make you happy. We men aren't like that."

❦

As Shayna sat at the desk beside her bunk, she was conscious, as always, of the swaying of the ship. She could never forget the hundreds of fathoms underneath the hull of the *Dauntless*. As she dipped the pen into the ink bottle, the *Dauntless* nosed down into the water. Instinctively she braced herself, waiting for the ship to return to an even keel. She had never told her father how she felt, but at night she would awake from nightmares of drowning, feeling herself pulled into the green depths of the ocean by forces that were too terrible to describe. The ship, however, did level off and resume its rhythmic swaying from side to side as she pursued her way northward.

The cabin was cold and Shayna had put on an extra coat made of sealskin, a gift from her father. Still her fingers were so icy that she had to flex them, rub them, then blow on them to get the blood flowing. Finally she took up her pen again and began to write:

> I have just told Trevor that there could never be anything between us. It gave me great pain to do so, for I know he cares for me—I have known it for a long time. But there was nothing else I could say. It has been unkind of me to let him go this far without telling him the truth. Now I have done it and that is over! I wish I could be as clear in my mind about Cathan as I am about Trevor, but how can I be so? Was I wrong in loving him? If you love someone, do you turn it off and go in the other direction of almost hating them? That seems to be what I have done. I can only write these words down, for I would never speak them aloud to a living soul—but I cannot forget the pressure of his lips on mine. I can't forget his arms around me and how I surrendered to them. It is sinful of me to say so, but I write the words down, hoping that by admitting the truth, I will be set free.
>
> I have seen him so few times, but something about

him is different, as I told Trevor. He has asked forgiveness
for his behavior and it is only right for me to forgive.
Still, is he honest? Does he mean it or is this merely
another one of his ways? I have to admit, as he himself
admitted, he had the wrong motives for pursuing me.
This is the same as saying he did not love me and I know
he does not.

As she looked at the words she had written, her heart was in
pain. When the ink was dry, she closed the journal and concealed
it in the bottom of the small trunk she had brought on board. She
did not want her father—nor anyone else for that matter—reading it.

Restlessly she paced the few feet allowed in her cabin. Then,
with willful energy, she took the fur cap down from a nail in the
bulkhead and pulled it over her ears, deciding to go on deck. As
she passed one of the hands, he said, "A little rough on deck, miss.
Be careful you don't fall overboard."

"I'll be careful."

She passed by, making her way up the ladder as the ship tilted
severely. The wind cut her with cold as she hung onto spars and
then onto the rail as she advanced to the bow. She was almost
halfway there when Cathan stepped out of the forward hold.

Surprised, Cathan stopped dead and nodded without speaking.
He was half turned when her voice caught him.

"Cathan?"

Stopping at once, he faced her, alert and waiting for her to
speak.

"There's something I must say to you. I was unkind when you
first gave me your apology and asked for forgiveness. I didn't mean
to be, but . . . I accept your apology."

"That's kind of you, Shayna, but you are always kind."

"That's not true."

"Then you never let me see it when you were not," Cathan said, realizing the two were alone for the moment, for the deck was almost clear and the lookout up on the mainmast was preoccupied with sweeping the seas. Cathan continued, "A man finds out what he is and sometimes it's too late. I wasted my whole life and I grieve the things that I've done. . . . I'd like to make it up to my parents, but I don't see any way for that."

Shayna, who was prepared to be angry, even suspicious with him, was moved by his open declaration. "It's not too late," she said. "You can make it right with them."

"I hope so—and I hope that you'll think kindly of me."

Shayna could not think how to respond. Her lips numb now with the icy wind, she said inanely, "It's cold, isn't it?"

"Very cold. I believe we're going to get some ice and snow."

The rising wind made a keening noise as it cut through the shrouds and ratlines overhead. Cathan watched Shayna, waiting to see if she would say anything else. When she did not, he bowed his head. "Thank you for your kindness," he said, then headed for the foremast. As he reached the shrouds and climbed up easily to take his place up on the yardarm, he looked like a strong, graceful Viking figurehead. Shayna watched, confused and pleased by the humility and gentleness that he had just exhibited to her. Then, realizing she had revealed more of herself to him than she should have, she went back to her cabin.

Once inside her cabin, she pulled her cap off, shook it, and hung it on a nail. Then she removed the journal from its secret place and again began to write:

> I've just seen Cathan and more than ever I am puzzled
> by him. I believe he has had a change of heart. There is
> something about him that was not in him before—what
> shall I call it? I would have to say a gentleness or

goodness. He was never that way before. I can only begin to believe that he truly has met with the Lord.

Capt. Honor Wakefield paced up and down the wet planking on the weathered side of the quarterdeck, noting that some of the moisture was freezing. "We'll have rough stuff to plow through if this keeps up," he said to himself. Gripping the hammock nettings, he stared out over the sea that was growing dark.

Looking down the ship he saw darker shadows moving, merging to receive their orders from Stillitoe and Peters. Even from where Honor stood, he could see the hands at work around the big guns. He thought of the state of the ship and the guns that were housed underneath the massive deck head.

The hands had been piped to an earlier supper since Honor had thought a storm was rising. Now he tested the wind and noted the violence in the sea. He looked up at the rigging, where the braced topsails flapped noisily, showing their displeasure at being so tightly reigned. He had slept little the previous night, for he was not a happy man. In fact, sleep had come only in fragments for the past week. Some of this, he knew, had to do with Shayna. He was concerned about her, and now as he stood there, the freezing wind cutting into every square inch of his flesh not covered, he thought, *I wish I could understand her better.*

"Deck there! Ship off the port bow!"

"Where away?" Wakefield shouted, his voice a trumpet in the wind.

"Two degrees off the port bow, sir!"

Straining his eyes against the fading light, Wakefield saw a mere speck of white, but he knew it had to be a sail.

"Stillitoe, send a good man aloft."

"I'll go myself, sir."

Wakefield watched as the lieutenant scrambled up the ratlines, arrived at the crow's nest, then pulled a telescope from his pocket. He steadied himself, then called down, "Deck there! A sloop, sir!"

"Tell me when you can make out who she is!"

But in the falling darkness the sloop could not be identified. "She's English," Stillitoe said. "I can tell by the cut of her!"

As the ship drew close, it was obvious she was seeking out the larger vessel. "Give them our number," Honor said. The signals were quickly sent up and acknowledged.

"Still can't make out who she is," Stillitoe said. He had come down the mast and now stood beside the captain.

"She's hailing us."

The two ships passed so close together that Wakefield could tell the captain was a big man. He shouted something, but the wind snapped it away.

Finally the sloop put about and Stillitoe said, "He's putting a boat down."

"Dangerous maneuver in this wind," Wakefield observed as the gig was launched and the captain clambered into it with a crew of six. They fought their way across the rising waves, skillfully bringing the small craft beside the *Dauntless,* which had reaped the sails in order to wait.

When the captain came aboard, he advanced at once, taking off his hat. "Capt. John Finney of the *Sprite,* sir."

"Welcome aboard, Captain. It's rough weather. Will you come down to my cabin?" Honor invited.

"I think I'd best do that, sir."

The two men went to the great cabin, where Capt. Wakefield asked, "Do you have time for a meal, Captain?"

"No, I need to get back to my ship. But I have news." Waving his large hands around, he began to speak. "I'm glad to find you, because I thought all was lost."

"What's happening, Captain Finney?"

"Early this morning I saw the *Matador,* the Spanish treasure ship. Why, she must have enough bullion to furnish the dons with money for ten years!"

"A nice prize. Why didn't you take her?"

"Because she's guarded by the *Formidable.*"

"A ship of the line?"

"Aye, a second rate of ninety-eight guns. She'd be a handful even for another ship of the line if what I hear is true. She's the pride of the Spanish fleet. Not that the dons produce such good sailors—they can't build a ship at all fit to sail in. But this one's a French ship. They captured her last year."

Immediately Wakefield's mind began working. If there were two frigates, it would be possible to challenge a mighty ship of the line, but they would be outgunned badly.

"Perhaps the two of us could do something," Capt. Finney suggested.

Wakefield restrained a smile. A little sloop with only twenty guns and most of them very small would be of little use against a massive ship such as the *Formidable.* "What would you suggest, Captain?"

"Suppose I were to sneak in and pretend to go for the treasure ship," Finney said eagerly. "The *Formidable* would see me and chase me away. But while she's chasing me you could run in with your ship. If you couldn't capture her, at least you might sink her. I would miss the prize money, but better at the bottom of the sea than that the dons have it."

Quickly Wakefield thought of the possibilities. On the negative side, his crew was ill trained and had seen very little action. He knew also that if a chance shot took the *Dauntless's* mast down, then the *Formidable* could come and pound them to pieces at leisure.

On the other hand, to sink a Spanish treasure ship! It would please the crown and he himself knew that capturing ships was the most effective way to strike against Napoléon and Spain itself. However, chief in his mind, although he tried not to let it interfere with his judgment, was Shayna. If the ship went down, she would go with it. If they were captured, he shuddered to think of what would happen to a beautiful young woman in the hands of the enemy. So he began to pray, asking for wisdom.

Finney knew nothing about Capt. Wakefield except the bits of information he had absorbed from other captains. Wakefield was a good sailor from all he had heard, but did he have courage for a feat like this? Not many captains would, Finney admitted. It was a difficult maneuver. Just one slip and it would be too late for Capt. Wakefield and his ship.

So Finney was startled when Honor said, "I believe we will have to attempt it, Captain."

"Yes, sir. Just give me my orders."

Honor felt a heaviness in his spirit, knowing he must do his duty to the Crown regardless of the cost. If it had been only himself or his crew, he would not have hesitated. But this time he was reluctant to bring his ship into action. However, he steeled himself and went over every detail with Finney. "We'll show them a thing or two, sir!" Finney said. "I must get back to my ship now."

Honor accompanied the captain topside and watched him climb into the dory and go bobbing away across the water. As he thought of the hours to come, Honor knew he was putting the *Dauntless* into the lion's mouth. If the captain of the *Formidable* was any seaman at all, he could make his ship do better things in heavy weather than the *Dauntless*. Honor could only hope the captain was not such a man.

Turning to his lieutenants, Capt. Wakefield said, "Gentlemen, we will be seeing action. Probably tomorrow. Come below and I will tell you what our plan will be."

A BITTER VICTORY

Praise God Barebones patted the huge gun he had been polishing, named "Kill Devil," then grinned crookedly at Cathan. "Ain't she a beauty?" Praise asked.

Cathan smiled back. "Some of the old guns had beautiful names."

"You mean like 'Kill Devil?'"

"No, I mean like 'Cannon-Royal,' 'Cannon-Serpentine,' 'Demi-Culverin,' and 'Falconet.'"

"I never heard of such names!" Praise said. "You learned a lot about the guns when you were in the army, didn't you, Cat?"

Cathan nodded idly. He had been checking to be certain that everything was in place. Somehow everyone on deck knew without being informed that there was action in the offing. Now he checked the breaching and the train tackle and then tugged at the lashings to be sure they were tight.

"Do you ever think about what would happen if the dons or the Frenchies sent a ball right through the port and smashed us all to jelly?" Praise asked, resting his elbow on the gun.

"I suppose we all think about that."

"I always say if the dons kill me, they can't kill me but once," Praise quipped. "And if they do kill me, they send me right to the arms of the Lord Jesus."

"That's the best way to look at it," Cathan said fondly. He glanced around the gun deck where men were lounging, then listened to the sounds of the water and the ship. Up on deck there was a complex orchestra of moaning sails and whipping lines. Beneath the deck there was the sound of wood under stress, groaning almost as if in pain. All these sounds continued, never slackening day or night while the ship made its way through the ocean.

Turning to Praise, Cathan studied the man who had been such a friend to him. Praise had taken out a piece of bone and was carving it, something he often did for his own amusement. He peered at it carefully with his one eye and seemed pleased with the result.

"Were you ever married, Praise?"

Barebones looked up. "Certainly I was married! I never told you about Annie?"

"No, you never did."

Sitting with his back against the bulkhead, Praise continued carving, looking up from time to time as he spoke.

"Well, she was a pretty thing when I first saw her, Cathan. Hair red as any you ever seen, eyes blue as the sky. I knew when I first saw her that I would have to have her for my own."

"Did you have a long courtship?"

"No, I married her two days after I saw her."

"That was quick," Cathan said. "Was she a good wife?"

"No, I can't say she was." Silence followed; then Praise continued. "I'm ashamed to say she took up with several men and finally ran off. Took me four years to find her."

Cathan asked gently, "Where did you find her?"

"She was in a bawdy house. One of me mates told me he saw her there so I went to get her. A proper mess she was. Nothing but skin and bones by then. She had been sick—mishandled, too. Lost her good looks. I took her home, I did. I had to just about carry her. She was sick enough to die. I thought she would for a spell. I had to nurse her like you would a baby." Praise carefully used the tip of his knife to remove a fleck of the bone, then smiled. "She got better, though, I'm proud to say, and she became a good wife, too."

"Where is she?"

"She went to meet the good Lord four years after I found her. We had some good times, me and Annie."

"Did it bother you to take her back after she had . . ."

"After she had been with other men? No, because I read in the book of Hosea that God told the prophet to do the same thing. So when I read that, I thought, 'If it's good enough for Hosea, it's good enough for me and Annie.' So I took her and led her to the Lord Jesus. Now she's in heaven waitin' for me."

"You still think of her then?"

"Think of her? I love her! Why wouldn't I think of the one I love?"

"That's a wonderful way to look at it, Praise."

"You never was married, was you, Cathan?"

"No, I never was."

"Well, you will be someday. Nothing like a good woman." Praise stood, slipping the knife into his belt. "Nothing like a bad one either, for that matter."

He would have said more, but Lt. Stillitoe came down the stairs calling, "Morgan, we've sighted the enemy. You'll be in charge of this gun deck. Use all the men on the port side when we bring to bear, then when we come about, give them a broadside from the starboard."

"Aye, sir, I'll do that." As Stillitoe disappeared, Cathan announced, "We'll be going into battle, men. We'll give them something to remember us by, right?" A cheer went up and Cathan grinned, his teeth white against his tanned face. But as he went from gun to gun, encouraging the gun captains, he was wondering, *How many of these fine fellows will be dead or crippled in a few hours?*

⌁

"You must go below, my dear."

"Yes, Papa." Shayna kissed her father on the cheek. Though her face was pale, she said clearly, "You mustn't worry about me. Do your duty."

After Shayna went below, Honor did his best to block her out of his mind. Instead, he watched the Spanish *Matador* as it continued to add sails.

"She can't run away from us," Stillitoe said. "It looks like your ruse worked. The *Sprite* seems to have drawn off the *Formidable.*"

"She had better, but I doubt if it will be for long. If that captain has any brains at all, he won't leave that treasure ship alone just on the hope of damaging a sloop."

"She almost made it. There's the coast of France over there," Stillitoe said, pointing east.

Somewhere along the French shore the treasure ship was seeking harborage. She would have made it, too, matched against some ships, but against the frigate *Dauntless* she had no chance.

"Set full sail!" Honor commanded. "We'll go in for a broadside, come about, and give her another!"

"No chance of taking her as a prize?" Stillitoe asked, then shook his head. "No, of course not. That ship of the line will be back long before we could do that."

The *Dauntless* cut through the water, bearing down on the *Matador.* Belowdecks Cathan yelled out a porthole, "There she is! A big one, but we'll put her on the bottom, men!"

He moved again from gun to gun, making sure all the guns were run out and ready to fire. "No one touches a gun before I give the order!"

"Don't worry," Praise called out. "We'll do it, Gunner."

Up on deck Honor watched the *Matador*. Although she had some eighteen pounders, she would be no match for the *Dauntless*. "Give the orders, Mr. Stillitoe. Never mind the sails."

"Aye, aye, sir!"

Running down the ladder, Stillitoe relayed the orders to Cathan, then returned to the upper deck. Lt. Peters was entrusted with seeing that the sails were set according to the captain's orders, so he ran about, screaming orders to the men who scrambled like monkeys up in the tops.

The *Matador* began to fire. The shots were badly aimed, for she was not manned, Honor assumed, by fighting crews. They depended on the *Formidable* to protect them.

"Bear two points east, helmsman!"

"Aye, sir!"

As it turned out, there was little battle at all. The *Dauntless* moved smoothly past the lumbering vessel and when they were even, the guns roared out. The sides of the *Matador* caved in and the portholes were destroyed. The marines from the *Dauntless*'s maintops poured fire onto the deck so fast that soon the Spanish ship wallowed helplessly.

"Put about! We'll give her a broadside from our starboard guns!" Honor said.

Beneath the deck Cathan shouted, "All right men, the other side! We'll sink her this time!" As they approached the vessel again, he yelled, "Fire!" and all the guns of the *Dauntless* exploded, filling the air with smoke. Sticking his head out the port, Cathan cried, "We got her that time! She's listing! She can't weather that one!"

Up on the deck Capt. Wakefield smiled grimly. "That did her in, Peters."

"I think you're right, sir," Lt. Peters said. "Look, she's going down. Must have knocked the whole side out of her. I think she was an old ship. I think—"

"Deck there! Ship off the stern!"

In the heat of the action most of the men had forgotten there was a man-of-war in the same waters. Honor suddenly realized he had committed the unpardonable sin of turning his back on his enemy. Now as he wheeled, he saw the *Formidable* rushing toward them, her sails bellied out with wind.

"Make more sail!" Honor screamed.

"Aye, sir!" Peters yelled to the hands aloft, but by then, the *Formidable* had come alongside.

Desperately Capt. Wakefield tried to put about, but as he did, he saw that he was on the lee shore.

At the same time the lookout hollered, "Rocks astern, sir!"

Then the first broadside of the huge ship came. The balls whistled past Honor's ear, tearing the sails overhead, as the *Dauntless's* own guns began firing. "Set the forecourse!" Honor yelled, but it was too late for action. The deck buckled sharply as hundreds of pounds of shot came on board.

As the battle continued fiercely, Dr. Trevor Wakefield labored mightily on the orlop deck. A huge jug of rum beside the table was liberally used to ease the agony of the men who were brought down.

"All right, next man," Trevor said, gesturing. But as he listened to the smashing of the balls as they rocked the ship, he thought, *We'll never weather this one.*

At that moment a sailor stuck his head in. "Sir, it's Lt. Peters."

"Where is he?"

"Up on deck. Can you come, sir?"

Trevor looked around in dismay. He was needed everywhere, it seemed, but Peters was one of the few officers left. "I'll be right back," he said. When he stepped onto the upper deck, he was half blinded by the sky, which was bright in contrast to the dark gloom of the hole.

"He's over here, Doctor."

Trevor stepped over bodies and broken spars until he reached

Peters. He bent over, took one look, and said, "He's dead! Why'd you bring me for this?"

"He wasn't dead when I left."

Shaking his head, Trevor began, "I've got to get back to the—" But he never finished his sentence, for a cannonball passed over the rail, smashing into the sailor who had come to get him and throwing him over the side. Trevor felt that he had twisted his ankle, but when he looked down he saw that the shot, or another one, had struck his foot and his shoe was gone. Quickly he pulled his belt off, making a rude tourniquet.

"Help me!" he cried.

One of the marines came over, laid his musket down, and said, "Is it bad, sir?"

"Bad enough."

By the time the marine had helped Trevor down to the orlop deck, the pain began. Trevor simply wound a bandage around the foot. *I'm going to lose that foot,* he thought, *but there's no time now, nor anybody to do it.*

"Next man," he said. "Here, hold me up. I can't stand on this foot." Two men held him up as he continued to operate.

Topside, Honor saw that the *Matador* had sunk completely. "Well, that's done at least," he murmured, then yelled, "Here they come again! Give them all you can, my good fellows!"

Down below Cathan Morgan was ready. More than half of the men were dead, but he had gathered crews enough for one more broadside. He looked over at Praise and said, "This is it, I think."

"You might be right. We may be in the presence of the Lord in the next five minutes."

What happened next no one ever fully explained. Cathan, of course, could see nothing except the broadside of the huge ship as she came alongside. He heard the crash of their guns and saw the sides of the *Dauntless* cave in. Then he said, "Fire!" and what guns were operative went off.

Up on the quarterdeck Capt. Wakefield gripped the rail to keep his balance, for the *Dauntless* was now tilted at a twenty-degree angle and was drifting, he knew, toward the rocks. He fully expected to be killed from the broadside the *Formidable* was about to give them. He wished he could go down to be with Shayna if she were still alive, but it was too late. "Give them the best you can!" he called, even though he knew the men at the guns could not hear him.

The *Formidable* gave her broadside with huge guns and the guns of the *Dauntless* replied with a pitiful popping sound. The *Formidable* had almost passed when suddenly there was a rumbling deep in her decks. Hearing it, Honor turned to watch. To his amazement, the sides of the *Formidable* bulged and then a ball of flame enveloped the entire ship. The wave of heat struck Honor in the face as he called, "Got her magazine!"

It was a terrible sight to behold. Honor knew that there was no hope any of the *Formidable*'s men could have survived that instant blazing inferno.

"Thank you, Lord, for delivering us from the hands of our enemies," Honor said aloud, then saw that the *Dauntless* was a dead ship. She was in among the rocks and he saw the shoreline clearly a mile away. As she struck, he was thrown from his feet. The deck tilted and he slid down, stopped only by the hammock rail. Struggling to his feet, he began to cry, "Get the boats out! Get the boats out!" He was well aware that most of his men were dead, but he made his way down the deck to the ladder. Down in the lower hold he found Shayna, who came into his arms at once. "You're safe!"

"What happened, Papa?"

"The ship is sinking. Come! We must get off!"

Refuge in a

1 8 0 1   **Part FOUR**   1 8 0 2

Strange Land

Seventeen

A Light in Darkness

The *Dauntless* was being ground to pieces, her bow having been rammed into the jaws of rocks that held firmly. The waves battered the rest of the ship, twisting and wrenching the timber so that huge gaps began to appear up and down the planking. The men's screams of terror struck against Shayna as she stepped out on deck. Then she almost fell as the deck careened wildly and water spilled over the rails.

"We've got to get a boat!" Honor shouted above the whistling wind. "The ship will break up! We've got to get off at once!" He looked wildly around and saw Cathan Morgan struggling to lift a fallen beam that lay across one of the shipmates.

"Morgan!" Capt. Wakefield yelled. "Can you launch a boat?"

Taking one look at the man under the wreckage, Cathan saw he was dead, his chest crushed. So leaping to his feet, Cathan clawed his way across the deck. "I think we might get the jolly boat free, Captain. I'll get what help I can."

"Cathan, have you seen Trevor?" Shayna called out, holding on to her father to keep from falling. She was drenched by the cold rain that had come down in slanting lines.

"No, he's probably hasn't come on deck yet. I'll go down and check."

"No, you get the boat launched," Honor shouted. "I'll go see about the doctor."

"I'll go with you," Shayna said, looking determined when her father protested.

So the two crept along the deck and then stepped downside. When they reached the lower gun deck they saw dead men everywhere. Those still alive were crying out for help. "I hate to leave them here," Honor said, but he knew there was no hope. "Come. We'll go to the cockpit."

They felt their way along, for the lanterns were out. When they finally found one that was still burning, Honor picked it up. When they reached the cockpit, he held the lantern up and saw Trevor on the floor, holding on to the tourniquet on his leg.

"Trevor!" Shayna cried, going to his side. "You're hurt!"

Trevor, almost unconscious, opened his eyes and whispered, "This is a bad one. Get off the ship. It's going to go down."

"We won't leave you," Shayna said.

"Let me fix that tourniquet so it will hold." Honor worked rapidly, tying the tourniquet tighter. Then, seeing that Trevor certainly could not walk, he said, "See if you can balance on one foot for a minute. Then I'll carry you."

They got the injured man upright for a moment; then Honor stooped to place his hands behind the back of the doctor's legs. But as Honor straightened up to carry him, Trevor suddenly went limp.

"He's fainted," Shayna said.

"Probably better off. Hold the lantern while I carry him."

The two made their way back down the passage. When they got to the ladder, Shayna went up first, holding the light. Gasping with the effort, Honor came up slowly, his legs crying out from the strain. Although Honor was a strong man, Trevor was a dead weight.

As soon as they got on deck, Cathan and Praise were there. "We'll take him, Captain," Cathan said and the two men quickly lifted Trevor's unconscious form.

"We've got the jolly boat over the side. Quick, miss, you first," Praise said.

They made their way across the sloping deck. When they reached the side, Shayna looked down and saw the jolly boat tied with two ropes, banging against the side of the *Dauntless*.

"Praise, you go down," Cathan suggested. "I'll hand the doctor to you and then the lady."

"Right you are!"

Praise moved to the opening in the rail and leaped into the boat, sprawling on the bottom. The boat was already full of water, but he jumped up and said, "On the next rise, lad!"

When the ship rose again, Cathan and Capt. Wakefield were ready. They heaved Trevor to the waiting Praise, who caught him and arranged Trevor so that he lay with his head on a bundle that was there. However, the fall had awakened Trevor and he whispered, "Barebones, tell them to bring my doctor's kit."

So Praise shouted up, "He says to bring his doctor's kit!"

"Let's get Miss Shayna into the boat first," Cathan said, "and then I'll go back and get it."

Shayna hung the lantern on a peg on one of the masts. It was darker now, almost night, and she could hear the faint cries of men struggling in the water. She stood there with Cathan's hand on one arm and her father clutching the other one. Again the waves lifted the jolly boat up and Cathan called out, "Now!"

Shayna felt herself half shoved, half thrown off the boat. But she did not have far to fall and Praise was waiting. He took her weight and staggered, but did not fall. "There, perhaps you can help the doctor now."

On the slanting deck of the *Dauntless,* Cathan said to Honor, "You go ahead, sir. I'll go get the kit."

Without giving the captain a chance to reply, Cathan grabbed the lantern from the peg and scrambled along the deck to the ladder. Holding the lantern aloft, he crept down the passageway.

Water was rushing in now and he knew it wasn't long before the ship would break up. A dead body floated beside him, but he splashed by it with no time to waste. When he got to the cockpit, he found a large empty case and began to scrape instruments from the table into it. Then he went to the cabinet and grabbed everything he could see—instruments, drugs, bandages—and stuffed them all into the case. Keeping a firm grip, he made his way back down the ghostly pathway and emerged on deck just as the back of the ship lifted. Scrambling across the deck, he could barely see the jolly boat in the darkness.

"Come on, lad, we'll pull you out! Jump for it!"

Cathan threw himself off the ship. His head went underwater, the weight of the bag pulling him down. But he was a good swimmer, so he came to the surface still clutching the bag. Knowing he could die if he did not get warm, he fought his way to the boat, not ten feet away. Shayna was on the side, holding her hand out.

"Here," he gasped. "Take the bag!"

Shayna pulled on the bag with all her strength and threw it into the boat; then she and her father reached down and grabbed Cathan. They hauled him aboard, where he sprawled full length, his chest heaving with the effort.

"We got to get away from here, sir!" Praise shouted. "We can man at least two of the oars if you will take a pull!"

"I'll do it," Cathan said, scrambling up and grabbing one of the oars.

Honor said, "I'll take another."

"I can pull a little," Shayna offered. She propped Trevor's head up against the sodden bag in the bottom of the boat and then took her place on the seat. The jolly boat was made to be pulled with eight oars, but the four of them, under Praise's direction, began to find some kind of rhythm. "There's the shore over there! We'll let the tide carry us in!" Praise shouted.

All of them pulled as hard as they were able. At times the boat was turned sideways and in danger of tipping over.

As they were halfway toward the shore, Cathan looked back in the last bit of light before total darkness. "There's the *Sprite!*" he yelled. "They've come to pick up survivors!"

Capt. Wakefield strained his eyes, considering trying to get the boat back. But the wind was against them and the tide was rushing them in. *Maybe the* Sprite *will stay till morning,* he thought, but he had little hope of that. After all, it was the French coast and it was unlikely the *Sprite* would try to land with the treacherous shoals.

Finally the jolly boat reached the shore, pushing them up on the sandy beach strewn with rocks. Praise and Cathan leaped out. Grabbing the rope tied to the prow, they pulled with all their strength until the boat was half out of the water. Leaping back in the boat, they went to Trevor. "Come along, Doctor," Cathan said, "we've got to get out of here."

With Trevor only half conscious, it took a massive effort to get him out of the boat. Then Cathan took his arms and Praise his legs and they staggered up on the beach.

"We'll have to get off the beach. They'll be searching for survivors," Capt. Wakefield warned. "We'll take turns carrying him."

Then the nightmare began. They were all soaked to the skin and freezing. As night deepened, the wind whistled more loudly, cutting through Shayna's garments like a knife. As she kept close to her father, who was shouldering the medical kit, she shivered violently. Honor took the lead, saying, "Maybe we can find a path or a road."

"What will we do? We can't let them find us," Shayna said.

"We'll have to hide and hope to find a way back to England."

As Shayna thought of the difficulties of this, and the cold, she began to pray, *God, help us out of this. Only you can do it!*

As they continued to walk, Cathan felt something bite his cheek. He touched it and strained his eyes. Another fiery bite—no, it was cold!

"It's snowing," he said, staggering with weakness, for the cold and the struggle to escape had drained him.

"We've got to get out of this," Capt. Wakefield said, gasping.

Cathan looked about. With only a sliver of moon for light, he could see very little.

"Here, there's a grove here, with bushes. It'll break the wind," Praise said.

Once inside the grove, the keening of the wind was muted. They lay Trevor down carefully and Shayna sat down and took his head in her lap. "I think he's unconscious."

"He'll die if we don't get him out of this," Cathan stated flatly. "I'll go see if I can find some shelter—a barn or something."

"How will you find your way back?" Honor demanded.

"I don't know, Captain. I'll do the best I can. God will have to be in it."

Even under the circumstances, Honor was impressed with this statement. It was something the old Cathan Morgan never would have said. He stared at the shadowy form of the Welshman, then said, "Go with God then. I think our lives depend upon it."

Cathan moved out of the thicket as quickly as possible. He could hear the sea behind him, so he walked straight away from there, stopping for breath from time to time. Then, when he was about to give up and turn back, he stumbled onto what was obviously an old road. *There's got to be a house on it somewhere!* he thought. He looked around for a landmark so he could find his way back. Directly across from him were two large trees standing side by side.

"They'll have to do. Two trees. Two friendly giants," he murmured. Then he asked himself, "Right or left?" If he went the wrong way, he might go for hours and find nothing. So he prayed aloud, *Oh, God, I don't know my right hand from my left. You know all things. Help me to choose the right one.* He stood there, waiting for he knew not what. Then, not knowing why, he took the right-hand fork. He had not gone more than two hundred yards when he saw it. "A light, by heaven!" he cried aloud. He continued another fifty yards and, sure enough, there, far back off the road to his left, was a large house surrounded by a stone wall with an opening. Cathan had no idea who lived there. It could be the chief of detectives of all of France, just waiting to make a capture. But it was also warmth and shelter—and that was what he had to have.

He turned and carefully retraced his steps until he came upon the two giant trees. Then he made an abrupt turn and went through the underbrush calling out, "Shayna? Capt. Wakefield? Praise?"

Praise met him. "Did you find something?"

"Yes, there's a house. I don't know who lives there, but we have to go."

They began their journey at once, Praise and Cathan carrying the unconscious physician. "It's only a few hundred yards down there," Cathan said, directing them. By now, their limbs had lost all feeling. Cathan could not even feel his feet. When they reached the opening in the stone wall, they turned down a driveway wide enough for large carriages.

Capt. Wakefield said, "This may be the wrong thing, but it's death to stay out here. Let me go first." He dropped the bag of supplies when he was halfway to the house and cried out, "Hello, the house!" Pausing, he lunged forward, crying out again. He was no more than ten feet away from the door when it opened. Through his almost frozen eyelids, Honor saw the figure of a man.

"Who goes there? Who's out in this night?" a voice demanded.

"Shipwreck victims!" was all Capt. Wakefield could say. He almost fell, then moved slowly forward. "We have a wounded man out here."

There was silence and then a woman's voice called, "Come inside out of the storm."

Honor staggered forward again, bracing himself against the front of the house. The woman came closer and put her hand on his arm. "Come inside," she said. "I'll get servants to help with your friends."

"Thank you, ma'am. I'd be most grateful," Honor said in a thin, reedy voice. As the women drew him inside the house, she called out for help.

The warmth was like a drug to Honor as he staggered inside and found himself facing a short man in a crimson robe. He stared at the man, his mind so confused he could not think. Finally, he said, "In the name of God, I thank you for taking us in."

"In the name of God—then you are English." The man's accent was clearly French. As he stepped closer, Honor saw that the white-haired man looked to be in his eighties. Now the man's dark brown eyes fastened on his unexpected guest. "You have a wounded man?" he asked.

"Yes, he needs help at once." Again there was a silence. "Will you turn us over to the authorities?"

The woman appeared. "No, we will not do that. Come, you must warm up at once and put on dry clothing."

"I'll see to my friends first, if you don't mind, ma'am," Honor said, noting that the woman, as best he could ascertain, was somewhere in her midthirties. Her hair was black, her eyes dark, and her skin olive. As she looked at his uniform, there was a strange expression on her face. "You are an English sailor?"

"Yes, our ship went down off the coast."

"We heard the sounds of the guns," the woman said as the servants came in, bearing Trevor's limp body.

"I am Capt. Honor Wakefield of His Majesty's ship the *Dauntless*. This is our surgeon, Trevor Wakefield, and this is my daughter, Shayna."

The woman's eyes traveled over them all, assuming the other two were servants since their names had not been mentioned.

"Come, we will see to the wounded man." As she gave quick, efficient instructions, Honor's head began to swim. Seeing this, the woman led him down a long hall.

"Madam, I don't even know your name," he murmured.

"Madeline de Fontaneau," she said. "Your host is Pierre Monbiere."

She pulled him into a room where a candle was burning and then went to a large mahogany wardrobe. She opened the door, pulled out items of clothing, and laid them on the bed. "I think these will fit you, sir. . . . They belonged to my husband. I have left them here since his death."

"I cannot thank you enough, madam."

"I'll have a servant kindle a fire. Change your clothes and go to bed."

"I must see to my friend Trevor."

"As you will, but get into the dry clothes first."

As she turned to go, Honor asked, "You realize you are taking in the enemies of France?"

Madeline de Fontaneau pivoted, a tense expression on her face. "Monsieur Monbiere had one son. He died in the service of Napoléon, who abandoned him. I can guess your feelings about Napoléon, but you will find in my father-in-law one who absolutely hates him. . . . And so do I." Moving toward the door, she said, "You may sleep safely here tonight. If searchers come, they will be turned away. Sleep well."

Honor stood in the middle of the ornate room. It was obviously a wealthy home to which he had come and the brief history he had just heard brought relief such as he had never known.

"We're safe here!" he exclaimed, beginning to strip out of his clothing. He knew that whatever happened next, they had found refuge for the night.

A FRIEND AND A
BROTHER

The next morning, Honor Wakefield came out of a sleep that was almost like a coma. He had been dreaming of home but became conscious of a slight sound. Opening his eyes, he stiffened, for he did not recognize the room in which he lay. Swiveling his head, he sat up to see a servant kneeling on the floor, kindling a fire in the marble fireplace. Then it all came rushing back. Drawing a hand unsteadily across his forehead, he expelled his breath. The sound caught the servant's attention.

"I'm sorry," the tall, gangly fellow said in French. "I didn't mean to disturb you. My name is Thomas."

"That's all right," Honor said, painfully aware that his French was abominable. Throwing the covers back, he stood on the floor.

The servant rose when the fire had begun to catch, saying, "Perhaps you might choose the buff trousers this morning. They are pure wool and very warm."

"I suppose that would do very well." Honor allowed the servant to help him select his clothes. Soon he was dressed in a fine suit.

"You are the same size as my former master," Thomas said.

"You served Monsieur Fontaneau?" Honor queried.

"Oh, yes, sir! He was a good man—a little quick of temper, but I didn't mind that. . . . Madame misses him dreadfully."

"I'm surprised she didn't remarry," Honor said. Then, realizing this came close to gossiping with a servant, he quickly said, "They fit very well. Thank you, Thomas."

"If you will allow me to shave you, I think you would feel much better."

Feeling the stubble on his face, Honor nodded. "That would be excellent." He sat down and waited until Thomas returned with hot water, a razor, and towels and was pleased to find that the servant was an excellent barber.

"I haven't shaved anyone else since Monsieur died. It brings back old memories." The servant shrugged, adding, "If you will follow me, I will take you down to the dining room. I expect the food has been kept hot."

Following Thomas, Honor was impressed by the quality of the house and its art. He was not at all certain what Monsieur Pierre Monbiere did for a living, but he did very well at whatever it was.

"In here, sir."

Honor stepped through the large, double doorway and saw that his hosts were already eating. He stopped in embarrassment, but Monsieur Monbiere rose, saying, "Ah, you are just in time. Sit down."

"Good morning," Honor said, smiling wryly as he took his seat. "I'm glad you both speak such excellent English. My French is almost nonexistent. I never know whether I'm saying 'How are you?' or 'The devil wears a red suit.' "

Madeline de Fontaneau, who was wearing an emerald brocade dress, laughed heartily at his remark. "You are feeling better this morning?" she asked.

"Yes, but then it would have been impossible for me to have felt much worse. We were in poor condition when we staggered into your home."

"Eat first, talk later," Pierre ordered and then snapped his fingers at an older man, evidently a butler. "Bring Capt. Wakefield's breakfast, Gerard."

The breakfast was excellent. It consisted of soft-boiled eggs, thick slices of bread with an assortment of preserves, thinly sliced ham and cheese, canned fruit, and several types of flaky pastries.

For a time Wakefield devoted himself to the food, for he had eaten almost nothing for the past forty-eight hours. Finally, savoring a fourth cup of hot chocolate, he held up his hand to his host, who was urging more food upon him. "No more, sir! I'm afraid I've already committed the sin of gluttony."

"I like to see a man eat heartily," Madeline said, smiling.

"I'm most grateful for all you've done for us," Honor said. "I'm concerned about my friend Dr. Wakefield."

"You shall see him shortly. One of my servants is tending to his needs even now." A frown creased the forehead of the Frenchman. "I am not altogether satisfied with his condition. Although I am not a physician myself, I can see that the foot is in bad shape."

"We would like to call a physician in," Madeline said, her warm eyes fixed on Honor. "But the only doctor in our area is a devout Bonapartist. He would inform the authorities at once if he found Dr. Wakefield here."

Disappointed, Honor shook his head. "Something must be done, but I'm not at all sure what. He can't be moved and even if he could, we would be apprehended immediately."

"Exactly," Pierre said, leaning back in his chair. "Your two servants are being cared for. They've already had a fine breakfast and are about. One of them came right away to see about Dr. Wakefield."

"That would be Cathan, I suppose."

"Yes, that was his name. He was very concerned. A faithful servant, I have no doubt."

"Well, not exactly a servant. He is . . . a distant relative—and the gunner on my ship, the *Dauntless.*"

"What happened, monsieur?" Madeline asked. "Did your ship simply founder on the rocks?"

Feeling he could trust these two and that he owed them an explanation, Honor plunged into a description of the events that had led to the loss of the *Dauntless*. He traced the history of the ship down to the sighting of the galleon, the sinking of it, then to the destruction of the *Formidable* and the sinking of his own ship. As he ended, he said regretfully, "It was a close thing. After we sank the *Matador*, we were taken unaware by the man-of-war. That was my own fault. She was on us before I knew. I was so taken up with sinking the Spanish galleon that I did not mind her approach."

"Two ships and one of them a man-of-war," Pierre said, admiration on his face. "That was a notable victory."

Shaking his head sadly, Honor said, "Most of my crew were killed. However, I have hopes that the smaller ship that brought us the news of the galleon rescued some of them."

"Some of the bodies washed ashore this morning," Pierre said carefully. "The army has sent a special troop here to search for survivors."

Honor looked up. "I'm concerned that we will put you in grave danger."

"There will be no trouble. I have some position hereabout and my word will be enough to assure the search parties. All that is necessary is that you and your friends stay in this house until they are gone."

"We must get back to England, sir. I don't know how—indeed it seems rather an impossibility."

"Nothing is impossible with God," Madeline said.

Pierre laughed aloud. "Be very careful or she will throw Scripture at your head until you will be drowned in it."

The remark interested Honor. "I would not mind at all. My

mother was the same way." Then, in a different tone of voice, "And so was my dear wife, while she lived."

Marking his change of tone, Madeline said quickly, "I am somewhat inclined to be . . . *preachy*. Is that the English word?" Then she laughed. "But I promise you that I will not ask you for a collection."

"If I had it, madam, I would gladly give it all," Honor said warmly. "I believe God must have led us to this place, for what other house would have received us with such hospitality—and dangerous hospitality at that?"

"I will leave you two to talk," Pierre said. "Madeline, you will want to take our friend to see the patient. I must go check the coast. It's likely I will encounter the searching parties and may be able to head them off even before they come on the grounds."

As soon as Pierre left, Madeline said, "You were exactly right. God must have led you to this place."

Honor had already noticed that she was a calm, thoughtful woman. And now he saw that she was not merely feigning interest in him but was genuinely concerned. "I would be devastated if I brought trouble to your house, madam."

"I think first names are in order. Madeline and Honor, is it not? A strange name, indeed, but a good one."

"I've had to explain it all my life," Honor admitted. "My mother was not English. She was what you would call a savage— that is, an Indian, from the New World."

Interest leaped into Madeline's eyes. "Indeed, I did see that all of your blood was not English. How fascinating! And did you grow up in America?"

"I did for much of my childhood."

"And did you live with the red people?"

"Yes, my mother was an honored member of the tribe." He smiled. "I learned to ride, to hunt the buffalo, to shoot with a bow and arrow. I was quite a young 'savage.'"

"And how did you come to be in the British navy?"

"After my wife, Rachel, died, I was not happy. We had our daughter, whom you have met, and I began going to sea more often—mostly, I'm afraid, out of despair."

Madeline studied him. "Your daughter is a lovely young woman. Does she favor your wife?"

"Very much so. I suspect that is why I find being around her so difficult. Back in those days, I was almost wild with grief after my loss. I kept seeing her face in Shayna's and I could not stand it. . . . But I was a coward to run away like that. I've regretted it since."

Impulsively, Madeline said softly, "You loved your wife very much, did you not?"

"Yes, I did."

"And even though she's been dead for some time, you're still in love with her."

It was an intimate conversation for two people who were practically strangers. Honor had never spoken so openly to anyone. In fact, he rarely spoke of his wife at all. But his memories were clear. And now, as he sat across from this tall, dark-eyed woman at the table, he began to speak of his wife.

Finally she asked, "Your marriage didn't last long?"

"No, only a few years. Rachel died when Shayna was six."

"You never thought of marrying again?"

Honor Wakefield dropped his eyes thoughtfully. When he did speak, the pain was evident. "I never found anyone to stand beside her," he said simply.

Eyes warm and approving, Madeline said, "Most men would not have spoken so honestly—or have maintained a love so faithfully."

As a private man, Honor was almost embarrassed by his openness. "I have never spoken to anyone like this. I suppose you're a very good listener." He tilted his head in an inquisitive gesture. "And you, Madeline. You never married again either?"

"No. Like yourself, I could not find a man to stand beside my husband. We are two of a kind, it seems."

As she sat back in her chair, Honor considered her frankly. He had never met anyone who had attracted and held his attention as quickly as this woman had. "I suppose we are the same," he said. "Perhaps too hard to please. I should have married again for Shayna's sake when she was young. She missed having a mother— she still does."

"Some people can do that sort of thing. Others cannot. I do not know why that is. It has something to do with who we are on the inside. I would have married had I found any man I could have loved." For a brief moment, Honor saw sadness in her eyes. But then the contented, resolute look returned. A thought flickered through Honor's mind: *What a waste of a fine woman. She would have made another man as good a wife as she did for her first husband.* He did not speak, however, for she said, "Most marriages fail because of individuality, I think."

"I don't understand."

"Individuality is the strongest thing in our makeup. It's the husk of personal life and it is a selfish, devouring element. It is all elbows," she said, gesturing with her elbows. "It says, 'Get out of the way. Give me room. This is my place!' Things like that, although we do not say them aloud or admit what we are really like." She smiled roguishly. "And I expect ship captains have more individuality than most others."

Despite himself and the pressures upon him, Honor laughed aloud. "I expect the crews of every one of His Majesty's ships would agree with that! We can have no 'discussions' aboard a ship. When the time for action comes, each man must know his station and there is no time for debate. It is a rough, hard life."

"I understand that well, for that is duty, but do you not see,

Honor, that it is the same in marriage? Men and women want their own way. They want to be the captain of the ship! And, of course, it is the man in our time and in our world whom society recognizes as the dominant one. But if a woman has a strong individuality—ah, there is trouble! I suspect my husband would have sentenced me for insubordination."

"I doubt that, Madam. You might be rebellious, but I am sure it would be in a most charming way."

"Oh, a cavalier!" Madeline threw up her hands. "But I can see it in your eyes. You are a captain not only of your ship but of any situation. You know," she said, growing thoughtful, "I think it is this continual insistence upon individuality that hinders the spiritual life in us more than anything else."

"Why, we *are* individuals!" Honor protested. "That is the way God made us."

"So we are and our entire lifetime is spent trying to find our place. But Jesus said, 'Blessed are the poor'—not the rich—and 'If you lose your life, you will find it.' So many Scripture verses speak of humility and yet it is the rarest of all graces."

"I cannot argue theology with you," Honor said, smiling. "You are too apt for me. What do you find love to be then?"

The question surprised Madeline and she tapped her chin, thinking carefully. "I think," she said deliberately, "that love is the outpouring of one personality in fellowship with another personality."

"That sounds profound, but I'm not sure I understand it."

"I think true love is wanting the best for the person you love when it means taking the worst for yourself."

Startled, Honor exclaimed, "Why, that's *exactly* what I've always thought—but I've never been able to say it. Yes, love is wanting the best for someone else while taking the worst, if necessary, for yourself."

Madeline sat for a moment, then said, "Come, we must see your friend Dr. Wakefield. He is a kinsman of yours?"

"Yes, a cousin. A very fine surgeon."

Arising, Madeline said, "I wish it had been one of the others who had had this injury. Then Dr. Wakefield could have cared for them. But I fear he cannot care for himself in this case." Turning so abruptly that Honor bumped into her, Madeline said slowly, "I've never talked to anyone quite as frankly as I've talked to you—certainly not on the first meeting. But we have talked of love, marriage, and the things of God. And I must say one thing, for I think it is as true of you as it is for me." Her lips softened as she spoke out of the depths of her spirit. "If I had found a man to love, I would have taken him. A woman," she said deliberately, "needs a man. . . ." Then her eyes met his evenly. "Just as a man needs a woman."

As Madeline left the room, Honor Wakefield knew that the cryptic sentence was her attempt to tell him something about himself. As they went down the hall, he moved alongside her, wondering what sort of fellow her husband had been. *He must have been a great chap for her to remain single, unable to find one like him. Perhaps I can find out more about him from her father-in-law.*

⚬

Cathan Morgan looked uneasily at Trevor's face. Cathan had come in, as he had done every day for the four days they had been hidden in the Frenchman's home. Now he sat down and, concealing his true feelings, asked cheerfully, "Well, how are you today, Doctor? You look well."

Trevor was sitting up in bed, but the constant pain from his mangled foot had etched lines in his face. "You don't have to lie to me, Cathan. I know what I look like. I've got a mirror."

"That foot must be very painful," Cathan replied.

Looking down at the foot that was wrapped in a bandage,

Trevor said evenly, "It's a misnomer to call it a foot. There's not enough left of it. It should have come off the same day it was mangled. I'd take it off myself, but that's impossible."

"Perhaps it will get better or perhaps we'll find a doctor."

"Neither is very likely."

Cathan knew enough medicine to understand the problem. The foot would never be of any use to Trevor Wakefield. It was too mangled and the bones were crushed. The most potent danger was gangrene. No one had spoken the word aloud, but it was in all of their minds. Now he said eagerly, "There's one thing we could do, although I haven't mentioned it. I could capture that doctor and blindfold him. I could bring him here, let him amputate, and then take him back to his home a roundabout way." The idea had been in his mind since the previous day and now a determined light came to his dark eyes. "It wouldn't be much of a trick. I speak French well enough to pass for a native, I think."

Trevor looked up with surprise. "That's the craziest thing I ever heard of in my life!" he announced. "You'd never get away with it."

"I think I could."

Seeing that Cathan was serious, Trevor managed a slight smile despite the pain in his foot. "Just one slipup and our hosts would wind up on the gallows."

"Maybe we could move you to another place and take him there."

As Trevor listened to Cathan's scheme, he could not help but think of how at one point in Cathan's life, he would have not risked anything for another human being. "I appreciate what you have done, Morgan," Trevor said. "Just getting me ashore was a miracle of sorts. I don't think we could have made it without your help. And finding this place—that was something I never expected."

"Well," Cathan said, shifting awkwardly, "God guided me. That night when I came to the road and didn't know whether to go right or left, I prayed. And I felt God was telling me to take the right fork." He laughed with some embarrassment. "At one time I would have said that wasn't God, that the thought was just my own imagination."

Just then Shayna came into the room, wearing a gown that neither of the men had seen before. Amused, Trevor asked, "Have you been shopping, Shayna?"

"No, of course not!" Shayna said, coming to sit beside Trevor. "It belonged to Madeline and she cut it down for me." Then she switched the subject. "How do you feel? . . . You must get sick of us asking that, but we're desperate to see you get better."

"I won't be getting better, Shayna," the sick man said bluntly.

Shayna's eyes darted to Cathan, who sat on the other side of the bed, then came back to Trevor's. "You mustn't say that!"

"We have to face reality. The foot should have come off at once. Sooner or later I'll have gangrene; then it'll have to come off or I'll die."

"We've got to believe in God," Shayna said.

"I do believe in God, but my faith is pretty small right now. . . . Have you told her how you prayed about finding this place, Cathan?"

It was the first time since the attempted elopement that Trevor had used Cathan's first name. In his sickness and weakness he had laid aside his authority, for since the ship had literally gone down, he had no office over Cathan. Warmed in his heart, Cathan answered at once. "I was just telling Trevor how when I prayed whether to go left or right, I felt as though God told me to go right. If I'd gone left, I'd probably have walked right into a patrol."

"And we would have died," Shayna said quickly. "I think that's wonderful and I think it was God." Then, turning back to Trevor, she said, "There must be something we can do."

"There is something," Cathan said. "I have a plan—"

"Don't listen to him, Shayna," Trevor protested. "It's a wild, impractical scheme."

"I want to hear it," Shayna said. "What is it, Cathan?"

Cathan outlined his plan. "It's very simple. There's a doctor here. I go capture him, blindfold him, and bring him to the patient. He does the surgery and I take him back blindfolded, leading him through a maze."

"Didn't I tell you it was insane?" Trevor said as pain wrenched his features. "Don't let him do this, Shayna. He could get himself arrested. Even worse, he could expose Pierre and Madeline. We can't risk that."

Seeing that talking to Trevor was useless, Cathan left the room while Shayna stayed. He went to Praise and laid the scheme before him. "Cat, that's quite an imagination you have there!" Praise said. "You don't even know the doctor. You might kidnap a shoemaker."

"I know it's not a perfect plan, but at least it's a plan. We've got to do something," Cathan insisted.

"Let's pray about it. That's all I know to do when things like this come about."

<hr/>

For two days Cathan tried to persuade someone to agree with him. He had presented his plan to Honor, who also thought it wild and impractical. In desperation he had pleaded for a chance to do something but had been voted down.

On the evening of the second day, Cathan found Honor standing at Trevor's bedside. The quick look Honor gave him made Cathan ask, "What is it?"

It was Trevor who answered the question. "Gangrene," he said flatly. He gestured toward the foot with utter futility. "If it weren't for risking our host and hostess, I'd join you in that scheme to kidnap the doctor," he said wryly.

A heated argument ensued then and Shayna arrived in time to hear some of it. But finally Trevor extracted a promise from Honor that no attempts at kidnapping the physician would be made.

Cathan shook his head but argued no more. Grieved, he knew he had done his best.

Then Trevor said slowly, "I've been thinking. There's one thing left to try."

"What's that, Trevor?" Shayna asked. "We'll do anything, won't we?"

"Of course," Honor replied. "Just say what it is."

"The foot has to come off. I can't do it myself, so someone else will have to do it."

Honor Wakefield was a man of courage who had seen violent action and immense bloodshed. But he was also squeamish about wounds, so to deliberately take a knife and cut into a man's living flesh was more than he could bear to think about. Swallowing hard, he said, "Trevor, that's impossible!"

"It probably is," Trevor said, his face gray. "But if there's someone here who's good with animals, even that would be a chance. If I didn't bleed to death, that is."

Shayna looked up at her father, a pleading expression on her face. Then she saw from his look that, despite his bravery, the surgery would be beyond him.

"I'll try it if you like, Trevor."

Cathan's voice broke the silence of the room. His face was pale, but his lips were set in a hard line. Looking at Trevor, he added, "I'm no doctor and I may make a mess of it. But if that's what you want, I'll try it."

Trevor was shocked. He had expected nothing like this. But as he looked up at the dark face of the Welshman, he remembered that Cathan had helped remove the foot of an injured sailor. "At least you've *seen* an operation," he said with hope in his voice. "If you've got the nerve for it, it might be done."

"I don't like the thought," Cathan said quietly, "but I don't like the idea of your lying there dying by inches. If you'll start right now and tell me everything over again until I've got it perfect, I'll try it."

Shayna Wakefield was staring at Cathan's face. She felt a sudden wonder that any man would attempt such a thing. She wanted to speak up, to say something encouraging, but she knew this decision was between Trevor Wakefield and Cathan Morgan. Because of the hatred that had existed between the two men, she knew it was a miracle that Cathan would even offer to do such a thing.

Trevor must have been thinking the same thing, for he said, "We haven't been friends, Cathan."

"I think we might be, and even brothers," Cathan said sincerely.

"All right," Trevor said, making his decision, "get a pen and paper, lots of paper. Bring all the instruments in. I'll have to see what you salvaged."

"Can I do anything?" Shayna asked.

"You can help drill Cathan on what has to be done," Trevor said. "I'll go over the operation step by step and when it finally comes, if he falters, somebody needs to be standing there to read him the next step. But it's not a pretty sight."

"I'll do it, Trevor. At least I'll try."

"We'll get Praise God to help," Trevor said. "It's time to go to school. You're going to become a doctor in record time, Cathan Morgan!"

***

Perhaps it was the intense study and thought that Cathan threw himself into—or the fact that every moment Trevor was awake he was drawing diagrams and going over the steps of the surgery.

But somehow talking about it had taken some of the horror out of it, for Trevor had made it as objective as possible. Shayna was always there, writing notes and taking the rough sketches that Trevor had made and improving on them, for she was a fine artist.

Two days went by. Upon being told about the upcoming surgery, Pierre and Madeline were at first shocked. "Only mad Englishmen would try a thing like this," Pierre said vehemently.

But then Madeline said calmly, "I don't agree, Father. It's simply a matter of courage and faith and evidently Cathan has plenty of both."

"I'll agree to that, but still, for an amateur to do an amputation . . . !"

"Have you noticed what's between Shayna and Cathan?"

Surprised, Pierre said, "Between them? No. What are you talking about?"

"Men are so blind!" Madeline said, feigning despair. "Don't you see how she looks at him and he at her? That is, when they don't think they're being noticed. I pried it out of Honor. He said they nearly eloped once but didn't."

"But he's only a sailor."

"There's more to it than that. But what if he is? It doesn't matter as long as they love each other."

Pierre laughed aloud. "I never know what's going to come out of you. Anyway, I don't have much hope for this scheme."

"I do. I believe God's in it," she replied strongly.

⚜

Trevor trembled on the table as Praise God removed the straps that had held his leg down. He had fainted twice during the operation, for the laudanum that had been overlooked during the previous battle had been strong indeed. Now he looked up at Shayna, who bent over him.

"How—did it go?"

"Wonderfully!" Shayna was smiling. Bathing his face with a damp cloth, she said, "I was so proud of Cathan."

"Where is he?"

"Right here."

Cathan's face appeared in Trevor's blurred vision. He reached up and whispered, "Give me your hand." When Cathan took it, Trevor said, "Congratulations, Doctor." Trevor knew he would never forget this operation, of which he had watched as much as he could before passing out.

Now as he lay there, his hand held by Cathan Morgan, he managed to whisper, "A friend—and a brother!"

"WE MUST LEARN
TO LET GO"

Looking around the blue, white, and gold drawing room in which he sat with Pierre, Honor was struck with how comfortable and how rich it was. He well knew the two things did not always go together, for often rooms that were created to display the wealth of the owners were stiff and uncomfortable—like being in a museum. However, this beautiful room, illuminated by a cheerful fire that crackled in the marble fireplace, invited relaxation, with its upholstered Chippendale chairs, gold serpentine sofa, and walnut corner cabinet filled with books and knickknacks.

"I love this room, Pierre," Honor said, leaning back from the ivory chess set that sat on a mahogany table between the two men.

"It's always been my favorite," Pierre said absently, his mind on the board. Then he reached out, lifted a piece, and, with a grin, plopped it down on the board, rattling the other pieces. "There," he announced triumphantly, "let's see you get out of this one!"

Glancing at the board, Honor asked evenly, "Are you certain that's what you want to do?"

"You can't bluff me this time! I've got you!"

Honor had come to treasure these nightly chess games with his host. The two men were unevenly matched, for their style of play was quite different. Pierre played almost by pure instinct, with little strategy in his moves. He threw his men into battle as a general might fearlessly, but sometimes foolishly, throw troops into the line. Yet it was amazing how many times the Frenchman was able to win against Honor, who played methodically, planning ahead.

"Well, if you're certain, then—checkmate!"

Staring down at the board, Pierre shook his head. "I see you have beaten me again." He laughed then, for he was good natured about losing. "Do you never get tired of beating your host? Would it not be more political for you to allow me to win?"

Knowing that Pierre desired nothing of the sort, Honor said with a smile, "All my training is to go for the kill." He picked up the cup of chocolate that the servant had brought and, after swallowing a mouthful, continued, "I don't think I've ever relaxed so completely in my life, Pierre. And that's strange, considering the danger all about us."

"Nothing can touch you here, Honor."

"No, I think not," Honor said, with a look of respect and admiration at his host. "It's like being in a castle. The drawbridge is up, the moat is full of dangerous creatures, and all that would harm me and mine is warded away on the outside. And although I know you dislike being thanked, I must tell you again how very grateful I am for all you have done for us."

"Nothing! Nothing!" Pierre waved his hand in the air as if commanding a physical object to disappear. "Suppose the tyrant and his henchmen find us and kill us. They can only kill us once, eh?"

Honor Wakefield laughed. "I like that very much. I shall employ it with my lieutenants the next time I lead a ship into battle."

"That will be soon, I trust. Napoléon cannot continue long. I was in Paris six months ago and saw the men. Their uniforms were as ragged as the lines they were forming and they were half starving. Bonaparte never thinks of trying to feed the men he compels to serve him and he pays them as an afterthought, if at all. He's putting forth the effort that only he is capable of, but it cannot go on. Wellington has won many battles and in the end it will be Wellington who defeats Napoléon."

"The blockade has been such a struggle for my country," Honor added. "But it's strangling the empire of the French."

"Yes, that will defeat him in the end. All of Europe, under his charge, is growing restive. They will begin to defect soon, one at a time, and he will not be able to stop it. One day very soon, please God, we will see peace in the world again."

As the two men continued speaking of the political situation, the flames of the popping fire cast wavering shadows on their faces. Finally Pierre led the conversation into a more personal vein, saying with regret, "I am sorrowful at times over Madeline."

Looking up, Honor saw that Pierre's face was not as relaxed and content as usual.

"She seems content," Honor replied.

"Oh, she never complains," Pierre said, "but I know she is unhappy." He paused, then began to speak quickly, as if the words had been bottled up. "I have never spoken of this to anyone else, but I have been concerned for a long time, my friend. She is a fine woman, who was very much in love with my son, And when he died, she went into deep grieving, as we all did. But grief must run its course and we must get on with life. Madeline has not been able to do that and it grieves me."

"You would like to see her marry again?"

"Yes. I would like to have grandchildren about my knees, even though they would not be of my blood. Yet Madeline is a daughter to me in all ways except that."

Honor sipped the chocolate, which was tepid now, then asked tentatively, "She is still in love with him?"

"Her love is very strong. Everything about Madeline is strong. You have noticed that, have you not?"

"Indeed I have. She's a most unusual woman. A very spiritual woman."

"Ah, yes, she is as strong in her religion as she is in her affections for those of us on earth. I think she loves me more than she loved her own father. He was not a warm person, nor was her mother. So Madeline has brought all of her affection to me, as I have given all mine to her." Then, looking directly at Honor, he said slowly, "So, yes, she still loves my son, but one cannot embrace a memory. A woman needs a man before she can be whole."

That remark is pointed at me! Honor realized. From all he had learned about Pierre, Honor knew that the statement "A woman needs a man before she can be whole" was a two-edged sword. *He's really saying,* Honor thought rapidly, *a man needs a woman before he can be whole.* Ordinarily such words would have angered him. He would have considered them an impertinence. But Honor could not take it so from the elderly man who sat across from him. He'd grown too fond of him. And besides that, he knew there was truth in what Pierre said. He had felt it many times over the years but had always shoved it to one side. Now he realized, *I haven't married because I've been proud of my earlier love. I've put Rachel in a shrine and worshiped there. But Pierre is trying to tell me that this is wrong for a man—as he is saying it is wrong for Madeline.* He sat quietly, aware that his host was regarding him intently, then said, "I think you are right, but men and women are not always wise in these things."

"Some things cannot be learned from books. You are a very logical man, Honor. You play chess logically, your head full of plans. And although we have not known one another long, I think you are the same in your relationships with others. You will always win more chess games when we play, but I will always enjoy the game more."

Again unspoken advice lurked beneath the surface of Pierre's words. *He's telling me to listen to my heart instead of my head. Perhaps he's right, but how does a man change his ways?* Honor asked himself. Although the question was unspoken, it was as if Pierre had heard it with his own ears, for he said, "Learn to trust your heart, my friend. Learn to trust your heart!"

<hr />

"Well, you're coming along well, Trevor." Madeline, accompanied by Shayna, had come in to change the dressing on Trevor's stump. The two women had worked together to remove the old dressing and now saw that the flesh was a healthy pink.

"I still can't believe Cathan did this," Shayna said, picking up a cloth and dipping it in the pan of warm water she had brought with her. As she bathed the stump, her face was still, but there was no sign of revulsion. In fact, it surprised her that she could handle a wound like this, which had been almost frightening to her at first.

Trevor sat up in the chair, his maimed leg propped up on a hassock, and watched. Then, somewhat embarrassed, he laughed. "I've probably got the two most attractive nurses in the history of the Western world." Now that he was getting his strength back, Trevor had discovered that he was able to handle his loss better than he had expected. Looking down at the stump, he said critically, "Yes, he did a fine job. I know a great many surgeons who couldn't do as well."

"Did you ever hear of such a thing before, Trevor?" Madeline asked, preparing the bandages. After Shayna had dried the leg and applied ointment, Madeline deftly began to put the bandages in place.

"I don't believe I ever have. Cathan could have been a surgeon if he had so chosen."

As the morning sun filtered through the high window, turning

Madeline's and Shayna's complexions rosy, Trevor realized how very different the two women were. Shayna had the beauty of youth and the feel of romance about her, although he knew her views had changed since her tragedy with Cathan Morgan. And yet Madeline had a deep, calm spirit that appealed to him. He knew also that she loved music and books and that she had been a member of a small Protestant sect before marrying. She had joined the Catholic church to please her husband, John, but Trevor suspected that at times she felt uncomfortable with the ornate ritual of her adopted church.

Trevor's thoughts snapped back to the present. "I didn't see Cathan yesterday."

Shayna started to speak, then shut her mouth. So it was Madeline who said, "You know, Trevor, I think he stays away from you because he doesn't want to be thanked."

"It's only natural that I should. He saved my life."

"You have thanked him and I believe you should say no more of it," Madeline responded as she finished the bandage and stood up. "That's fine. It won't be long before we can begin thinking of making you something to get around on."

"I'll bring you some breakfast, Trevor," Shayna said, leaving the room. As she made her way toward the kitchen, she thought of the days that had passed since the operation. She had noted that Cathan went out each day to hunt and then mostly stayed with Praise God. *Could he be avoiding me?* she thought, troubled, and hurried more quickly toward the kitchen. But as she and Elise, the cook, began putting their heads together to create a good breakfast for Trevor, her mind was still on Cathan Morgan. *What's wrong with me? At one time I didn't ever want to see him again and now I find myself wanting to. I hope I'm not the foolish, romantic girl I was in those days.* But as hard as she tried to cover her thoughts with cheerful conversation, she kept wondering what would happen in the future.

Cathan enjoyed the crunching of the snow underfoot as he made his way through the woods, wondering if he had been missed. Shortly after the operation he had sought Pierre Monbiere's permission to hunt in the woods and his host had merely said, "Since you speak French it will be all right. Wear old clothes and try to stay away from the roads."

Cathan had gone out each day, sometimes bringing in the rabbits that abounded in the woods and once, a hungry, under-sized deer. However, it was not the game that drew him there but something in his own heart. He and Praise had spent a great deal of time together, but aside from the sailor he found himself unable to be comfortable with the other members of the household. Although Pierre and Madeline had never shown him any un-kindness, they were aristocrats and he was a poor man. They would not think of inviting him in for a meal any more than they would invite one of their own servants. Trevor had spoken of this once, saying, "I'm sure they don't mean to be impolite."

Cathan had just grinned and shook his head. "They've got the right of it, Trevor. To them, I am a servant. But that's all right—I don't mind."

A flight of rooks circled above him, then flew off. "Go on, get away from me, you worthless creatures!" Cathan said teasingly. He was feeling very good, for he had made several difficult shots and now the bag on his shoulder was heavy. As he shifted it, he remembered the times he and his father, Ivor, had gone hunting. *We were so close then,* Cathan thought sadly. *And I've violated that relationship. He should have knocked me on the head when I was fifteen.*

Making his way to the creek that wound between the hills, he stopped at the water's edge. It was skimmed over with plates of ice that magnified the stones in the creek. Stepping forward, he kicked the ice and watched as pieces broke and floated downstream, knowing they would wind their way to the sea. Thinking of the sea, Cathan was reminded that someday they must leave this place. Although he was grateful for their escape, it seemed as if they were now hiding from life. He knew Trevor felt the same way, but he wasn't sure about Honor.

Just then a rustling attracted his attention and he turned quickly, his hand automatically closing on the trigger of the loaded musket. But he relaxed his grip and dropped the muzzle toward the ground as Honor Wakefield appeared. He'd been walking alongside the creek.

"Cathan!" Honor said, looking startled. "I didn't see you!"

"Good afternoon, Captain."

"Have a good day?"

Cathan lifted the bag and smiled. "Enough to feed us, although they don't need it in that house."

"I always did like rabbit stew, but I could never shoot well enough to bring home a bag full."

"You do better with the guns on ship, Captain."

Wakefield smiled at the way Cathan had returned the compliment. Then both men were silent, for although they were no longer on a ship, they were still separated by their positions in the British navy. Even more, there was the issue of the past. But Honor had been waiting for an opportunity to speak of the walls between them, so he said, "I've been meaning to say something to you, Cathan."

"Yes, sir?"

"We've had our difficulties and there was a time when I felt like shooting you," Honor said with a wry grin. "I don't often feel like that, but one day when you have a daughter and you think she's being misused, I believe you'll understand."

"I understand already, Captain," Cathan said, meeting Honor's eyes. "I behaved like a rascal and would have gotten exactly what I deserved if you had shot me."

Pleased with Cathan's straightforward reply, Honor was reminded of Gareth Morgan, Cathan's grandfather. When Honor, in his early days in England, had first met Gareth, it had seemed to him that Gareth Morgan was exactly what a man of God should be. Now he saw that same quality in Cathan. "You've changed a great deal. God has done something in you."

Cathan nodded. "Well, God didn't have a great deal to work with. When I was in prison, I gave up hope, but I also saw what a rotter I had been. It was Praise who led me to Jesus. You know, sir, I don't think I ever would have been converted if I hadn't gone to prison."

"Well, you know what your grandfather would say," Honor responded.

"My grandfather?"

"He would say, 'Why, that's just God's hand working on you and all things work together for good to those who love God.'"

Cathan laughed aloud. "That's *exactly* what he would say, sir! You must know him very well."

"I don't know any man I admire more."

"It's very generous of you to say so," Cathan said, face glowing.

"Not generous at all. Just the plain truth. . . . I'm very pleased to see this change in you, Cathan. Not just for your own sake, but for your father's and for your grandfather's. They'll be very pleased when they hear what I have to say to them."

"That's very kind of you, Captain."

"Well then, shall we go back?" Honor said, pleased that they had finally had this conversation and that the walls had broken down. Perhaps because during his childhood he had had no one except his mother, Honor had a strong sense of family. He loved the honor of the Wakefield name and was proud of the Welsh strain from the Morgan side of the family. *I must tell Shayna about this conversation. She'll be pleased,* Honor thought.

They had not gone very far when Cathan asked, "Captain, have you had any thoughts about getting back to England?"

"I've had little else, but they go nowhere. My head's in a swim, it seems. But now that Trevor's mending, we must do *something!* We're putting Pierre and Madeline in great danger. . . . Why do you ask?"

"I can't see any way of getting back except crossing the channel by ourselves."

"Exactly right! I had hoped we might see a British ship and row out to it, but that's far fetched. They won't come this close with the French patrol ships so active."

"What sort of a ship or boat would it take to cross the channel, do you think?" Cathan queried.

Honor Wakefield halted, interest in his gray blue eyes. "Not as much as you might think. One captain sailed almost two thousand miles in a boat no more than thirty feet long."

"Well, Captain, I've covered this coast pretty well in my wanderings. There's a small inlet that feeds into the sea, and an abandoned boat there. It's in bad shape, but—"

Honor began to fire questions at him: How big was the boat? How badly was it damaged? Did it have a sail? And then he demanded, "How far away is it, Cathan?"

"About three miles."

"Come. I must see it!" Honor said, hope springing alive.

As he kept pace with Cathan, he prayed, *God give us wisdom and let us find a way out of this place before our friends are injured.*

When they reached the inlet, which was little more than the culmination of several creeks that had created a stream some twenty feet wide, Cathan motioned. "There she is, Captain."

Eagerly Honor moved toward the bank and evaluated the boat. It was obviously old, but at once he said, "It will do, Cathan! We'll have to add a new mast, a sail, and do some caulking, but in the right weather we can go back to England in this craft!"

When Trevor saw the pleased look on his visitor's face, he asked, "Well, Cathan, what have you been up to?"

"We've found a boat—we're going to get away from here!"

The words tumbled out of Cathan as he related how he had found the old boat and how the captain had been firm in his declaration that it would do to get them across the channel.

"Wonderful!" Trevor exclaimed as he sat in a chair by the window. Then he shook his head woefully. "I won't be any help getting it ready."

"There's no problem about that. Praise and I can make it shipshape. . . . How's the leg?"

"The foot that's not there itches," Trevor said. "It's not unusual, though. I just have to bear with it and it'll pass."

"We'll have to fit you out with a new foot, or a peg at least."

"I've already been thinking about that," Trevor said eagerly. "It shouldn't be too hard."

"We'll get Praise working on it. He's good at making things."

They talked longer about completing the boat; then Trevor said carefully, "We've come a long way, haven't we, Cathan? I mean, we've had our troubles, but after all, we're family. For my part, I say, let's bury the past."

"Agreed," Cathan said, a look of awe on his face.

Honor and Madeline sat together on a couch, looking at a book. When the clock began to chime, Honor looked up and said incredulously, "Why, it's ten o'clock! We've been here for three hours!"

Indeed, they had stayed in the drawing room long after Pierre had gone to bed. Madeline had brought out some of the books she treasured most and they had drifted into a conversation about something in Scripture. She had gotten out an old Bible, well worn, to check some passages. And then they had begun to talk of eternity.

"You see," Madeline said, smiling, "we're so conscious of time. Here we've spent just a few hours and we think that's a long time."

"I suppose that's true, although it doesn't seem long to me." Honor was enjoying the company of this charming, intellectual woman. "But it *is* hard to think about eternity."

"Yes, it is," Madeline replied, her dark eyes matching her dress. As the lamps threw their golden beams over her, softening her olive skin, she continued, "But sometimes I think back to the years gone by, before the worlds were made and the stars were fashioned. Back when the universe slept in the mind of God. All was yet unborn. I think about God, the Creator, living alone with everything sleeping within him. All creation resting in his mighty, gigantic thought. I try to go back, and back, and back, ages upon ages. I go back till it seems that whole eternities have passed and yet that's not the beginning."

"That's very deep, Madeline," Honor said.

"Do you know what I think of often? How that before the worlds were made, or the suns, or the planets, or the moons, before anything was ever made, God chose us. He chose me and he chose you. Back when universal silence reigned. Not an angel had been created. Without the song of an angel or the attendance even of a cherubim. Before the living creatures were born, or even the wheels of the chariot of Jehovah were fashioned. Even then, in the beginning was the Word, and in the beginning he chose us to eternal life." Her eyes bright and lips gentle, she said, "That's marvelous, isn't it, that God loves us?"

Breaking the mood, she said, "Oh, look! Snow is falling!" and hurried to look out the window. As he came to stand beside her, he murmured, "I've never known a woman like you."

Startled by how close Honor was standing, she said, "I suppose my thinking *is* rather strange."

"Not at all. It's good to hear talk like this."

Looking into her eyes, Honor felt something stirring that he thought he had locked away long ago. Drawn by the richness of her beauty and her deep spirit, he reached forward and put his arms around her. She did not resist, for the same urges had touched her. As she lifted her face and their lips met, they were conscious of nothing except their desire to love and be loved.

Finally Madeline put her hand on his chest. "I suppose," she whispered, her lips trembling, "we're entitled to one mistake."

"A mistake? No, it was not a mistake," he said huskily. "You stir me just by being who you are."

As Madeline de Fontaneau stood in the embrace of this tall, strong man, she realized how dry her heart had become. Now old thoughts and memories surfaced. "We are two lonely and vulnerable people, Honor."

"All people are lonely and vulnerable," he said, holding her closer and inhaling the sweetness of her hair. As they stood together, she clung to him and began to weep.

"What's the matter?" he asked gently.

"I suppose I'm more lonely than I thought." She pulled back then and turned away. "You'll be leaving soon."

"I must. It's too dangerous for us here, but I will miss you."

"I will miss you, too," she said, her tears shining like diamonds. He reached for her again, but she shook her head and left, shoulders shaking.

Honor Wakefield stood alone in the room. He had steadily withstood the fire of the enemy, but now his breathing was uneven, for he could still smell her perfume and taste the softness of her lips. Even as he shook his head, as if to clear it, he realized that this woman had touched him in a way he could never escape.

Twenty

THE PRESENCE

Neither Honor nor Madeline spoke of the moment when he had taken her in his arms, though both of them knew they had crossed over into a new relationship. As the days passed, Praise and Cathan devoted their energies to the boat that would take them back to England. And from time to time Honor went out to see how the work was progressing.

Trevor's health improved rapidly and he grew impatient waiting for the time when his stump would be able to support his weight on an artificial foot. During this period, Madeline spent much time sitting beside him, reading from the large selection of books that she and her father-in-law had collected. They were, for the most part, devotional books. And as she continued to read, Trevor grew more and more to appreciate the deep spiritual life of Madeline de Fontaneau. He said as much once to Shayna and her eyes had brightened.

"Yes, she is a very fine Christian. Perhaps the finest I've ever known. I wish I could be more like her."

Trevor responded quickly. "You've changed a great deal, Shayna. You're not like the young woman I knew even a year ago."

Shayna did not answer directly, but later in the day she went to her journal, one of the few possessions she had managed to take with her from the shipwreck, and wrote:

Trevor says I'm not the same and I hope he's right. Perhaps all of us, when we look back over our lives, can find foolish acts, things we wish we had never done. Looking back over my own life, I see that I've been too much taken by drama. Now I think that romance is wonderful but it's only a part of life. Love has to be more solid than the foolish characters I've always read about!

She put down the pen, thinking again of Cathan Morgan. It had become almost a habit with her each day to try to understand her feelings for him. She knew that they were far different from when she had first met him and that his changed life was responsible for her own emotional transference. Still, she did not trust herself, thinking that if she made a mistake once, she might do it again. Finally she closed the journal with a sigh.

Thirty

Honor faced Madeline, who was dressed in a green, Grecian-style gown and was sitting beside him on the couch. *I remember the last time we were in this room together; it turned into a kiss,* Honor thought. He had not forgotten that embrace. He had been alone for so long that he had forgotten how wonderful it was to have a woman to share his thoughts with. Glancing at the woman beside him, he thought, *I've never known anyone so easy to be with.* Then, unbidden, visions of his wife arose and guilt filled him. However, as he thought of Rachel, he knew she would have been happy to see him find a companion.

"You're not listening," Madeline said, putting her finger on the place in the book. "I think you've had enough theology for one day."

"No, it's not that," Honor said quickly. "I was just trying to—" He broke off, knowing that he had allowed his thoughts to wander. "Well, I confess," he said, pulling the book closer to him, "that this is a little deep for me."

"Deep? Why, it isn't deep at all," Madeline protested. Honor's hand rested on hers for a moment and she smiled at him. "This book, *Practicing the Presence of God* by Brother Lawrence, has influenced my life more than any other, except the Bible."

"Well, from what you've told me about him, he ran away from the world, went to a monastery. That's no way to face life."

"Not for most of us, but it really wasn't that simple," Madeline said. "Actually, Brother Lawrence was as busy in the monastery as he was outside. He went there to give himself to God, knowing that most monasteries offered shelter from the world. But they put him to work in the kitchen and you can imagine what a noisy place that was!"

"It doesn't sound like he accomplished much."

"Oh, but he did!" Madeline said, her eyes glowing. "Brother Lawrence set out to find the presence of God. And he learned he had to find it not just when he was alone in a room but while he was busy in the kitchen. He says: 'I engaged in a religious life only for the love of God, and I have endeavored to act only for him; whatever becomes of me, whether I be lost or saved, I will always continue to act purely for the love of God. I shall have this good at least, that till death I shall have done all that is in me to love him.' Isn't that wonderful?"

"Not many of us can achieve that."

"Why, don't be foolish, Honor! Do you think that God has favorites?" Madeline scolded gently. "It's in our hands how close we come to God. Brother Lawrence found out the hard way that practicing God's presence must become a regular and disciplined way of life until we can keep ourselves in the presence of the Lord no matter what happens."

Shifting uneasily on the couch, Honor admitted, "I'm just a sea captain, Madeline. I can understand a preacher doing that, or maybe a monk or a nun, but I don't see how the average human being could possibly do it."

"We can't—not perfectly, for even Brother Lawrence never achieved that. But instead of panicking, he prayed for God's grace and then went on again. It took him a long time to get to the point where he could live in God's presence in the middle of busyness. But even after his death, his testimony is still helping people, as it has me."

"It always seemed to me that some people are more conscious of God than others."

"That's true," Madeline agreed. "Being saved is one thing, but being aware of Jesus as a person, well, that's something else again. But I think that once you have really known the presence of Jesus Christ in your heart and in your life, the world will never appeal to you again. At least that's the way it is with me."

As the two talked further, Honor was amazed that he could be so happy talking about God with anyone. He had always been a rather nominal Christian, but Madeline had shown him a higher plane. Finally he said, "I wish I could be as close to God as you."

"Oh, Honor, you can!" In her intense desire to see this man prosper, Madeline unconsciously took his hand. "One of my favorite Scriptures is 2 Timothy 4:2. It says, 'Be instant in season, out of season.' I didn't know what to make of that for a long time, but I came to understand that it simply means we ought to be faithful to God whether we feel like it or not. There are times in our lives when we don't feel like praying and there are times when we do. Honor, have you ever prayed and felt the presence of God close to you in your prayers?"

"Yes, a few times. Not often."

"Have you ever tried to pray when it seemed the heavens were brass and no one was listening?"

"Yes!" Honor said fervently. "Quite often that's my experience."

"Well, which one of those do you think pleases God the most?"

"Why, when I was fervent and felt his presence."

"No, I don't think so," Madeline said, smiling. "Anyone can pray under circumstances like those. I think it pleases God the most when we pray when it's difficult and we have no sense of anyone hearing. That's the proof that we are rightly related to Jesus—when we do our best whether we feel inspired or not."

Astonished, Honor stared at Madeline. "I never thought of that. Usually I stop praying when I don't feel inspired."

"And that's just the time when we need to give ourselves to Jesus and pray more."

Realizing her hand was on his, he covered it gently. "You are a wonderful woman, Madeline. I can't tell you how much it has meant just to be with you. I think I've learned more about God since I've been here than I have in all my life."

Aware of the warmth and strength of his hand on hers, Madeline blushed and bowed her head. "As Christians, we need to help each other along the way, Honor." Then, suddenly flustered, she withdrew her hand and rose. "I'd better go see about dinner."

As she left, Honor thought with regret, *I thought I'd be happy to get back to England. But it's going to be hard to leave here.*

───────────

Cathan was so engrossed in his work on the boat that he did not hear Shayna's footsteps.

"Hello, Cathan!" she called, startling him.

Whirling hastily, he jumped to his feet, holding the hammer.

Moving toward him, she asked, "What are you doing?"

"Caulking the joints," he said, speaking quickly to cover his awkwardness. "This boat's been out a long time and the caulking has gotten old and has to be redone."

"Is this what you fill the seams with?" Leaning over, Shayna picked up something that looked like rope.

"Yes. It's not like the oakum we use on a ship of the line, but it's close enough."

"Show me how you do it."

Turning back to the boat, Cathan picked up a bit of the caulking material and placed it in a seam. Then, picking up a chisel, he tapped it in carefully with a wooden mallet. "Not much to it," he said. "Just have to be careful. Too much oakum will force the seam to part and too little will produce a leaky seam. But if you do it just right, it will not only keep the water out of the hull but make the boat stronger."

"Could I try?"

"Of course." Cathan handed her the mallet and chisel and watched as she awkwardly pounded some caulking into the seam and then hit her finger.

As she let out a cry, he said gently, "Well, that goes with the job, I suppose. Maybe you'd better let me do the caulking."

"I wish I could help," Shayna said, putting her finger in her mouth to take the sting away, "but I never was any good with tools. I couldn't learn to sew very well either because I was always sticking myself with the needle."

"I was about ready to take a break anyway. We'll fix some tea." Praise and Cathan had begged a kettle, mugs, and tea from the cook for their long hours of working on the boat, so it wasn't long before Cathan had a fire blazing and the teakettle was on the little grate.

They talked for a time about the ship as Cathan explained what had to be done. "Of course, I just do as I'm told," Cathan said, grinning. "Praise is the architect. He knows a lot about ships. I'm just the apprentice on this job."

"Do you really think we can get all the way across to England in this little boat?"

"Praise thinks so. He says God can do anything. And I guess he's right about that. It's human beings who mess things up."

It was a revealing statement, Shayna thought—something he would never have said back in the days when they first met. "Let me make the tea," she offered. "I can do that at least."

Ten minutes later they were drinking tea from the mugs. "This is good!" she exclaimed.

"Anything tastes better when you are out in the open air. When I was in the army, we had awful cooks. But when we were on the march, anything tasted good."

"Did you like the army, Cathan?"

"It was adventurous for a time, but it's a lonely life."

"Would you ever go back to it?"

"Not much chance of that. I was drummed out of the regiment. That sort of thing gets around."

"What would you do if you could do what you liked?"

Cathan thought for a minute, then shrugged. "I have no idea. Of course, I'm in the navy under your father's command."

"Would you like to continue in the navy?"

"I don't think so. I can handle the guns, but that's about all. Besides, it's a lonely life too."

"Yes, I know all about that," Shayna said quietly, thinking of how rarely she had seen her father in her growing-up years. "It is a hard life. . . . But my father is very different now."

Cathan glanced at her. "Different in what way?"

"He's thinking more about God. He's been a Christian for as long as I can remember and he always goes to church when he isn't at sea, but he's never talked much about God."

"What's changed him, do you think?"

"Oh, it's Madeline. She's very devout."

"Yes, she is. A fine woman." Then, seeing Shayna was troubled, Cathan asked, "Do you think your father is interested in her—as a woman?"

"I know he is. I've never seen him like this," Shayna said. "Of course, a lot of women have wanted to marry him. He's handsome and has money and a title. For as long as I can remember, women have shoved their daughters at him." Then, eyes sparkling, she continued, "And some have even shoved themselves. You should have seen some of the schemes they developed. They were all nice to me because they wanted me to like them."

"Did you like any of them?"

"I wasn't impressed with any of them."

Cathan took a sip of tea. "Would it worry you if your father married again?"

"It would be strange."

"Well, I haven't been very close to the lady, but it seems to me that any man would be fortunate to have her. She's very attractive and, as you say, a fine Christian," he said encouragingly.

"It would be different having a mother now, when I'm grown," she said hesitantly.

"It might be a comfort to your father. One of these days you'll marry and he'll be left alone—except for the grandchildren, of course," he said, grinning.

Startled, Shayna looked up at him. They had been sitting on a fallen log and now she got up and brushed her skirt. Seeing that his remark must have bothered her, he arose, saying, "I didn't offend you, I hope."

She turned toward him suddenly. "Back when we first met, Cathan, I made a terrible mistake. I was so full of romantic notions that you swept me off my feet. I wouldn't want to make a mistake like that again. But now I don't know. I haven't been able to think too well, it seems."

Above them a bird started singing, but neither of them looked up. They were caught in the moment. Cathan said carefully, "I don't think you'll make that mistake. You've gained a lot of wisdom since then." Then, throwing caution to the wind, he said impulsively, "Shayna, I've wanted to say this, but I've never known how. I've felt so guilty and miserable about the way I treated you that I thought it would not be fitting."

"What is it, Cathan?" she said softly.

He reached for her hand. "I've told you that I was wrong about the way I treated you, but I know now that it wasn't all greed. Even when I was selfish and looking out for my own miserable advantage, I saw something in you that I've never seen in another woman."

"What did you see?" Shayna whispered, conscious of her hand in his.

"I saw a sweetness and goodness that all women should have and very few do." He lifted her hand and kissed it gently. "They're still there, Shayna. They will always be there. If you live to be a hundred, you'll still have the goodness I see in you now."

As Cathan stood there looking down at her, Shayna did not know what to say. For so long she had been confused and now she saw an honesty and goodness in him that she could not mistake. "Thank you, Cathan. I'm glad you see those things in me whether they're there or not."

"They're there. I couldn't be mistaken about it." He kissed her hand again and then, to lighten the moment, said, "I'm getting to be quite a courtier, all this hand kissing!" Then he grew serious again. As he released her hand, he said simply, "You're a fine woman, Shayna Wakefield, and I hope that when you do marry, you'll find the man who can make you as happy as you deserve." Then, as if he had embarrassed himself, Cathan said brusquely, "I'd better get back to caulking the seams."

As she made her way toward the house, Shayna knew that the two of them had found their way through what had been a terrible situation. Although she could not explain it, the sky seemed more blue—and suddenly it was not so terrible that her father was falling in love with Madeline.

Twenty-One

UNDER THE STARS

W hen winter had almost passed away and the spring of 1802 dawned near, Trevor watched with apprehension as Praise God Barebones fastened the last strap of the new wooden foot. He had been waiting for this moment for the several months since his surgery, for it had been more difficult for him than for the others. Praise God had gained weight as a result of Elise's cooking. He and Cathan had busied themselves putting final touches on the boat. And as for Capt. Wakefield, Trevor was aware that he had spent most of his time with Madeline. Shayna, on the other hand, had made it a point to spend time with him.

"Let's see if you can navigate with this new limb," Praise said, stepping back.

Sitting on the edge of the chair, Trevor moved his leg back and forth. Now that the moment had come, he was fearful. Although he longed to get around without being a burden, he realized that he might not be able to manage. Determinedly he heaved himself up, but as soon as he let go of the chair arm, he began to sway.

"Let me give you a hand!" Cathan said, grasping Trevor's arm and noting the paleness of the doctor's complexion and the slight film of perspiration on his forehead.

"I don't know if I can do it," Trevor murmured.

"Of course you can," Cathan said cheerfully. Holding lightly to Trevor's arm, he said, "Come now. Just give it a try."

"The room is moving around," Trevor said, gasping. "It's worse than being on a ship in a storm!"

Actually to him, the room did seem to be heaving, but he knew in his mind that this was to be expected. As he looked toward Praise, who stood a few feet away, his jaw hardened and he gritted his teeth. "All right. Here I come. If I fall—let me fall."

Tentatively Trevor stepped forward. But soon he discovered that walking was now altogether different. "I can't do it!" he said. As he started to fall, Praise and Cathan grabbed him, maneuvering him back to the chair. Trevor scowled.

"Don't worry," Cathan said encouragingly, patting him lightly on the shoulder. "Take a rest and we'll try it again."

This was the beginning of a process more difficult than any of them had foreseen. It was a matter of some days before Trevor managed the weakness that beset him. Then, as soon as he had learned to make his way across the room, they found things wrong with the wooden leg. Several times Praise had to alter the length of the leg and the pitch of the leather tip. As Trevor walked, the stump on which his weight rested grew inflamed and was sometimes too tender for him to use. Other times he fell over, causing himself dreadful pain. But eventually the skin that grew over the stump became calloused.

"I think if the boat's ready, I can make it," Trevor finally told Honor.

"We can wait a little longer," Honor said. In truth this was not altogether for Trevor's benefit. Honor had found himself more and more reluctant to leave the Frenchman's house because of Madeline. But at the same time he realized that with spring, there would be more and more opportunities for someone to spot the visitors at the house. The snow was gone now and the boat was finished. So he said to Trevor with a laugh, "It's been a hard time for you, Trevor, but for the rest of us, well . . . I believe it's been the most pleasant time I've had in years."

Trevor smiled knowingly. "It's been royal living all right. The cooking, I'll miss that."

"Yes, and Pierre has become a good friend."

"And Madeline, too, of course."

Seeing the grin on Trevor's face, Honor got flustered. "Well, yes, she's a charming woman."

"Very charming," Trevor said solemnly, but his eyes were laughing. "When do you think we should try for it?"

"In a few days. We'll have to leave at dusk so we can get as far offshore and out of the way of the patrol boats as we can before morning. There will be a bit of luck involved with it." Then, smiling, he added, "Madeline says that it's not luck at all, that God's in it."

"I'm beginning to think she's right. We all could have died in that wreck, Captain. It's a miracle we didn't."

"I know. My heart's been grieved for all of the men who did perish," Honor said, shaking his head sadly.

"Well, I'm ready when you are," Trevor said, tapping the tip of his wooden leg on the floor. "I don't think I'll be any handicap to you now."

<hr/>

Four days after his conversation with Trevor, Honor made up his mind. He spoke to Pierre, saying, "We're going to be leaving."

"We'll be sad to see you go, Captain."

"That's generous of you, Pierre, and I'll be sorry to leave. But it will be better for you and Madeline. We're nothing but a danger to you while we're here."

"We do not think of that, my friend. When do you think of leaving?"

"Day after tomorrow. We'll have to impose on your generosity to stock the boat with enough food."

"What about arms?"

"We can't put our hope in arms. Any kind of a patrol boat would have a cannon that could blow us out of the water if we don't surrender," Honor said honestly.

"Tomorrow night, then, we will have a special meal together."

The dinner *was* special. Elise had outdone herself. As Honor looked down the table, he proclaimed, "What a feast!" The meal consisted of steaming bowls of turtle soup, thin biscuits with caviar and heavy cream, quail stuffed with liver paté, and thin slices of dark bread. Afterward came the cheese and fruit plates, followed by steaming cups of dark, rich coffee.

Although the food was exquisite, Honor could not join into the spirit of the thing. He noticed that Madeline, who looked lovely in a plum-colored satin dress, said almost nothing during the meal. He himself ate sparingly, forcing himself to take part in the conversation. Even Shayna had little to say. *She looks a little pale,* Honor thought. *No wonder, after this experience.*

Trevor, who was seated beside Shayna, also noticed she had said little. "It's been quite an experience, hasn't it?" he murmured.

"Yes, it has."

"I think our lives are punctuated with memories that never leave. Most days go on and nothing out of the ordinary happens, but I'll remember this time here with Pierre and Madeline as long as I live."

"I think we all will." Shayna managed a smile, then turned to Trevor. "It must be hard having lost your foot."

"Oh, I suppose I will miss some of the things I can't manage. I won't be able to walk easily through the woods as I once did, but on the other hand I still have both knees. That makes a big difference, you know, and I can be just as good a physician as I was before. Maybe better," he added. "I'll be able to understand my patients better."

Meanwhile, Madeline had said softly to Honor, "It will be a quiet house after you've gone."

"My thoughts will return here often," he said, feeling foolish at his understatement and noticing, with a pang, how beautiful she was.

Pierre's questions about the voyage across the channel were a welcome interruption, for Honor could give the details of the plan at some length.

Finally the dinner ended and the party broke up. Madeline got up quickly and left the room.

"I will see that all the provisions are ready. What hour would you like to leave tomorrow?" Pierre asked.

"At dusk tomorrow night, I think. We'll trust for a good wind."

After lingering for a time with Pierre, Honor left his host and headed down the hallway. As he glanced into the library, he was surprised to see Madeline there. Stepping inside, he said almost roughly, "That was the best food—and the worst dinner party I've ever been to. I hate to leave, Madeline."

"It is a grief for me, but I expect you know that," she said, her eyes darker than usual with emotion.

"You made my stay here so wonderful." Then, noting that her lips were pressed tightly together, he asked, "What's wrong, Madeline?"

For a moment he thought she would not answer. Then she said evenly, "Honor, I never expected to find love again, but I have." Seeing the surprise on his face, she continued, "I know it's not socially proper for a woman to say such a thing, but I will not see you again, so I must say it." She reached up and laid her hand on his cheek. "I love you," she said softly. Then pulling him close, she put her arms around his neck and kissed him with passion, grief, and almost anger. As she held him tightly, fearing he might move away, he clasped his hands around her, returning her kiss with ardor.

When she stepped back, she said, "You will never marry, for love for your wife is too strong." Then immediately she whirled and ran from the room, not looking back.

⁂

The next morning Praise God and Cathan were busy loading supplies and putting them in exactly the right place. "I hate to leave this place, Cat," Praise said as they stowed the food in a locker in the prow of the boat. "Better than any ship I was ever on."

"You need to marry that cook, Elise," Cathan said, grinning. "She knows how to treat a man." To Cathan's surprise, Praise did not laugh. Instead he stood up slowly, and said, "Well, stranger things than that have happened. She's a fine woman."

"But she's French."

Praise winked at him, a merry look in his good eye. "Yes, but it wouldn't be too hard to transplant her, my boy."

"I wouldn't put it past you, Praise, to marry a woman just to get a good cook," Cathan said, amused.

In the afternoon, Cathan walked through the hills for the last time. When he got back, Shayna was waiting for him. "I was afraid you had left for good," she said.

"No, that would be desertion. I'm just nervous. I wanted to take one last look at this country. It's beautiful."

"I'd like to come back here after the war is over and visit with Pierre and Madeline," she said intently. Then she added quickly, "I think Father wants to see you."

The two made their way to where the small crowd gathered by the house. It would be dark in another hour, just time enough to get to the boat, and apparently it had been decided that Pierre and Madeline would not be seeing them off.

Noticing how drawn her father's face was, Shayna glanced at Madeline, whom she had not seen all day. It was obvious that she, too, was unhappy. Going to her, Shayna said, "Madeline, you've been so good to all of us. How can I ever thank you?"

"It was God who brought you here," Madeline said, gathering the girl into her arms. "And I will miss you more than I can say."

Turning, Honor Wakefield saw his daughter in Madeline's embrace. Without preface, he walked over to them, took Madeline's hand, and kissed it. "God bless you, my dear Madeline. You have made this place a heaven for all of us."

Ordinarily Madeline might have jested, but the only words she could say were, "You are most welcome, my dear Captain." Then she stepped back as they started down the trail toward the boat.

"Madam is very unhappy," Cathan mentioned to Shayna.

"I know," Shayna said sadly. "Father is too. I can tell."

Out of the corner of his eye Cathan saw Praise hug the cook, Elise, and whisper something in her ear. As she smiled, Praise wheeled and ran to catch up with the group.

As they made their way to the boat, Trevor said, "Look at that! I congratulate you on your craftsmanship, Praise." Praise had fastened a flat piece on the crutch so that the tip did not puncture the ground.

Praise nodded cheerfully. "You'll be hunting grouse one of these days, mark my words, sir!"

Once they reached the boat and got in, Praise and Cathan shoved with long poles to get the boat started and Honor took the tiller. As they moved away from shore, the naval air fell on them and Honor was again the captain.

"Unfurl the mainsail, Barebones," Honor ordered.

"Aye, sir!"

Since there was only one sail, which by definition meant that it was the mainsail, Cathan smiled a little. Nevertheless, when he looked up and saw the breeze puff the canvas out and felt the boat stir under his feet, a thrill went through him. His eyes met Shayna's. "On our way home, miss."

❦

"God has been with us," Cathan said as he sat by the tiller, looking up at the sky from time to time. They had been two nights and one day and soon morning would roll around. It had been an easy voyage, although the wind had forsaken them. They had seen no patrol boats—indeed, no boats of any kind during the daylight hours. Once Praise thought he saw a light moving during the early part of the evening, but it had moved on and they all drew a sigh of relief.

Shayna looked at the three men, none of whom had slept at all the first night or during the day. She had slept some and now felt refreshed.

"You know, Cathan, for the first time I think we're going to make it. Somehow I was always afraid that we'd be caught, but now I don't think so."

"I believe you're right. Madeline said so anyhow," Cathan said confidently.

"You talked to her?"

"Yes, she came by to see me before we left."

"What did she say?"

Cathan said nothing at first, for there were things that Madeline de Fontaneau said that he did not wish to repeat to Shayna. He remembered Madeline's words: *The young woman loves you. Do not miss love, Mr. Morgan.* Now he savored those words as he had when she spoke them, but he knew it was no time to speak of that. So looking up at the stars, he said, "I wish I knew the stars as well as sailors do."

"Why don't you tell me what she said?" Shayna said, puzzled.

"Well, among other things she said that God told her we would reach England safely. And I believe her. Sometimes I think that

264

woman is like Moses. I read in the Scriptures the other night that God talked with Moses as a man speaks with his friend. It would scare me spitless if a thing like that happened," Cathan confessed.

"Me, too," Shayna said, shivering in the early morning air. As she drew her coat closer around her, Cathan said, "Here, hold the tiller."

"I can't! I'll get us lost!"

Cathan laughed. "You're not going to get us lost that quickly." He moved forward, opened one of the boxes, and come back with a blanket. "Here," he said, "let me put this around you." He arranged the blanket over her shoulders, then pulled it around so that it completely enveloped her. "Is that better?"

"Much better."

As Cathan took the tiller again, he said, "I know that star. That's Polaris, the North Star. That's what all the sailors steer by, so Praise tells me."

"Cathan, tell me what Madeline said."

Amused by her persistence, he said, "You always were stubborn. Can't a man have a conversation with a lady without reporting every word of it?"

"Please tell me," she said pleadingly. "I want to know."

"She talked about you. What a fine woman you are. She seemed to think I needed to know it, but I told her I already knew."

A sudden rustling from the forward part of the ship caught their attention and then Honor's tall form blotted out part of the sky. "I'll take the helm, Morgan, so you can get some rest."

"Aye, aye, sir!" Cathan said, glad of the chance to escape Shayna's questioning.

Taking his seat beside Shayna, Honor peered at her in the gloomy darkness. "Aren't you tired?" he asked.

"I suppose so, but I can't sleep."

"I couldn't much, either. . . . It's been a strange time, hasn't it, Daughter?"

"Yes, but God's been good to us. We're safe and I believe we'll be back in England soon."

They were silent for a time, then Honor said, "I never met a woman like Madeline."

"She's very unusual," Shayna said, encouraging her father to talk. But when he did not respond, she blurted out, "Are you in love with her, Papa?"

The moon came out from behind a cloud and poured its silver light over Honor's face. He had been trying to understand his own heart and now discovered that he did not. "I can't say. I thought of your mother for so many years as the only woman I'd ever love. It's hard to put that aside."

As the boat rose and fell gently over the waves and the wind popped the sail from time to time, Shayna was glad of the darkness, for she, too, had questions in her heart for which she had no answers.

Twenty-Two

A MATTER OF FAITH

Shayna pulled the wooden box containing the food out from under the shelf in the prow of the boat. The spring wind was cold and the rain that fell in long, slanting lines bit at her face and fingers as she carefully lifted the lid. Peering inside in the falling darkness she squinted, trying to make out the condition of their larder. Finally she straightened up and said, "It's dinnertime. How does chicken sound to everyone?"

"It sounds good to me," Trevor said. He was sitting hunched over, his coat sodden with the rain, but he added cheerfully, "Chicken's always been my favorite."

Shayna flashed him a grateful smile. Trevor had been cheerful even through the difficulties of the journey. All of them had been hopeful that the weather would be good and that they would find a breeze that would take them across the channel, but it had not developed that way. The wind had come all right, but it had been contrary and they were forced to tack constantly. Shayna had not even known what it meant to tack until her father explained that it meant sailing almost at right angles against the wind.

Unwrapping the paper, Shayna said, "Come on, let's eat it before it gets soaked."

Cathan was at the tiller, steering. Shayna divided the baked chicken, handing pieces to Honor, Praise, and Trevor. She did the same with the bread, then said, "Oh, I forgot the butter. Would you get it, Praise?"

"Yes, Miss Shayna, I'll take care of that." The sailor hopped down to the box, opened it, and after rummaging around, brought back another package wrapped in cloth. Shayna buttered several large chunks of the bread and passed them out.

"I wish it would stop this confounded rain!" Honor grumbled as he tore a large bite off a drumstick. It was tough, but he chewed it thoroughly, adding, "I wouldn't be surprised if we didn't get a blow out of this." He looked with apprehension at the darkening skies.

Holding her cloak over the food in her right hand, Shayna moved over toward Cathan and sat beside him on the wide seat. "Here it is," she said, "wet and cold, but . . ."

"That's all right," Cathan said, the rain running down his face and neck in rivulets. None of them had weatherproof coats and he, like the others, was soaked to the skin. He did not seem to mind it, however.

Shayna watched as he bit into the chicken breast, then added a large bite of bread spread with butter. "Like eating under water," he said, smiling, "but it's good."

"Do you think we'll get there soon?" Shayna asked, nibbling on the chicken.

"You'll have to ask your father—he's the sailor. Or maybe Praise."

His words were punctuated by a flash of lightning that clawed its way out of the ebony sky. Shayna heard Cathan counting, "One—two—three—four—" and then the thunder clapped.

"What were you counting for?" she asked, her eyes still dazzled by the lightning's brilliance.

"To see how far away the lightning is."

"How can you do that?"

"If you count slowly, as I did, you can tell how many miles away that lightning was. I counted to four, so it's only four miles from here."

"How do you know about that?" she asked, amazed.

"My father taught me."

She shivered a little as the wind whistled through the mast and popped the sail. "I hate the nights out here because they're so dark."

"But there's no way we could show a light," Cathan replied. "Even if we could keep one going, the wrong ship might see us."

"I've been praying for a ship to find us."

"Better pray for an English one then. If a French one finds us, well, we couldn't outrun it."

"All right, I'll pray for an English ship to find us."

"Good," Cathan said, wiping the rain from his face to watch the horizon. Seeing flashes in the distance, he knew that soon they would be in a rainstorm.

"I wish you had some dry clothes," he said.

"I'm no wetter than you are!" she said defensively.

"I suppose not, but if we had to do it over again, I would have built a small cabin to give you some shelter. I don't know why I didn't think of it."

It was a nice thought and Shayna felt warmed by it. She sat beside him for a time and talked of the days they had spent at Pierre and Madeline's house. But soon she could tell that Cathan's mind was not on the conversation, so she moved away and sat down across from Trevor, midway down the length of the boat. Praise saw to the sail, making adjustments when it was time to tack.

"I'll take the tiller, Morgan," Honor said.

"Aye, sir. I've been watching that lightning. We're going to be in the middle of some bad stuff, I think."

"I believe you're right. I hope it doesn't get too bad. This craft is pretty old. You and Barebones did a good job of patching it together, but if the waves get too rough. . . ."

As Honor took the tiller, it was so dark that he could not see the prow of the boat now. Only when the lightning flashed could he make out the occupants, huddled miserably in their wet clothes. He was soaked too, but years at sea had hardened him to this kind of thing. As the hours passed, Honor kept doggedly at the task of tacking the boat, checking his pocket compass from time to time when he could read it by the flashes of lightning. Soon the sky was filled with whips of light and the boat began to toss.

"Hang on," Honor said, to those who were awake. "We'll weather this one!"

"That we will, sir," Praise God called out. He had just shifted the sail over and looked up at the mast that he and Cathan had made out of a tall pine tree. "I'm not sure the mast will take the strain, Captain."

"Better reef it a bit, Barebones."

"Aye, aye, sir!"

Shayna was holding on, pressing her back against the planking of the boat and bracing her feet against the board that ran down the middle. Fear washed over her as she realized how tiny and insignificant the boat was in the midst of this endless ocean of tossing waves.

As she prayed, lightning flashed across her face. Seeing her anxiety, Praise leaned over and said, "Don't be discouraged, miss. The good Lord's going to get us out of this."

"Thank you, Praise," she answered, summoning a smile.

When the storm reached a crescendo, it seemed as if the boat would be plucked out of the frothy waves, tossed upside down, and sucked down to the depths. It was all Honor could do to hang on to the tiller and keep them all afloat. Praise and Honor knew how close they were to disaster, but neither of them voiced their fears.

Finally the wind died down and the lightning faded off into the west. Honor stood up, bracing the tiller against his knee. "Well, I think that's the worst of it."

"I believe it is, Captain," Cathan said as he stood by the sail. "I believe the mast might take a little more strain now if you could get a direction for us."

"Yes, I think so." Peering at his compass as Praise God and Cathan unfurled the sail to its full capacity, Honor said, "We'll tack four points to starboard and hold that for half an hour."

"Aye, sir!" Cathan replied and soon the ship was sailing over waves still rough from the storm.

⚓

The night wore on until all aboard thought it would never end. Finally Praise said, "I think I see a little light over in the east. Morning's not far away."

As they eagerly looked in the direction Praise indicated, they saw a tiny ray of light. It wasn't much, but it illuminated the darkness enough to give them some cheer.

"We'll have some breakfast as soon as it gets a little lighter," Shayna said.

Ten minutes later the light had grown, and feeble though it was, Shayna made her way to the stern to get food from the box. She was interrupted when Cathan called out sharply, "Ship ahead, sir!"

"Where away?"

"Off the port bow!" It was difficult to see anything, for though the morning had come, a thick fog was beginning to roll in.

"I don't see anything!" Honor called out. "What sort of a ship is she, Morgan?"

"I couldn't make her out, sir. Just caught a glimpse of the sails. I think—wait, there she is!"

This time Honor Wakefield saw the flash of a sail. He put the tiller over and said, "We'll see if we can intercept her."

"What if she's French?" Trevor asked.

Honor shook his head. "I can't answer that. We'll hope that she's British. We should be far enough out of the range of the French patrols by now," he said hopefully, but there was no certainty in his voice.

"There she is again! A sloop!" Cathan said.

"Can you make out what she is, Morgan?" Honor called sharply.

"I can tell you," Praise said with alarm. "That's a French sloop. Look at the cut of her. Bear away, Captain!"

Instantly Honor threw the tiller to his left and Praise shifted the boom of the mast so that the wind caught at the vessel and wrenched her into a new course.

"I think she's seen us," Praise said. But his words were unnecessary, for Honor already knew that she had, for he had seen her sails trimmed and the vessel turned about.

"Can we outrun her, Captain?" Trevor asked, wondering if they would spend the rest of the war in a foul French dungeon.

"No, there's no chance of that," Honor said realistically. "We can only hope this fog gets heavier and we can lose her."

"I wish it was as thick as pea soup and then as thick again," Praise grumbled. "Not even a pistol to defend ourselves."

The sloop bore down on them rapidly. When it was almost alongside, a voice called out in French, "What vessel is this?"

"Answer him, Morgan," Honor hissed. "Tell him we're fishermen."

Although he knew no fisherman would be out this far from shore, Cathan obeyed. "We're fishermen," he yelled in perfect French.

"Come aboard after we come about" was the order that crackled across the waters.

The wind had picked up, giving Honor hope. "Listen carefully," he said quietly. "This is what we're going to do. She's going to put about. If she turns to port, we'll turn starboard. And if she turns starboard, we'll go to port. We can turn much quicker than she can and maybe hide ourselves in this fog. Watch now and be ready."

Honor almost held his breath, waiting to see which way the sloop would turn. The instant he saw the stays pull the sails around, he knew what she intended to do. "Hard to port!" he called and threw the tiller over, catching the bite of the water. The wind had come up enough to drive the small boat through at a fast pace and he watched eagerly as the sloop bore to starboard while his own craft whirled and entered the fog banks in the opposite direction.

"Now," he said, "we must be quiet. She'll be coming around and looking for us. Our only chance is that she'll miss us in the fog."

No one answered, for they all knew that their freedom depended upon how well this strategy worked. Now that the sail was set, there was nothing Cathan could do. So he moved over and sat down beside Shayna, finding her trembling.

"It'll be all right," he whispered, reaching for her hand.

"I'm afraid, Cathan," she said, grabbing his hand with both of hers. "Do you think they'll find us?"

"I'm praying they won't. All it takes is a grain of faith the size of a mustard seed. That's what Praise says."

As Shayna held his hand tightly, his presence took the fear away. She was quiet for a while, then asked, "What's that?"

"That's the Frenchy coming after us. You can hear the creaking of the mast. He's right over there."

"It's nice to have someone to lean on at a time like this," she said gratefully, her face soft in the fog.

"Yes, it is."

Shayna had meant *him,* but Cathan had quite naturally assumed she meant God. He smiled at her and whispered, "That's it. Don't let it get you. We're in God's hands now. He's never failed any of his people."

Back at the tiller, Honor heard the French sloop coming toward them. "We're going to put about now. She's coming. If we can get over just a few yards, she won't be able to see us. Put the sail around."

Instantly Praise God and Cathan put the boom around and Honor pushed at the tiller. The boat heeled over, apparently just in time. The French ship had put lanterns high as they hunted for their prey in the fog. As the ghostlike ship floated not fifty yards away from them, Honor thought, *It's a good thing we put about. Thank you, Lord.*

"All quiet now," Honor said and the little craft made its way silently through the waters as they all held their breath.

Cathan could hear the French officers calling to the lookouts to be alert. Conscious he was still holding Shayna's hand and that she was clinging to him, he was glad he was able to give her this comfort. *If I can never give her anything else, I can give her this,* he thought.

The game went on for over an hour, with the French ship going back and forth through the waters as Honor shifted directions, heading away from the noise that the larger ship made. Finally it was over. Honor waited until he was sure and then said in a voice tinged with triumph, "There, she's making away! We're safe!"

Shayna suddenly realized she had been holding Cathan's hand so hard that her own hand was cramped. Embarrassed, she pulled it away, wanting to express her thanks, but he went to help with the sail.

"That was a tight one, Cat," Praise God said as they shifted the boom and changed direction. Honor had peered at his compass and given them a new steering.

"God has taken care of us," Cathan said.

"He always does." Now that the boom was shifted, the two men moved forward to better distribute the weight on the ship. Cathan sat loosely on the bench next to his friend. "I'm glad the Frenchies didn't get us. It wouldn't be so bad for us, but I'd hate to see Miss Shayna in a French prison."

"So would I."

Relieved and in a talkative mood, Praise began speaking of their first meeting in prison. "Who would have thought the first time I saw you come down into that foul hulk that we'd wind up out here in the middle of the channel dodging French warships and God delivering us from them?"

"It seems like a century ago."

"Aye, time's always like that. The only thing that's real is the moment. That's what I say. Right now we are out of sight of the Frenchy; we've got food, a good captain, and a good craft. Soon we'll be in old England again."

"You're always an optimist."

"I'll always believe what Romans 8:28 says. 'All things work together for good to them that love God.'"

"Hard to see *all* things can work for good. What about the bad things?" Cathan asked. "I've done a lot of rotten things. How did they work for good?"

"You didn't love God at the time," Praise said simply. "But God can use even those things for good. Think of Joseph. His brothers threw him in a pit and sold him into slavery. That was bad, wasn't it?"

"Certainly."

"Well, it was God working in it. Joseph said that at the last. Remember? Joseph said to his brothers that they had meant it for evil but God meant it for good."

"I like it the way you say it," Cathan said, grinning.

The fog continued to roll in so that when the sun rose, it was merely a luminous blur in the sky.

"It's a good thing your father has a compass," Trevor said. He was eating the bread and jam that Shayna had dug out of the larder and passed around. "I can't tell up from down in this blasted fog."

"No, I can't either," Shayna said, sitting beside him.

"Just think. It won't be long until we're in England again. I suppose you're ready, aren't you?"

"Of course. Aren't you?"

"Yes. Things have changed a lot since we first set foot on the *Dauntless*," Trevor responded, tapping his wooden foot with his hand. "I'll always have this as a reminder of our adventure. But it's little enough price to pay. I'm glad it wasn't one of my hands, for then I couldn't continue my work as a surgeon. So God has been good to let me keep both hands. You know, when the ship was going down, I thought we were all going to die."

"So did I," she said, handing him another morsel of bread loaded with Elise's strawberry jam. "What did you think about during that time?"

"Oh, the usual, I suppose. I was afraid to die. Not of what would happen afterward but of the process itself."

Shayna laughed loudly, drawing the other's attention. Clapping her hand over her mouth, she said more quietly, "That's what I thought of."

"I suppose it's what everyone thinks of, but mostly I thought of the time I'd wasted."

"Trevor, you haven't wasted any time! You've worked all your life!" she said, shocked.

"That was the trouble," he replied. "I've done nothing *but* work. I don't suppose there are many men on their deathbeds who say, 'I wish I had worked more.'"

"Why, I don't suppose so," Shayna said, wonder in her voice. "I never thought of that."

"Well, *I* thought of it and I decided then that if I ever got back home to England, I would do things differently."

She looked at him curiously. "Things like what?"

He thought for a minute, then grinned at her rashly. "I'd read more romances."

Shayna's face colored. "You're making fun of me."

"I'm not making fun of you at all," Trevor protested. "I think people ought to read romances."

"Look at what it got me," Shayna said, her voice brittle.

Trevor took her hand. "It's not reading romances that's wrong. It's reading too many of them and confusing them with real life. For instance, it's not wrong to take walks in the fall to smell the leaves. But if you don't do anything *but* walk, that's a problem. I think the most significant Scripture for Christians may well be the one that says to do all things in moderation."

"I've never thought about that before."

"God's given us so many good things," Trevor said. "He gave us food, but when we eat too much, we ruin the good intents our Creator had for us. So, I'm going to read some romances; I'm going to go for some walks." Then he added roguishly, "I'm going to write love poetry. Fall in love with some woman and make a fool out of myself for a while. That ought to be part of life too."

"I can't imagine you writing a love poem."

"Well, I can do it. I'm going to learn to play a guitar and go caterwauling under her window."

"Trevor," Shayna said, laughing, "I could never see you doing those things."

"Well, maybe not like that. But I'm going to make room in my life for those things people call romantic. A man's life is pretty hollow if he doesn't have some of that in it. Why, when I think about it, I've known many a marriage that could have been saved if the husband had just shown a little romance in his spirit!"

Shayna's eyes widened. "I've often thought that myself, but I didn't know anyone else did."

"Well, I wouldn't have before all this. But, like you say, we've been changed. I may have lost a foot, but I've gained a little wisdom, I think."

Later on, as Shayna sat beside her father, who maintained his station in the stern, holding on to the tiller, she related to him what Trevor had said. To her surprise, her father nodded. "I think that's good sense. Trevor's always been too hard a worker. He didn't leave any time in his life for fun."

"I think some might say the same of you."

"You're right. I haven't been very playful, have I?"

"Do you remember when I was five or six and you and I had tea parties on the floor? You even helped me name my dolls as we played with them."

"Yes, I do remember. That was a long time ago." Honor hugged his daughter close. "But I wish I'd done more of that. If you give a party now, I promise to come," he said, smiling. "Our world's been turned upside down, hasn't it?"

When she did not answer, he asked, "What about that young fellow there?" He indicated Cathan. "He's changed, too. Trevor lost a foot, but Cathan Morgan lost something too."

"What, Papa?"

"He lost himself—that wild, reckless, young man who never thought of another soul except himself. That's all gone now."

"Do you really believe that?" Shayna asked quietly.

Honor did not answer except to grunt an assent; then he suddenly called out, "Look! A ship!"

Immediately Praise turned in the direction Honor indicated. "I see it, sir!"

Shayna went over to Cathan and took his arm. Surprised, he turned and asked, "Shayna, what is it?"

She took a deep breath. "I hated you for so long that it's hard for me to say this," she said, tears in her eyes. "But I don't hate you anymore. In all truth I—I've come to care for you very much." Then she whirled, not wanting to hear his answer, and made her way back to her father.

"Here she comes," her father murmured. "She looks English to me, but the French have captured so many of our ships that it could be manned by a French crew."

At that very moment an English voice called out, "What ship is that?"

Honor tightened his arm about Shayna and whispered to her with exultation, "English! She's English!" Then he lifted his voice. "This is Capt. Honor Wakefield of His Majesty's ship *Dauntless.*" When silence fell, he said to Shayna, "God has delivered us, my daughter."

But Shayna did not look at the ship that loomed out of the fog. Instead, she was looking at Cathan. He had not moved since she spoke to him. Dropping her eyes again, she listened as a voice from the English ship said, "We'll receive you on board, Captain. We heard you were dead."

"God has kept us, sir." Honor's voice sounded loud and clear over the waters. When he looked down at his daughter, he was astonished to see her weeping. At first he thought it was tears of joy, but then he saw she was sobbing with distress. As he put his arms around her, he caught Cathan's eye. It was then that he realized what was wrong with Shayna. *She's in love with that fellow,* he thought, *and there's nothing I can do about it.*

Twenty-Three

"HE CAME TO HIMSELF. . . ."

C aptain Honor Wakefield stood looking at the *Defiant,* wondering if he would come forth from the court-martial a private individual. Court-martials were required of all captains who lost their ships, no matter under what circumstances. There had been sad cases of captains who had been judged ineffectual and therefore were dismissed from the navy for their behavior. But the thought of such a fate did not trouble Honor, particularly since he had considered this possibility seriously on the return voyage to England. Yet, looking at the magnificent ship of the line, he wondered if he was fitted for any other sort of life. Sensing this, Shayna had said to him the day before their arrival in Portsmouth, "Don't worry, Papa. There's plenty to do at Wakefield. You can be a country gentleman, maybe become a member of Parliament."

That wouldn't be so bad, Honor thought, as he got in the jolly boat. *No more long absences from England. I could do something with my ideas about breeding animals. A man could live a good life like that.*

As the six sailors rowed him to the *Defiant,* he was taken with their shore-going rigs—wide-brimmed white hats with red streamers, blue jackets with brass buttons, black silk handkerchiefs, and white duck trousers. *Maddox likes a colorful crew,* Honor thought. When they reached the side of the towering warship,

Honor realized that Paul Maddox, commodore of the *Defiant,* could change his future.

As Honor mounted the ladder and then stepped on the deck, a hoarse order sounded and the marines, in their scarlet tunics, presented arms. Despite the fact that he was coming aboard to face a court-martial, he was still a captain in His Majesty's navy, so the officers doffed their hats. He moved forward, noting that the warrant officers and midshipmen were dressed in their best blue-and-white uniforms.

A lieutenant stepped forward. "Welcome aboard, Capt. Wakefield. If you will come this way, sir, I believe the court is assembled."

Honor followed the lieutenant along the deck, then stepped inside the great cabin that had been cleared to make room for the many lines of chairs. To his surprise, the chairs were all filled. Honor briefly wondered why so many would come to witness his court-martial, but he had no time for further thought. Heads turned to watch his entrance and then the spectators rose as the members of the court entered and seated themselves against the stern windows. Commodore Paul Maddox, serving as Judge Advocate, said, "Be seated. You may begin, Mr. Smith."

Mr. Smith, the prosecuting attorney, began to present the case. It was simple enough, he explained: Capt. Honor Wakefield had lost his vessel in an action against the enemy. He laid out the simple events of the loss of the ship, then shrugged as if to say, *Well, that's all there is to it,* and stepped back.

Silence fell across the cabin as every eye turned to the Judge Advocate. They knew that Maddox, a short man with dark eyes, would now set the tone for the court-martial. Those familiar with such things, including Honor Wakefield for he had served on many, waited to hear whether it was to be a driving, harsh sort of affair or the Judge Advocate would be lenient.

"I'm interested in how you managed to make your way back to England, Capt. Wakefield."

Relief washed over Honor Wakefield, for the Judge Advocate had, in effect, waved aside the loss of the *Dauntless*. Suddenly it was clear that the court-martial was merely a perfunctory duty in the eyes of Commodore Paul Maddox.

"Yes, sir. I am happy to oblige," Wakefield said. As he described the escape from the ship itself, he was interrupted once as the Advocate said, "I take it these two men, Morgan and Barebones, were quite helpful?"

"I cannot say enough about these two members of my crew, sir. Without their help, it is entirely unlikely that my daughter, myself, and Dr. Wakefield would have escaped." He went on to praise the efficiency and courage of the two men. When he had finished, the Judge Advocate said, "We are impressed. It is the sort of thing one likes to see in English seaman. Pray, continue."

As Honor spoke of the time spent at Pierre Monbiere's house, he found himself again talking about Cathan and Praise. Finally, he ended by saying, "It was these same two men who fitted out the ship on which we were able to make our escape."

"I take it you would like to see these two promoted?"

"Indeed I would, sir. They are fine sailors, reliable, courageous, and inventive to an extreme degree."

"I will leave their promotions in your hands," Maddox said, looking around the courtroom. "If you will wait outside, Captain, we will call you when the court has reached a decision."

Honor stepped outside briefly, then was called to return. When he was back inside the cabin, Maddox smiled. "The court finds that you behaved in the best interest of the service. We not only find you innocent, but we commend you and your crew for their service toward His Majesty."

"Thank you, sir."

"It is my privilege to appoint you as Vice-Admiral to the Red."

For a moment Honor Wakefield thought he had not under-stood. *Vice-Admiral to the Red. They are making me an admiral!* He swallowed hard and said in an unsteady voice, "It only remains for me to give you my heartfelt gratitude, Commodore Maddox."

"The two men, Morgan and Barebones, will be happy to hear of your promotion and of their own. Are they here?"

"Barebones is here in the city, sir, but Morgan has gone on leave to see his parents."

"He will have good news for them."

"Yes, indeed, sir," Honor replied. He was thinking, however, that the best news for Cathan's family would not be that he had done well in the service but that he had found God.

Shortly after receiving individual congratulations from the court members, Honor left the ship and traveled toward Wake-field. The shock of the promotion occupied his mind for most of the journey, but by the time he arrived at Wakefield, he had become accustomed to it.

As he stepped from his carriage and walked up the steps, Shayna raced out and threw herself into his arms. He caught her and spun her around.

"Papa, tell me! What did the court say?"

Holding her in the circle of his arms, Honor Wakefield smiled down at his daughter. "Complete exoneration."

"I knew it would be so!" she cried, and hugged him hard.

"But that's not all. You are now holding in your arms a Vice-Admiral of the Red."

"An admiral? They made you an admiral?"

"Yes, they did."

Filled with joy, Shayna laughed aloud. "You should have lost the ship a long time ago."

As Honor marched inside with Shayna, he said, "Not every

captain who loses a ship gets promoted. Come along. I want to tell you about it."

It was late that night when Shayna finally got to bed. She had enjoyed to the fullest the result of the trial, seeing that her father was happy. It had saddened her, just for a time, to think he would not be staying at home, as she had hoped. He would be gone again, sometimes for long months or maybe even years, with Napoléon still on the march. But Shayna knew that sailing was what her father loved and she wanted him to be happy.

When she had undressed and prepared for bed, she pulled out her journal and began to write:

> Papa has been totally cleared of all charges by the
> court-martial—and he has been made an admiral! I'm so
> happy for him that I can hardly write these words. He loves
> the sea and, though I will miss him, it is the life he has chosen.

She wrote happily for a time, then grew sorrowful as she began to write of Cathan.

> I cannot understand Cathan. On the voyage home he
> did not speak to me, not even once. I know that he is a
> member of the crew and I am the daughter of a captain,
> but he could have found some way if he had wanted to!

Agitated, she stopped writing and put the journal away. But when she got into bed, her thoughts were not on her father's promotion. They focused on Cathan Morgan. *Will I ever see him again?* she wondered as sleep eluded her.

The chapel was small and only three-quarters filled. Those who did attend were primarily older people, for the church had been mostly forsaken by the younger generation. A newer, larger, and more imposing structure had been built only ten miles distant, so now during the evening service the congregation had no trouble finding seats.

The minister, who had joined in the singing, tapping time on his knee with an arthritic hand, was somewhat stooped. He reminded one of a board that had been left out to weather. Now in his eighty-fifth year, Gareth Morgan had done most of his preaching in the rain or in fields and time had taken its toll. But even as he rose to speak, there was still vigor in his voice and a sparkle in his dark eyes. As he began to read the Scripture he knew and loved so well, he noticed that a latecomer had slipped in through the door and taken a seat at the back. Gareth's eyes were not what they had been, so he could only make out that the man was tall and had dark hair. As always, however, Gareth Morgan thought of those who sat under his preaching as the objects of Christ's quest.

"I take my text today from Luke's Gospel, chapter fifteen. Most of you are so familiar with this that you could quote it from memory, and well you might, for in my mind it always has been one of the clearest pictures of the love of God for sinners such as us. It begins, "A certain man had two sons. . . . ""

As Gareth quoted the drama of the Prodigal Son, his eyes kept going to the latecomer in the back. He wished his vision were as sharp as it had been when he was a young man, for it was his habit to observe the faces of those under his preaching, for then he could discern their hearts. Finally he came to the end of the story: "But when he was yet a great way off, his father saw him, and had compassion, and ran, and fell on his neck, and kissed him. And the son said unto him, Father I have sinned against heaven, and in thy sight, and am no more worthy to be called thy son."

Stretching his hands out eloquently, Gareth Morgan cried out, "What would we expect a father to do? Many would have turned him away saying, 'You are right. You are not worthy to be called my son.' But what does the father of this parable do? He says to his servants, 'Bring forth the best robe, and put it on him; and put a ring on his hand, and shoes on his feet.'"

The voice grew stronger as Gareth spoke of God's love and the fact that all men and women are prodigals. Tears came to his eyes as he spoke of his own youth. "I well remember, as if it were only yesterday, when I flouted God, when I turned away from his offers of mercy and went the way of this poor lad in the parable. He had nothing on me, for I tasted rebellion to the dregs. But when I came back, I saw Jesus on the cross and one look broke my heart, dear, beloved friends. I fell on my face before God and cried out as this young man did, 'I have sinned against heaven.'"

Although the pointed sermon was not long, Gareth's voice was raspy by the time he said, "I have no deep theology to offer any of you who are away from God. In John chapter three, verses fourteen through sixteen, Jesus said of himself, 'And as Moses lifted up the serpent in the wilderness, even so must the Son of man be lifted up: That whosoever believeth in him should not perish, but have eternal life. For God so loved the world, that he gave his only begotten Son, that whosoever believeth in him should not perish, but have everlasting life.'"

As Gareth concluded, the room was quiet. But Gareth heard a sound he had heard many times in ministry, that of someone trying to choke off sobs. Glancing toward the visitor, Gareth quickly dismissed the congregation with a prayer. Then he stepped from the pulpit and moved down the aisle toward the tall man who sat with his head bowed, face in his hands.

"My dear brother, may I be of help to you?" Gareth said gently.

As the man slowly raised his face, Gareth whispered in shock, "Cathan!" He put out his hand and touched the young man's face. "Is it really you or are my old eyes playing tricks?"

Cathan stood to his feet and took his grandfather by the

shoulders. Tears were running down his face, but he was smiling. "It's me, Grandfather. I've come home and I have good news for you."

As Gareth stared at his grandson, for whom he had prayed faithfully, joy leaped within his heart. "I can see it in your face!" he exclaimed. "You are a different man. Not the same rebellious boy who ran away."

"Yes, and it has been yours and my parents' faithful prayers that have kept me safe."

"Come. Sit down. I want to hear everything."

For the next half hour Cathan traced his experiences since finding God. When he finished, he said, "I've come home to do what the Prodigal did in the story you just read. I've got to go to my parents and confess that I have sinned against them and ask their forgiveness."

Gareth gripped Cathan's shoulders hard with happiness. "I know what they will say. They will say, 'For this my son was dead, and is alive again; he was lost, and is found!'"

Ivor Morgan and his wife, Lydia, were sitting at the table, finishing the evening meal. As they sipped their tea, Lydia said, "I miss the noise of all the children. It's so quiet here now, Ivor."

"That it is," Ivor said, squeezing his wife's hand. "But we'll have the grandchildren with us next week. That'll put some noise in the place."

"I'm so glad," Lydia began, as a knock at the door interrupted them. "Who could that be at this time of the night?" Lydia asked.

"One way to find out," Ivor said. Standing up, he moved swiftly to the door and threw it open. "Why, Father," he said to Gareth, "what are you—" Then he stopped, speechless for a moment, because he saw the young man standing beside his father. Then he cried out, "Cathan, it's you!"

Lydia leaped to her feet. She ran across the floor and threw herself into Cathan's arms, crying, "My boy! My boy!"

Gareth Morgan moved slightly to one side and watched as the two hugged and kissed their son. Finally Gareth said, smiling, "Well, are you going to ask us in?"

"Come in. Have you eaten?" Lydia cried, holding tightly to Cathan's arm.

"I didn't come to eat," Cathan said. As he faced his parents, guilt swept over him as he remembered how badly he had treated this couple who had never shown him anything but love. Then he said quickly, "Grandfather preached on the Prodigal Son tonight and a very apt sermon it was." He hesitated, then said simply, "I have found the Lord Jesus and I've come to ask your forgiveness for the grief I've brought into your life."

As Gareth had foretold, there was joy in the Morgan household. Ivor and Lydia had prayed years for this young man and now he had come home again.

After that, Cathan sat at the kitchen table and retold everything while his mother supplied them liberally with tea and food. Lydia, not content with general description, wanted infinite details. Finally, two hours later, Cathan threw up his hands and said, "Mother, that's all I can remember!"

"What about Shayna?" Lydia demanded. Although Cathan had said as little as possible about Shayna, Lydia had a mother's heart. She had gone at once beneath the surface of his words. "How do you feel about her now?"

Cathan glanced at the three who, he knew, had literally prayed him into the kingdom of God. "It doesn't matter much how I feel about her," he said quietly.

"Why do you say a thing like that?" Ivor asked. "Do you love her?"

"Yes, I do."

"Then if you love her, fight for her," Ivor insisted.

"I don't have a thing to offer, Father. She's the daughter of a nobleman and I have nothing."

"You have yourself," Lydia said stoutly, "and that's just what a woman wants."

"Your mother's right," Ivor said. "I had nothing either, except myself, but she was good enough to take me and make me a happy man."

"If this young woman loves you, she'll not care what you have. And besides, you're a young man. You can make your way. God will do something in your life. I gave you to him the day you were born and have prayed every day since that God would use you mightily," Lydia said confidently.

Cathan Morgan could not speak, for his heart was full and he had to blink away the tears. He felt unworthy of their love—and of Shayna. Still, looking over at his grandfather as if asking a question, he was glad when the old man said, "Obey your father, my boy. If you love her, fight for her!"

Twenty-Four

A TIME TO EMBRACE

S hayna made her way down the path that had been carved between the banks of roses. Although watching the flowers bloom had always delighted her, in the early summer of 1802 they did not seem to smell as exquisite as they had in previous years. As she made her way through the garden in the brilliant sunlight, she stopped to examine a particularly healthy blooming plant. Reaching out, she touched the bush, inadvertently driving one of the thorns into her thumb.

"Oh!" she exclaimed, releasing the bush. She tried to bite the thorn out with her teeth, but it was embedded. She turned to go back inside for help when a voice caught her attention.

"Shayna?" Turning, she saw her father walking toward her. When he saw her expression, he asked, "What's the matter?"

"Oh, I jabbed my thumb with a thorn."

"Let me see." Taking her hand, he examined the thumb. "It looks like it's broken off. Do you have a pin?"

"Yes, I have one here somewhere."

"Let me have it."

Taking a pin from her blouse, she handed it to him and he began to extricate the thorn.

"I wish Trevor were here," Honor remarked. "He could do this much better."

"A successful London surgeon wouldn't stoop to a little operation like this," Shayna replied, smiling. "Did you read the letter I got yesterday?"

"Yes, I'm very proud of that young man. He didn't let the loss of a foot stop him from living, not a bit. Who's this young woman he keeps talking about?"

"I have not met her, but from his glowing letters I think something might come of it—Ouch!"

"There, I think that got it."

"Thank you, Papa."

"Would you like to go to London?" Honor asked. "I must go to the Admiralty day after tomorrow."

"All right."

Disturbed by Shayna's lack of enthusiasm, Honor said, "I think it would be good for you. You haven't done a thing for the last two months, not since we got home."

"I suppose I'm just tired from our adventures," Shayna said. "I'll just stay here if you don't mind, Papa."

"You ought to get out more," Honor said encouragingly. "It's not good for you to be here alone. You never go anywhere, except to church and to the market once a week."

Finally Shayna said, more for his sake than her own, "I'll go with you, Papa."

"Fine! Fine! Maybe we could go shopping and I could help you pick out a new dress. Who knows, we might even find a ball or two to go to?"

"That would be nice," she said quietly.

Dissatisfied with her reaction, Honor said quickly, "I'm going to look at the new bull I bought. Would you like to come?"

"No, thanks," Shayna said, smiling a little. "When you've seen one bull, you've seen them all."

"There's the voice of one who doesn't take any interest in cattle breeding," Honor said, laughing as he walked rapidly away.

After he left, Shayna noticed that some of the roses needed trimming, but she had no interest in tackling the task. Then, feeling uncomfortable with her mood, she went upstairs and changed into her burgundy riding habit. Once she was in the stable, Michael Devon saddled a gray mare. As Michael gave her a hand up, he said cautiously, "Watch her now, Miss Shayna. She's kind of a handful."

"I will, Michael," Shayna promised. She touched the mare with her crop and shot out of the stable yard, turning the horse firmly toward the low-lying hills to the north. As the afternoon drew on toward evening, the hot air cooled with the descent of the sun. Turning the mare's head back toward the house, she allowed her to pick her own pace.

When she reached the stables, Michael Devon asked, "Did you have a good ride, Miss Shayna?"

"Very nice, thank you." Shayna said. Tired from the ride, she walked slowly across the grounds toward the house, stopping to look at the artificial pool that contained fish. Sitting down on a rock, she began to toss pebbles in. When some of the fish rose to investigate, she remembered how tiny they were when she and her father first stocked the pool. Now some were over a foot long.

Although the sky grew darker, she was still unwilling to go into the house and change. She knew that tonight would be like all other nights—she would eat dinner with her father, they would play chess or read, and then she would go to bed. Since their return to England, life had been dreary and she remembered her time at Monbiere's with pleasure.

When footsteps approached, she rose and turned, thinking it was one of the servants. "I'm coming in," she began to say. And then she could not finish, for there, striding across the yard, was Cathan Morgan. For a moment she thought she was dreaming, for he was not wearing his sailor's uniform but instead was wearing a suit, boots, and hat. "Cathan," she said, "I'm surprised to see you."

Cathan removed his hat and tossed it on the grass. His face was not as tan as she remembered it and he looked as if he had lost weight.

"I had to come and see you, Shayna," he said quietly and tensely. "I would have come before, but I wasn't sure if you would be glad to see me."

"I'm so glad you've come!" Shayna burst out, realizing this was why she had been so unhappy being back at Wakefield. The very sight of him recalled the days when he had kissed her and she had felt herself so in love. As she remembered her days of reading romances and how silly her thoughts had been, she knew that what she felt for Cathan now was not that but something much deeper. Her color rose as she remembered that he had never answered her when she told him on the boat that she cared for him. Embarrassed, she stood there, waiting for him to speak.

"I had to get things straight in my mind," Cathan said carefully. "I spent a lot of time with my grandfather, Gareth Morgan." Then he impulsively reached out and took her hands. "I've come prepared to be told I'm a fool, Shayna."

"A fool? Why should I tell you that?"

"Because I've come to tell you that I love you, that I have for a long time now. I've come to ask you to marry me."

Time stood still for Shayna as her face drained of color. She could not believe Cathan was asking to marry her. Conscious of his strong hands holding hers, she couldn't say a word. But her eyes fixed on him as he continued.

"You'd be a fool if you did marry me. You have everything here, Shayna—money and position. And I don't have one blessed thing! But you said, when we were in the boat, that you cared deeply for me. I couldn't believe it then and even after I did, I couldn't ask you to marry me because I had nothing to offer. But my mother says that a man can offer himself and that's what I've come to do. It's all I have, Shayna, and I want to share my life with you."

"Oh, Cathan," Shayna whispered brokenly as she swayed toward him. As he swept her into his arms, he savored the moment, knowing that this was what he had hoped and prayed for. Lifting his head after their kiss, he said, "Will you marry me, Shayna?"

"Yes!"

"That's all? Just yes? Do you understand you're marrying a pauper?"

"You can do anything you want to, Cathan Morgan!"

"I'm glad *you* think so."

"Where have you been these past two months?" she asked, clinging to him. "I've been so lonely. I thought surely you would write or come to visit."

"It would have done no good to come. I had to fight my feelings out and I decided only yesterday that I'd at least tell you how I felt."

As they shared another kiss, Shayna said, "Have you talked to Father yet?"

"No. What if he says no?" he asked, watching her face. "What will you do then, Shayna?"

"Where's your faith, Cathan Morgan?" Shayna demanded. "Didn't you learn any more about faith from Praise God Barebones than that?"

He laughed then, picked her up, and swung her around. "Do you know where he is?"

"Probably out looking at his new herd of cattle. He's fascinated with them."

As they walked down the path that led to the pasture, they found Honor Wakefield there, just as Shayna had said. When Honor looked up, he straightened, his eyes growing alert.

"Well, Morgan, you've come at last," he said in an even tone. Realizing he was holding Shayna's hand, Cathan started to drop it. Then he changed his mind and held on, knowing there was no way to soften this blow. "Capt. Wakefield, I would like to ask for your daughter's hand in marriage."

Honor Wakefield blinked and his mouth opened. But he was so surprised that he could think of nothing to say, so he just stared at the pair.

Finally, Shayna said, "Well, Papa, say *something!*"

And then Honor Wakefield looked directly at his daughter. Although this man might have had a bad past, a misspent youth, and did not come from the aristocracy, those things suddenly seemed like nothing compared to the life and joy in his only child's eyes. "I think I know enough of you, Cathan, to understand that if I say no, that will only make you more determined," Honor said.

"I'm ashamed to admit it, but that's true, sir. I know I don't have anything and Shayna has everything. I know what people will say when she marries a pauper. But I love her and will care for her as long as I live."

"And you, Daughter. This is what you want?" Honor queried. "Yes!"

Honor Wakefield took a deep breath. "Then, so be it. This girl of mine has been mooning for you like a sick calf ever since we got home."

"Papa!" Shayna protested, her cheeks flushing. She looked up at Cathan, who grinned at her. "Don't believe a word of it!"

"I have to take the word of my captain and my future father-in-law," Cathan said. Then, more seriously, he added, "I don't know what the law is, but I do understand I'm still under your command. So what will your orders be?"

"Do you want to go back to sea, Cathan?"

"It was an exciting time," Cathan admitted, "and I know that for some men such as yourself, sir, it's the only life. But truthfully, no, I'm not anxious to go back to sea."

Looking around at the spacious fields, Honor thought quickly. Since he himself would be at sea and not at Wakefield for long periods of time, he had hoped Shayna might marry a man who could take care of the land. Now she had a man, so he asked abruptly, "Do you think you could learn to manage a place like this?"

Cathan was stunned. "You mean Wakefield?"

"Of course Wakefield! I'll be going to sea relatively soon. We won't have much time. You two will have to get married and have a short honeymoon. Then I'll teach you all I can about the place." Seeing the surprise on Shayna's face, he said to her, "You make a husband out of him and I'll make a stock raiser out of him. Would that suit you?"

Shayna let go of Cathan's hand and came forward to hug her father. "I have the best father in the whole world!" she said, then whispered in his ear, "He'll make you proud. I just know he will!"

Cathan said huskily, "If you'll give me a chance, sir, I'll try to show you what a man can do."

"Very well, come inside. You can have him during dinnertime, Shayna, but after that we'll begin the most boring part of being lord of a manor— going over the books."

As the three walked together, arm in arm, back toward the house, Honor thought of all the Wakefields who had been born, lived, and died in this place. Looking at his daughter and soon-to-be son-in-law, he lifted a prayer to God, saying, *Watch over them, Lord, and prosper them!*

⁓⁂⁓

The announcement of Shayna Wakefield's engagement to Cathan Morgan had been a hurried affair in the opinion of many. There had, of course, been the usual behind-the-hands scoffing at the idea of a titled young woman marrying a nobody. But all of this had made little difference to Shayna, although Cathan had been forced to bite his tongue many times.

But they had endured and, during the short time that had passed since Honor Wakefield made his offer, he and Cathan had spent many many long hours together. Honor had been pleased at how quickly Cathan took to the business of managing a large estate. Cathan had a quick and penetrating mind and had inherited from his father a love for land. By the time the two men had spent a week together, Honor knew he had done the right thing and said so to any of his acquaintances who dared challenge his daughter's choice.

Now Shayna and Cathan's wedding day had arrived, but Honor had mysteriously disappeared. When Shayna asked the steward where her father had gone, he denied any knowledge of the master's whereabouts. "But he'll be here for the wedding, never you fear that! He's been looking forward to giving his daughter away."

The morning wore on and guests, such as Cathan's family, began to arrive. Indeed, his own grandfather, Gareth Morgan, was to perform the ceremony. And others, anxious to get a look at the unlikely young couple, had come from miles around.

Shayna was in her room, nervously pacing the floor until her maid, Lucy, lost patience with her. "You're going to wear your shoes out! Don't worry, the master will be back!"

"But where could he have gone on my wedding day? I can't believe it, Lucy!"

She paced for another ten minutes before a knock sounded at the door. When Lucy opened it, there stood her father.

"Where have you been, Papa?"

Honor Wakefield's face held an odd smile and he merely said, "Come along."

"Where to? Is someone sick?"

"No, no one's sick," he said, taking her arm and propelling her down the hallway into the drawing room. "I see, Cathan, that they found you."

Cathan was as puzzled as Shayna. "Yes, sir, they said you wanted to see me at once."

Honor Wakefield said, "I know you've both been anxious about my absence, but I went to pick up a guest who wanted to attend the service."

"A guest? Who is that, Papa?"

"Wait right here and you'll see."

Honor left the room with long strides, leaving Shayna and Cathan to look at each other helplessly. "Do you know what he's talking about, Shayna?"

"I haven't the foggiest clue! He's behaving peculiarly. It's not like him!" she said.

In a few minutes, footsteps came down the hall. Both Shayna and Cathan turned toward the doorway as Honor entered, a woman behind him. Honor smiled. "Here is the lady who is so desperately eager to see your wedding." He stepped aside—and there was Madeline de Fontaneau.

"Madeline!" Shayna cried, racing forward to hug the woman.

"You are surprised? Well, so am I," Madeline said.

"It took some dark sailing to get them . . . I mean . . . her to England," Honor said, with a broad smile. "And now I owe an old navy friend an immense favor. It appears that both sides pay little attention to small fishing vessels in the channel waters."

Cathan came at once, took Madeline's hand, and kissed it. "I'm so glad to see you, Lady Fontaneau."

"But surprised, is that not so?" Madeline said impishly.

"Well, to be truthful, yes," Cathan said.

"This surprises you?" Honor said, his eyebrows raised in an arch. A mischievous light came to his eye. "Well, I shall surprise you even more." He turned to his daughter and said, "I know it is a little late, but you're going to have a new mother. I've asked Madeline to marry me and she has agreed."

"Papa, that's wonderful!" Once again she embraced Madeline and then flew to her father to kiss him on the cheek. "That's the best news I ever heard!"

"I have another surprise for you," Madeline said. "Wait right here." As she disappeared, Honor refused to answer any questions. Again the sound of footsteps came down the hall. Elise, whose cooking they remembered so well, appeared. Immediately behind her, looking happy but awkward in a new eye patch and suit, stood Praise God Barebones.

Cathan immediately knew what had happened and began to laugh. "You rogue!" he said. "You said you would marry this woman and now you've done it!"

Praise God Barebones grinned. "Well, the Bible says he that 'findeth a wife findeth a good thing, and obtaineth favor of the Lord.' Well, that's what I've done."

All of them laughed then as Honor said, "Praise, you always have a Scripture to fit everything."

"Indeed I do," Praise said, nodding with enthusiasm.

Then Madeline took over. "Come," she said to Shayna, "I must help you dress for your wedding." Touching Honor Wakefield's arm in a possessive manner, a roguish look came into her fine eyes and she whispered, "You watch carefully so you won't make any mistakes when you go through it in a very short time."

⸺◈⸺

The wedding was over now and Cathan and Shayna were riding toward Bath, where they were to spend a week. As the carriage rocked along, Shayna held tightly to Cathan's hand. Looking out at the sky, she said, "Look how beautiful the moon is."

"I've got something more beautiful than that right here in this carriage," Cathan said, pulling her closer to him. "Now you're mine and I don't have to ask anyone's permission to do this." He kissed her so thoroughly that she squirmed free, gasping happily. "So," Cathan said, smiling, "how does it feel to be a bride and a wife?"

Shayna said timidly, "It has only been a few hours, but it feels wonderful."

He grinned at her, then said, "I was reading in the Bible about the Year of Jubilee—the time the Hebrew slaves in the Old Testament were freed. But there's one thing I don't understand. It said that if a slave loved his master so much that he wanted to stay with him, they did a rather strange thing." He put his arm around her again. "He became what was called a love slave and they took an awl and pierced his ear. I don't know whether they put an earring in it or not, but from that time on, he belonged to that master because of his love, not because of law."

"I think that's wonderful, Cathan."

"That's what I want to be to you. You want to put a ring in my ear?"

She grabbed his nose, tweaking it playfully. "How about in your nose so I can lead you around like Papa does his prize bulls?"

They began to wrestle on the seat until suddenly, using his greater strength, Cathan pinned her, kissing her until she could scarcely breathe. "Is that enough romance for you?" he asked passionately.

Shayna Wakefield relaxed in his arms. "You're all the romance I'll ever need, Cathan Morgan!" she whispered as the carriage rolled on.

THE END